'Miss Louisa...' The words were spoken in a masculine voice low enough to send an ice-cold chill down her spine.

Her hand froze. She kept her gaze downcast and willed the stranger to go. She could not be so unlucky as to encounter Jonathon Ponsby-Smythe here. In Newcastle. He was a habitué of London clubs, fashionable salons and Almack's—not provincial concerts with second-rate singers.

Louisa forced the breath into her lungs. This man, this friend of Miss Daphne's nephew, was someone else. This man was not the man who had destroyed her life.

And she was no longer the same naive girl who had believed a man's whispered endearments of eternal love.

What was the proper etiquette for greeting the man who had taken your innocence and destroyed your girlish dreams?

# AUTHOR NOTE

When I first started writing COMPROMISING MISS MILTON, Daisy's friend Louisa Sibson was supposed to be a throw-away character. A few lines, nothing more. However, Louisa had other ideas. She arrived, and refused to budge from my mind. She was determined to have her story told. Luckily my editor agreed with her, and allowed me to write Louisa and Jonathon's story. Because Mrs Blandish and her daughters were also very determined characters, they also had a part to play in this story. Hopefully you will enjoy it.

Louisa's story was inspired in part by reading *Other People's Daughters: the Life and Times of the Governess* by Ruth Brandon, *The Victorian Governess* by Kathryn Hughes, and Miss Weeton's *Journal of a Governess*, both volumes: 1807–1811 and 1811–1825. If you are interested in the actual experiences of governesses, the books are excellent sources.

As ever, I am always delighted to get letters from readers. I can be contacted via post to Mills & Boon, through my website, www.michellestyles.co.uk, or my blog http://www.michellestyles.blogspot.com

# BREAKING THE GOVERNESS'S RULES

Michelle Styles

All the characters in this book have no existence outside the imagination of the author, and have no relation whatsoever to anyone bearing the same name or names. They are not even distantly inspired by any individual known or unknown to the author, and all the incidents are pure invention.

First published in Great Britain 2011
Harlequin Mills & Boon Limited,
Eton House, 18-24 Paradise Road, Richmond, Surrey TW9 1SR

© Michelle Styles 2011

ISBN: 978 0 263 88245 2

Harlequin Mills & Boon policy is to use papers that are natural, renewable and recyclable products and made from wood grown in sustainable forests. The logging and manufacturing process conform to the legal environmental regulations of the country of origin.

Printed and bound in Spain
by Litografia Rosés, S.A., Barcelona

Born and raised near San Francisco, California, **Michelle Styles** currently lives a few miles south of Hadrian's Wall, with her husband, three children, two dogs, cats, assorted ducks, hens and beehives. An avid reader, she became hooked on historical romance when she discovered Georgette Heyer, Anya Seton and Victoria Holt one rainy lunchtime at school. And, for her, a historical romance still represents the perfect way to escape. Although Michelle loves reading about history, she also enjoys a more hands-on approach to her research. She has experimented with a variety of old recipes and cookery methods (some more successfully than others), climbed down Roman sewers, and fallen off horses in Iceland—all in the name of discovering more about how people went about their daily lives. When she is not writing, reading or doing research, Michelle tends her rather overgrown garden or does needlework—in particular counted cross-stitch.

Michelle maintains a website, www.michellestyles.co.uk, and a blog, www.michellestyles.blogspot.com, and would be delighted to hear from you.

**Previous novels by the same author:**

THE GLADIATOR'S HONOUR
A NOBLE CAPTIVE
SOLD AND SEDUCED
THE ROMAN'S VIRGIN MISTRESS
TAKEN BY THE VIKING
A CHRISTMAS WEDDING WAGER
 (part of *Christmas By Candlelight*)
VIKING WARRIOR, UNWILLING WIFE
AN IMPULSIVE DEBUTANTE
A QUESTION OF IMPROPRIETY
IMPOVERISHED MISS, CONVENIENT WIFE
COMPROMISING MISS MILTON
THE VIKING'S CAPTIVE PRINCESS

BREAKING THE GOVERNESS'S RULES
features characters you will have already met in
COMPROMISING MISS MILTON.

To India Grey,
who has the unfailing knack of brightening my day.

# *Prologue*

*1833—Warwickshire*

Pain consumed Jonathon Ponsby-Smythe. Every breath seared his lungs. His limbs refused to obey his command. Jonathon fought against it and the heavy blackness that called to him and invited him into its embrace—to death. Jonathon knew he was far from ready to die. His life mattered.

'Louisa, Louisa.' The words escaped from his lips, a plea for life, for salvation. With Louisa at his side, he *could* accomplish anything. With his last ounce of strength, he lifted his hand towards a shadowy female shape. 'Louisa, help me. I want to live.'

'Jonathon, oh, my poor, brave Jonathon, you must rest. You are not allowed to die,' an overly sweet voice cried.

'Louisa…not you…' he croaked at the woman with her English-rose complexion and immaculately golden curls. 'Get her now! Louisa!'

'Who is this Louisa?' the woman asked, less sugary and far more imperious. 'Should I know her?'

'He wants that little nobody, the governess, Louisa Sibson,' the brisk tones of his stepmother rang out. 'Put her from your mind, Clarissa. She is beneath your notice.'

'Not governess. Fiancée. Find her.' Jonathon ignored the sudden stab of pain that racked him and forced his body to an upright position. He stared at the pair. They would do as he commanded. 'I want her here. Now. Louisa. Must marry.'

'Jonathon is marrying the governess?' Clarissa shrieked. 'But you said…Mama said… It is all arranged and has been since we were babies. *I* am the right wife for him.'

'Have licence. Marry Louisa today.' Jonathon frowned. How much time had he lost to the black pain? A few hours? Days? He shook his head to clear his mind. 'Tomorrow.'

'He has hit his head, Clarissa, and raves. A good wife knows to allow these indiscretions. Men are like that,' his stepmother said. 'Jonny is lucky to be alive, to be given a second chance. I pray he makes a better fist of it.'

'But this Louisa? I will not have her here. This is my house! I forbid it! He is not allowed to be in love with her!'

'He will forget her. She is nothing. A trollop who had ideas bigger than her station.' His stepmother snapped her fingers. 'Patience and fortitude will win the day, my dear. Remember that and he will always come back to you.'

Jonathon summoned the last of his strength. Forget

Louisa? Never. Louisa was his life. His lodestar. 'Find Louisa.'

'Rest, my darling, later.'

Jonathon searched his memory and met the heavy curtain of blackness. Something had happened to Louisa. Dead? Injured? His fault? Pain shot through him as Jonathon rejected the notion. She had left. They had quarrelled and she had refused to come with him in the curricle, said that he drove too fast. So he had driven the horses faster to show her. 'Clarissa, fetch Louisa to me. Now.'

Clarissa backed away and glanced over her shoulder. 'She is not here. I don't know where she is. But I promise I will see you back to health, Jonathon. Then…then you can find her if you wish.'

'Find her!' He bit his lip and pain pounded on his lungs and skull. 'Please.'

'Jonathon,' his stepmother said in her brisk voice, 'Louisa Sibson is not coming. Not now. Not ever. Clarissa will nurse you back to health.'

'Never?' Jonathon searched his memory. Had he gone back and insisted that Louisa come with him? He had wanted to. Louisa hadn't been in the curricle when it had overturned, had she? Every breath was fire and the pain in his head screamed worse than ever. He felt the memory of the crash slip away from him and become lost. 'Was she in the curricle? Clarissa, you would not lie to me. Did I kill her?'

Clarissa turned away, sobbing, unable to meet his eyes.

'No one is lying, Jonny,' his stepmother said with great precision.

'Venetia, where is Louisa? What has happened to her?'

'She has gone for ever from our lives, Jonny. You had to indulge in your needs and to go against my advice.'

'Dead.'

His stepmother was silent for a long moment. 'You will not see her again. Jonathon, you were spared. No one but a fool would have left a cart on a blind bend.'

Louisa had died in the accident. His stepmother had admitted it in that roundabout way of hers. The knowledge hammered against his chest. The one person in the world he loved, that bright shining girl, dead. He had sworn to protect her, but instead he had destroyed her.

'It would have been better if we'd never met.'

'You can't turn back the hands of time, Jonny.' His stepmother gave him a fierce look. 'You can only go forwards. It was providence that led you here to Clarissa's. If the farm manager had not found you, I shudder to think.' She put a cool hand on his shoulder. 'You have everything to live for.'

Jonathon collapsed against the linen-covered pillows and willed the darkness to take him to Louisa. His body refused to die.

He turned his head and met his stepmother's icy gaze. 'You are wrong, Venetia. Without Louisa, I am beyond redemption.'

# Chapter One

*Four years later, August 1837—Newcastle upon Tyne*

'Miss Daphne Elliot.' The three words were said in a warm masculine voice, but they were enough to send an ice-cold chill down Louisa Sibson's spine.

Her hand froze on the soft folds of Miss Daphne Elliot's woollen shawl. Louisa kept her gaze downcast and willed the stranger to go. She could not be so unlucky as to encounter Jonathon Ponsby-Smythe here. In Newcastle. He was an *habitué* of London clubs, fashionable salons and Almack's, not provincial concerts with second-rate singers. Louisa forced the breath into her lungs. This man, this friend of Miss Daphne's nephew who had sponsored the concert was someone else. This man was not the man who had destroyed her life. And she was no longer the same naïve girl who believed a man's whispered endearments of eternal love.

Dimly she heard Miss Daphne answer with delight

in her elderly voice and the low rich voice answer again.
And she knew her luck in England remained resolutely
poor.

Louisa concentrated on the shawl.

What was the proper etiquette for greeting the man
who had taken your innocence and destroyed your girlish dreams? Particularly when one of the women most
responsible for giving her a new life was enthusiastically
greeting him?

And, most importantly, how had she missed his name
as one of the sponsors of the Three Choirs concerts?

Louisa weighed her options. Cutting him dead would
be the height of rudeness and would distress Miss
Daphne no end. Neither could she turn and flee. There
had to be a solution, but her mind refused to offer it.

'Miss Sibson, are you quite the thing?' Lord Furniss,
Miss Daphne's nephew, asked. Before Louisa could
reply, Lord Furniss swallowed her hand in his gigan-
tic paw. 'I can see from a glance something is wrong.
You have gone pale. It is not allowed to have a beauty
fainting.'

Louisa withdrew her hand and looked up into Lord
Furniss's broad genial face. 'There is little danger. I leave
the fainting and attacks of vapours to the débutantes.
They are the experts in these matters, after all.'

'As ever, your wit slays me, Miss Sibson, but you
do not have to be brave.' Lord Furniss's ruddy cheek
became a deeper shade of red. He cleared his throat.
'Chesterholm, we shall have to leave you. The esteemed
Miss Sibson protests far too much. She is unwell.'

'My health is robust.' Louisa planted her feet more

firmly, and her gaze locked with the clear blue-green of her worst nightmare, and her forbidden dream.

'How delightful to meet you again, *Miss Louisa Sibson.*' He held out his well-manicured hand. It was then that she knew her prayers were destined to remain for ever unanswered. 'A highly unexpected occurrence.'

Louisa twisted Miss Daphne's shawl about her fingers. By rights, he should have grown fat. Or have his face be marked with scars, something to show his wickedness. However, Jonathon Ponsby-Smythe's countenance was as fair as ever—golden brown hair contrasting with intense blue-green eyes. Once she had thought his face with its dimple in the chin angelic, but now she could see the sardonic twist and the hardness that lurked behind the smile, the heartless seducer of women.

*Gentlemen must be allowed their little indiscretions as long as they do not interfere with the household.* She could remember Mrs Ponsby-Smythe's precise intonation as Jonathon's stepmother explained why she was dismissing Louisa immediately without reference, and not allowing her to wait for Jonathon's return.

Louisa took another steady breath and squared her shoulders. She had found her solution. She would get through this unasked-for encounter with dignity and poise. She would demonstrate to him and the rest of the world that he meant nothing to her. She had learnt from her years in Italy. Let him prey on some other gauche governess who might believe his lies. She was now a woman of means, with standing and a good reputation.

'Mr Ponsby-Smythe.' Louisa inclined her head. Even

now, a traitorous part of her remembered how his fingers had skimmed along her skin, sending quivers of delight throughout her as they bid each other goodbye despite the quarrel. Naïvely she had thought he offered the world, and instead it was one night. For when does the first-born son marry a governess with no family, except in a fairy tale?

'Lord Chesterholm, Louisa,' Miss Daphne squeaked, her withered cheeks flushed an excited pink. 'You have not been paying attention. Young Jonathon has become the fourth Baron of Chesterholm and changed his name to Fanshaw out of respect to his late uncle. *Chesterholm,* Louisa.'

Louisa crossed her arms and mentally kicked herself. Such a simple thing as a name change. She had not even considered the possibility when she quickly scanned the list of subscribers to the concert. If she had known… she'd have invented a dozen reasons why she could not attend the concert and why she had to leave for Sorrento immediately, even if Miss Daphne had not finished her sentimental journey back to her childhood haunts. 'Why did you change your name, Lord *Chesterholm*?'

'It was my late great-uncle's wish. He wanted his name to carry on.' An arrogant smile crossed his features. 'It suited me to please him, Miss Sibson.'

'Why should the reason matter?' Miss Daphne asked, bewilderment in her tone. 'You are being very bold, Louisa, my girl, with a man you have barely met. Are you certain that you are not sickening? I have never seen you act this way before.'

'Hasn't the esteemed Miss Sibson confided about our friendship? That was remiss of her.' Jonathon's blue-green eyes burned with a fierce light as his fingers captured her hand and brought it to his lips. '*Miss* Sibson and I are acquainted. Old friends. Is that not true, *Louisa*?'

Even after all this time, a warm pulse went through her as he used her first name, rolling it slightly on his tongue and making it sound like no one else had ever done. Louisa ruthlessly quashed the feeling.

'I had the pleasure of *teaching* Lord Chesterholm's younger sister several years ago…before I departed for Italy.'

'That is true. You were my sister's governess, among other things.' His fingers tightened and caressed the soft inside of her wrist where her glove gapped.

Louisa tugged at her hand. Surely he had to let her go. It was beyond the bounds of all propriety. He knew why she had left. The coward. He had not even bothered to answer her letters—not the one after the dismissal or the other even more desperate one four months later informing him of her delicate condition. Instead he had left the task of irrevocably severing relations to his stepmother.

She could hear Venetia Ponsby-Smythe's cut-glass tones echoing down the years. Her relationship with Jonathon was a misalliance. Mrs Ponsby-Smythe daily expected the announcement of her stepson's forthcoming marriage to the Honourable Clarissa Newton to whom he had been betrothed since they were in the cradle. Louisa and the child she carried must stand aside and forge a new life…for the good of everyone. Venetia Ponsby-Smythe had said that while she sympathised with Louisa's plight, such things happened when women behaved lewdly. The knowledge of a child would not bring him back, Mrs Ponsby-Smythe had advised, and could Louisa even prove the babe she said she carried was Jonny's. Then, when Louisa had been ready to storm out, Venetia Ponsby-Smythe had waved her hand and offered to provide Louisa passage to Italy as she did feel responsible for her stepson ruining one of her former employees. Her one condition was that Louisa should never return, never contact her again. Faced with starvation, Louisa had accepted the offer with tearful gratitude. She had even kissed the woman's hand.

'Fancy you knowing Aunt Daphne's delightful friend, Chesterholm.' Lord Furniss's voice rang out, recalling her to the present. 'Who'd have supposed it? Miss Sibson, you have been keeping secrets from me.'

'Miss Sibson keeps her secrets very well.' Jonathon's eyes pinned her. 'Some day, Miss Sibson, you must tell me how one can rise from the dead. I visited your grave not more than three months ago.'

Miss Daphne and Lord Furniss exchanged shocked glances as the entire Assembly Hall fell silent. Louisa wanted to sink down beneath the floorboards and hide. Everyone was looking at her as if this mess was somehow her fault.

Dead? A gravestone with her name? Louisa fought against a wave of dizziness. She had suffered a sort of death. She had even forbidden her friend Daisy Milton to tell Jonathon where she was if he should ever ask. But it was not what Jonathon meant. He had thought her dead. In the ground. Buried.

'But you are gravely mistaken, Chesterholm. Miss Sibson is happily very much alive,' Lord Furniss boomed into the silent void. 'She nursed my late great-aunt through her last illness. She is a pillar of strength to Aunt Daphne. Words fail me to think of her dead. Who could have been so cruel as to give you misinformation? You must have had the wrong person.'

As Lord Furniss finished, suddenly the room was filled with noise.

Louisa shot Lord Furniss an admiring glance. He had taken her part. The tiny gesture meant so much. She was far from alone. She had friends.

'Rumours of Miss Sibson's demise appear to be with-out foundation,' Jonathon said in a clipped tone. 'They are to be regretted.'

'I remain as I always have been—alive,' she said through gritted teeth. 'I know nothing of a gravestone. It must belong to someone else.'

'Nevertheless, it is a surprise.'

'I trust a welcome surprise,' Miss Daphne said, flut-tering her fan. 'Louisa is such a treasure. My sister looked on her as the daughter she never had.'

'I had not expected to see Miss Sibson again in this lifetime.' His eyes slowly examined her from the top of her carefully constructed crown of copper-brown plaits to the bottom of her mauve-silk evening gown, slowly, as if mentally taking off each garment.

Louisa fought against the rising tide of heat. She was over him. Every time she woke at night with the memory of their passion lingering in her brain, she gave the same promise—Jonathon meant nothing to her and her rules guarded her reputation. Never again would she be that impetuous woman who was so desperate for love that she believed a rake's promise of love was for ever.

'Nor I you, Lord Chesterholm.' She graciously inclined her head. Two could play at this game. The rules for winning were simple—icy politeness and never to allow any of her inner turmoil to show.

'Four years, Louisa,' he said in that slow seductive voice of his, the one which even now made warm tingles run along her spine. 'Where did you hide?'

With an effort, Louisa closed that particular door of her memory and concentrated on filling her lungs with life-giving air.

The woman she had once been was dead. Long live the reborn Louisa—the one who believed in schedules and rules, rather than following her desires. Jonathon—indeed none of the Ponsby-Smythes with their smug words and self-satisfied manner—had any power over her. This time she had money and a position of sorts in society, maybe not as grand as the one she had dreamt of in those halcyon days but it was one she had on her own merit and one she would keep as long she remembered the rules of conduct.

She tugged one last time and he let her go with such suddenness that she had to take a step backwards. A faint smile touched his lips. He had done it on purpose and was enjoying her discomfort. 'In some ways, Lord Chesterholm, it has been but a moment, but in others a lifetime.'

'You never speak, Louisa, about your past,' Miss Daphne said, putting a frail hand on Louisa's shoulder and looking at her with faintly accusatory eyes. Louisa shifted uncomfortably. The last thing she wanted was to cause Miss Daphne distress. 'I had no idea you were friendly with the Ponsby-Smythes. Young Jonathon's mother was the only niece of Arthur Fanshaw, the late Lord Chesterholm. Did Mattie know? She would have been very interested, I am sure.'

'Did you offer references, Miss Sibson?' Jonathon asked with an arrogant curl of his lip. 'Or was it a little detail you neglected, Louisa? Miss Sibson was never very good on details.'

'Your sister, Miss Daphne, was always considered an excellent judge of character. She interviewed me and was satisfied. More than satisfied.' Louisa ignored Jonathon's barb. She knew what game he was playing— trying to drive a wedge between her and Miss Daphne. Not content with ruining her once, he wanted to ruin her again. Hopefully Miss Daphne was not suddenly going to become difficult and demand particulars. Here. In public. The last thing Louisa desired was a reliving of her dismissal for improper behaviour with the very reason towering over her.

'Mattie...yes, she had an instinct for character. One I sadly lack. I trusted her judgement on such things.' Miss Daphne ducked her head like a child, her grey ringlets hanging in submission.

Louisa's heart squeezed. She had been far too quick to judge. Miss Daphne had a kind heart, far kinder than most people's. While Miss Mattie knew about the failed love affair and its aftermath, Louisa had never confided the full story to Miss Daphne. Obviously Miss Mattie had done as she had promised and kept the confidence. The thought made Louisa miss the elderly lady with her vinegar tongue all the more.

'You have been in Italy,' Jonathon said, his lips becoming a thin white line.

'Yes, Italy. Sorrento, in the Kingdom of Two Sicilies, to be precise.' Louisa fixed a polite smile. The next round in the match had begun. Italy had been his step-mother's idea of precisely the right place for an incon-venient governess in a delicate condition to go. Within moments of Louisa agreeing, Mrs Ponsby-Smythe had produced a ticket for the mail coach and one for a packet leaving London and bound for Naples. And Venetia Ponsby-Smythe had been correct. Eventually Louisa had found a far better life than in the gutters of Warwick. 'The air there has been more conducive to my health than Warwickshire's.'

'And now you have returned. Is England to have the benefit of your company for long?'

'I have returned to the north-east. Not to Warwick-shire. And only temporarily. Miss Daphne wished to visit those places she remembered from her childhood.' Louisa swallowed hard, hating the way her breath caught in her throat. She curled her hand about her fan and concentrated on taking calming breaths. 'You must remember me to your sister, Margaret. When will she have her first Season?'

'Next Season, if my stepmother gets her wish.'

Louisa took another deep breath. Icy politeness, talk-ing about inconsequential acquaintances. But equally she had to know—what had happened to her rival. Had he married her? 'And Clarissa Newton?'

'We married a year after you…disappeared,' Jona-thon said in a measured tone. 'Clarissa nursed me back to health and everyone agreed that it was the correct thing to do. Chesterholm needed an heir.'

They had married. Mrs Ponsby-Smythe had told the

truth. Louisa's insides churned as she forced her back to be ramrod straight. Clarissa had been everything that she was not—well connected, accomplished and possessing looks that were in fashion. With the little misalliance out of the way, he had married Clarissa, no doubt in a huge wedding with all the *ton* in attendance.

'And is Lady Chesterholm with you?' Miss Daphne asked.

'Regretfully, Miss Elliot, Lady Chesterholm died eighteen months ago. She contracted a fever and died hours after giving birth.' Jonathon inclined his head and his face showed genuine sorrow.

*Died.* Louisa's retort withered on her lips. Clarissa was dead. Despite everything that Clarissa had done, all the petty remarks about governesses getting above their stations and all the boasting about how she'd rule the *ton* as Jonathon's wife and how they had been betrothed in the cradle, Louisa had never wished for the woman's death.

'I am sorry for your loss,' she whispered.

'As am I,' Miss Daphne said, putting a handkerchief to her eyes. 'It is so tragic when a young woman loses her life in childbirth.'

Louisa silently put the shawl about Miss Daphne's shoulders. If she was very lucky, she would be able to escort Miss Daphne home now. Miss Daphne loved a good weep. This night and her meeting with Lord Chesterholm would be behind her. Tonight demonstrated how easily she could lose everything she held dear if she failed to keep to her rules.

'And now, my dear lady, it is my turn to offer condolences.' Jonathon captured Miss Daphne's hand, and prevented Louisa from leading her off. 'Lord Furniss informs me that your sister recently died. You both visited Furniss several times at Eton for the Montem celebrations.'

'How good you are.' Miss Daphne's eyes shimmered. 'We always brought iced buns. They were Rupert's favourite.'

'My dear mama always forbade them as she thought it bad for my figure,' Lord Furniss said, puffing up his chest. 'But there is something glorious about an iced bun—sugar on the top and soft dough underneath.'

'And now you have returned to the land of your birth, Miss Elliot,' Jonathon said.

Louisa frowned, trying to work out why Jonathon was determined to prolong the painful encounter. Silently she willed him to give up and go.

'For a fleeting visit. Dear Louisa wishes to return home as soon as possible.'

'I am hoping to persuade them both to stay in the country,' Lord Furniss said, reaching for Louisa's hand.

Louisa avoided it. Tomorrow, she promised silently, tomorrow she would check the steamship timetable.

'I regret, Lord Furniss, our schedule…' Louisa said, inclining her head.

'How long are you here, Miss Elliot?'

'Louisa took charge of all the arrangements, even though England holds few good memories for her. She has a wonderful talent for scheduling and making sure all the details are sorted.' Miss Daphne gave a tremulous smile. 'But then you know Louisa, how kind she is and what a wonderful eye for detail she possesses.'

'Yes, I do know her.' His eyes shone like cold emeralds. 'I will take your word for her kindness. And I'm pleased to learn her eye for detail has improved.'

Louisa flinched. Once he had proclaimed her the kindest of women and told her that he'd love her until he died. She refused to let his words have any lasting sting. They were only words. And she wanted nothing from him. She needed nothing.

'I think it might be best if I checked on the carriage, Miss Daphne. We would not want to put the schedule in jeopardy.' Without giving Miss Daphne a chance to answer, Louisa marched away, clinging to the remnants of her temper. It was better to leave than to fight.

'Don't forget my shawl…Louisa.' An elderly voice floated out over the crowd. 'You promised…'

Jonathon watched the swinging mauve skirt of the very much alive Louisa Sibson disappearing into the crowd. He wanted to shake her insolent shoulders for vanishing in the way she had. For years, he had thought her dead, religiously visiting her supposed grave on the anniversary of her death, but she was alive and far more beautiful than his last memory of her.

Why had his stepmother allowed him to think Louisa was dead? That he had accidentally killed her? Even with his stepmother's legendary efficiency she could not have achieved the deception without Louisa's active co-operation. Louisa had to have participated in the deception.

For months he had lain, staring at the white walls of the Newtons' sickroom, waiting to heal, willing his body to prove the doctors wrong and to walk again. And the first thing he had done was to walk to Louisa's supposed grave. He had taken such pride in standing in that windswept graveyard, solemnly vowing to live his life as she would have wanted him to. But the entire thing had been a monstrous lie.

Now, he wanted answers, answers from the one person who could give them—Louisa. She was not going to find it that easy to dismiss him. With a few quick strides, he reached Louisa and caught her by the elbow. 'Oh, no, no more disappearing tricks. You are staying.'

'What do you think you are doing, Lord Chester-holm? Unhand me!' Louisa pulled away from his grip, but Jonathon tightened his hold. 'Jonathon, please, people are beginning to stare! For propriety's sake!'

'We are going to have a conversation, Louisa,' he said through gritted teeth as white-hot anger seethed through him. 'One we should have had four years ago. We can have it here in this public space or we go into one of the private card rooms, but we will speak. You may begin by explaining why you faked your death.'

'I have nothing to say to you!'

'But I have things to say to you.' Jonathon kept a leash on his temper. For years he had thought about what he would have said to her if he had had one more chance.

The woman had never been dead. She had left, leaving others to heal him and his broken heart. And now she had returned, more desirable than ever. The innocent promise of four years ago had blossomed into a sensuous combination of rich, autumn-red hair, amber eyes and dusty-rose lips—all staring provocatively up at him. 'And you will listen.'

Without giving her a chance to protest further, he led

her to a small room that was often used for card games when balls were given and shut the door with a distinct click, then turned to face his adversary.

She crossed her arms and her amber eyes blazed with fury. 'You have precisely two minutes before I scream, Lord Chesterholm. We finished a long time ago.'

'You may have finished, but you neglected to inform me personally.'

Her mouth opened and shut several times. 'Your step-mother served as your emissary. The Kingdom of Two Sicilies was her suggestion. She paid for my passage. It was a chance for me to start again.'

A red mist settled on Jonathon. 'You asked my step-mother to help you rebuild your life?'

'She was my employer. What reason did she have to lie? There was nothing for me here, as she so help-fully pointed out. You were engaged. I was an unwanted reminder.' Her crown of auburn hair quivered with indig-nation. 'I shall leave now. Miss Daphne will worry.'

'Furniss can guard his aunt.' Jonathon held up his hand, stopping her. Louisa was going to stay and they would speak under his terms, not hers. 'Why did you return to England?'

'To allow Miss Daphne to visit the places of her youth. She wants to see them one last time.' Her lips turned up in a false smile. 'You need not worry. I intend to depart from these shores as quickly as possible. England is anathema to me.'

'A pity. And what charms does Italy hold?' He looked her up and down, noting how she no longer tried to hide behind demure high-necked gowns but chose instead to wear a *décolleté* gown that barely skimmed her breasts, proclaiming she was a woman of the world instead of the naïve and somewhat gauche governess who blushed so charmingly. 'For a woman like you.'

The beauty-spot mole in the corner of her mouth flashed. 'A marriage proposal. To a baronet. Think of that. Sir Francis Walsham wishes to marry me, honourably, with a large church wedding.' She snapped her fingers. 'I have rebuilt my life, Jonathon. Give my regards to your stepmother. Her instincts were correct. Italy has been far better to me than England ever was.'

'When rebuilding anything, Louisa, you should have a care that the foundations are not made on sand.'

A crease appeared between her perfectly arched brows and for the first time, she appeared less certain. 'You have lost me, Jonathon.'

'You admire plain speaking.'

'Wherever possible.' A smug smile crossed her lips. She tilted her head upwards. She believed she'd won.

Jonathon waited, savouring the moment.

'Unlike some I could mention, I am an admirer of the unvarnished truth,' she said with absolute assurance.

'Your besotted beau's proposal might prove difficult to accept.'

Her eyes narrowed and her smile trembled. 'Why?'

Jonathon leant forwards, his breath brushing her cheek. 'I have a prior claim.'

# *Chapter Two*

*A prior claim*. Claim to what? To her? To her hand, or her body? Louisa stared openmouthed at Jonathon as the words echoed around her brain. His hooded eyes held a sensuous promise and his lips were a mere turn of her head away.

She stumbled backwards, away from him, away from his body, narrowly missing a gilt-edged chair.

Louisa put out a steadying hand and grasped its back, shifting the chair so it was between her and Jonathon. She attempted to get her emotions under control. Emotions and dreams were the enemy. They had destroyed her before. They could again. Once she had longed to be married to him and to belong body and soul to him. She had considered them already married, soul mates, and had disregarded all the warnings and well-meant advice to wait until the wedding night. She had mistaken a young man's lust for all-conquering love and had paid a heavy price. But she had finished paying, years ago.

'Do you agree I have a prior claim, Louisa?' His

hands closed over hers, pressing them against the gilt-edged wood.

'Words said in jest can destroy a person's reputation, Lord Chesterholm.' Louisa gave a light laugh to show that his betrayal no longer had the power to hurt. It was in the past and she no longer pined for him or her girlish fantasies. She had rebuilt her life on rock-solid foundations. She had learnt from her mistakes. Her heart might bear scars, but it was whole and safe.

'I am deadly serious.' He released her hands and moved the chair so it sat squarely between them. 'Perhaps you chose to disregard such things. But will your intended? Does he know that you bolt? Does he know you are promised to another?'

'Hardly promised. What was between us ended years ago.'

'We were engaged, Louisa,' his voice purred. 'We were as close as a man and woman could be, but forgive me—when did you sever our relationship?'

*Just after your stepmother informed me you were engaged to another woman, and had been promised to her for months before. You seduced me when you were not free.* Louisa kept her breathing steady and wished she had not done her laces up so tightly. 'Your memory is indeed failing. You never returned.'

'I was in an accident. It was nine months before I could walk any distance, before I was released from my sickroom.' An ironic smile played on his full lips. 'Forgive me for being remiss, but then I was otherwise occupied—attempting to survive.'

'Nobody told me,' Louisa whispered.

'Did you ever ask?' His words were intended to cut, but instead they gave her strength.

She pushed away from the chair and drew herself up to her full height, regretting that she only reached his chin. 'I am a respectable person. I always have been, despite what passed between us. Despite your stepmother's dismissal for loose morals.'

The covered tables and gilt-edged chairs with their air of north-east respectability seemed to leer at her and mock her—as if they too knew about her lapse and how, in her headlong rush towards matrimony, she had ruined her prospects for ever. And no matter what happened in this room, society would deem it all her fault and turn its collective back, just as it had done the last time.

'You had a choice, Louisa. You knew my habits, my friends, yet you contacted not a single one.'

'And risk further humiliation?' Louisa gave a strangled laugh. Even the innocent girl she had been knew the sort of company he kept and how women were passed around like gaily wrapped parcels. She had had their child to think of. No child of hers was going to be abandoned in a foundling home while she warmed another man's bed. 'I think not, sir.'

'And do your swains know about your past? Did Miss Elliot?'

'Do not threaten me, Lord Chesterholm. I have paid for my sins.'

'Surely you know me better than that.' He brushed an imaginary piece of dust from his cuff. 'I never threaten. I make promises and I always keep my promises.'

'And that is supposed to make me quake in my evening slippers?' she asked scornfully.

'You may do as you like—go dance around St Nicholas's church in your petticoat if it pleases you, but answer my question. Why did you conspire to fake your death?'

'You should be careful of your accusations. I have never abandoned anyone, nor have I ever pretended to be anything but alive.' Louisa gripped her reticule tighter. Dance about St Nicholas's church dressed only in her petticoats? The man was insupportable. 'Simply repeating lies over and over does not make them suddenly become the truth.'

'I never lie. Can I be held to blame if people choose to misinterpret my words?' A muscle tightened in his jaw and Louisa knew she had scored a hit.

Once she had readily believed the words that had tripped off his tongue. *I will love you for ever, Louisa. You are the only woman in the world for me. You are my wife in truth. What is a licence but a piece of paper? I will return. I know how to handle the ribbons of a curricle. I will always find you. Your life will be one of luxury.* Instead she had discovered the humiliation and degradation of trying to find work without a reference and what it was like to be pregnant without a friend to turn to. It was then she had stopped believing in happily-ever-afters.

'Piecrust promises, then—easily made and easily broken. Your servant, Lord Chesterholm, but there is no claim on either's part.' Her self-control amazed her, but he did not deserve to know of her heartbreak or the baby. She had decided that long ago. She had her pride. She gave a perfunctory curtsy. 'You will forgive me, but I have other business to attend to.'

He took a step towards her, brushing aside the chair. It fell to the ground with a thump. 'In the village church-yard where you grew up, there is a stone that bears your name. I have placed flowers there every year on the anniversary of your death.'

'Your stepmother engineered my disappearance, as you call it.' Louisa retreated and found herself pinned between the table, a pile of two chairs and the wall. 'Why would I seek a life of shame? How could I stay after I had been dismissed? A governess has little choice in such matters.'

The shadows deepened in Jonathon's eyes and his advance stopped. There was the faint hint of hesitation in his mouth as if he had never suspected his stepmother might do something like that. Louisa's stomach lurched. He did know. He had to have known what Mrs Ponsby-Smythe had done, what she was capable of doing. A tiny whisper resounded in the back of Louisa's brain—perhaps he hadn't known.

She quashed it.

'I was an innocent, Jonathon. You were infinitely more experienced.' She paused and controlled the faint tremor in her voice. 'You knew what you were doing. I had no idea, but I knew you were disappointed in me. We quarrelled. You broke with me. It was a late summer romance and then the chill winds of autumn came.'

'You are wrong, Louisa, very wrong.' Jonathon banged his fists together and took a step towards her, his face contorting in anger. 'I wanted you.'

'You may wish to live in fantasy worlds, Lord Chesterholm, but mine is solidly grounded in reality.' She kept her voice steady and her eyes on a spot somewhere over his right shoulder. Dignity and hard-won poise would see her through this ordeal, rather than weeping uncontrollably or shouting. 'You discarded me because I no longer excited you.'

A faint smile tugged at his mouth. 'Interesting—that is not my recollection of the night. Untried, yes, but passionate and willing to learn.'

Louisa focused on the dust-sheeted furniture, forced herself to remember the awful words Venetia Ponsby-Smythe had said when Louisa had proudly boasted that she would marry Jonathon. 'You left your stepmother to sort out the mess just as she had sorted out every other scrape from the Earl's wife to the little dancing girl at Covent Garden.'

'Which Earl's wife? What dancing girl from Covent Garden?' Jonathon tilted his head to one side, his lips a firm white line. 'What fustian nonsense are you spouting, Louisa? Why would I ever ask Venetia to do something like that?'

'The women that your stepmother had to pay off. She showed me a list of your women...'

Jonathon's mouth dropped open and his eyes were wide with disbelief and horror. The expression vanished in an instant. He slammed his fists together. 'I have *never* asked for any assistance from anyone in my family with managing my women, as you call them. I never would.'

'You married another woman, a woman who was far more acceptable to your family. You were engaged to her when you made love to me,' Louisa continued on, refusing to allow him and this pretended outrage to distract her. 'You never looked for me.'

'One does not look for the dead amongst the living, Louisa. Clarissa and I only became engaged after I thought you were dead,' he said slowly, running his hand through his hair. A small shiver ran down her spine. He was serious. He had thought her dead. 'As much as I wanted to believe otherwise, I thought you dead—a fact you have not until now bothered to correct.'

'I refuse to dignify that remark with an answer.'

'What were you so frightened of that you had to disappear?' His voice held a new note, a plea for something. In many ways, it was worse than his anger. Anger she could react against. 'Did our love-making frighten you? There was so much passion between us.'

She gazed up at the ceiling, noticing the swirls and stains from the burning tallow candles. He was right in a way. She had been frightened, frightened of losing him, particularly after their bitter quarrel in the curricle as they had journeyed back to the house. Her cases had been waiting for her in the vestibule as Mrs Ponsby-Smythe had discovered her lie about her ill friend. And Jonathon had departed before she could ask for his help. Very quickly the enchanted afternoon and night had become a nightmare.

His stepmother had said the very words Louisa had half-expected to hear drip from Jonathon's lips on his return from his great-uncle's. *She had been a mere plaything and had served her purpose.*

A great weariness invaded Louisa's being. This battle was four years too late. Taunting him was beyond her. Venetia bore some of the blame, but she had put her past behind her.

'Your stepmother would have made a good general.

She leaves nothing to chance. And never gives any quarter to her enemies. Should haves and could haves serve no purpose. What was between us ended and you married another while I began my life again.' She smoothed the folds of her mauve silk gown, a small action, but one that served to remind her of her independence. Jonathon might threaten and bluster, but ultimately she would survive. 'Let me go, Jonathon. It is over between us.'

In the silence that followed, Louisa could hear the concertgoers moving around outside the room. A woman had lost a glove, another wanted to find her carriage, little snippets of ordinary conversations that reminded her there was another life out there, waiting for her.

He took a step towards her, his blue-green eyes flashed and his fingers flexed as if only through the greatest act of will-power did he refrain from wringing her neck. 'No, it is not over.'

'Four years ago we parted,' she said and hated the way her voice squeaked. She always promised herself that if they ever met she would be calm and collected. She would act as if nothing had happened and as if the grave in Sorrento did not exist because he had no right to know. And now there had to be a way of making him understand, of getting through to him before he did something that they both regretted. 'The girl I was, the young man you were…they are gone. Dead, if you like. Unwelcome memories.'

He stopped, fingers outstretched as if he had been about to capture her and pull her to him. A small traitorous part of her was disappointed. Louisa quickly silenced it. Jonathon Ponsby-Smythe, now Fanshaw, Lord Chesterholm, had played her for a fool four years ago. His touch might feature in her dreams, but on waking she remembered the aftermath.

'You are wrong, Louisa.' He lifted a hand and brushed her cheek, a butterfly touch, but one that sent pulses of warmth throughout her body. 'My memory of you is far from unwelcome.'

'I have put the sordid episode behind me. I suggest you do the same.'

She waited. If anything, his eyes glittered more dangerously. The silence threatened to press down on her soul. He had to believe her. All she had to do was to stick to her rules. They were simple and straightforward.

'The past has nothing to do with my future, Jonathon.' Louisa started to push past him, but he stepped in front of her, blocking the door. The cut of his evening coat made his shoulders appear broader than ever. 'Neither of us wants or desires a scandal. Society has rules for a purpose and I for one intend to keep them...this time.'

'But scandals can be enjoyable.'

Louisa ignored the sudden prickle of heat that coursed through her. It was simply a reminder of why Jonathon was dangerous. He lived and breathed sensuality in a way no man had before or since. In the intervening years she had not been tempted or felt one ounce of breathlessness. But now she spent a few moments in his company and the hot pounding of her blood started again. This time she was wise and mature and recognised it for what it was—a remembrance. She refused to give in.

'Remove yourself from the door and allow me to be about my business.'

His hand reached out and grasped her waist gently, but firmly enough to keep her there. The prickle of heat threatened to become a flame. Louisa concentrated on breathing slowly. She had survived such things before. Jonathon would be no different than the major who had had too much to drink at the Trasemeno hotel. Her rules had worked then. They would work now.

'About my business?' The lights in his eyes deepened. 'And what exactly is my business?'

She moved to the next stage. 'Unhand me, sir.'

'My hand is off you.' His fingers hovered above her waist, and somehow it was worse because her body ached to have the small caress. 'You are free to go.' He leant forwards so his forehead touched hers. 'But before you do, Louisa, do you think about what we experienced together? How your lips felt against mine? At night when you lie in bed?'

'Never,' Louisa breathed. Her heart thudded so loudly in her ears that she thought surely Jonathon must hear. It bothered her that she remained attracted to him, but that had always been her problem. Even the first time she had seen him, her pulse had beat faster. This was simply an echo from the past. Everything to do with being this close to a man for the first time since…since the last time she had been with Jonathon.

She swallowed hard and grasped her reticule to her bosom. It was not the same. She had changed. She knew the pain men were capable of inflicting on her soul. She knew why the rules existed. She had learnt her lesson well. 'You have vanished from my mind.'

'You were always a poor liar, Louisa.'

Before she had a chance to move away, he lowered his mouth and captured hers. The kiss was designed to evoke a response—small nibbles at her mouth, swiftly followed by a more lingering meeting as her lips gave way to temptation.

Louisa's backbone melted as small tongues of fire leapt from his hand to her skin. Her hair tumbled about her shoulders and she remembered how Jonathon had once run his hands through it, proclaiming it softer than silk and infinitely more precious. She knew she should stop, but her body luxuriated in his touch.

Abruptly he released her and she stumbled away from him.

'Is that the best you can do? Seek to dominate me with the physical?' Louisa automatically began to straighten her gown, but she knew her chest rose and fell far too fast. 'I never think about such things. They have vanished from my mind.'

A smug look appeared in his eyes. 'We are far from finished, Louisa. We have only just begun, and this time, it will end when I say it does.'

Louisa paused with her hand on the door. She gave him a quelling look. 'I decline your offer of marriage. We would not suit.'

'You should wait until you are asked, Louisa.' His face became all planes and shadows.

'Then I decline whatever you are offering.'

Louisa pulled the door open and slammed it behind her. Never again would she return to being that woman who melted at the slightest touch from Jonathon. That woman no longer existed. She had died when they had prised her baby daughter's lifeless body from her. Born too soon, the baby had failed to draw even a single breath. It had been a judgement from God and she would do well to remember that.

* * *

'I want this letter in the first post,' Jonathon said, handing the sealed note to his valet.

'Very good, my lord.' Thompson gave a bow and left Jonathon alone in the library of his Newcastle town house on Charlotte Square.

Jonathon swirled the untouched ruby port in his glass. His stepmother would come to Chesterholm and she would bring his half-sister Margaret. Before he confronted Venetia over Louisa, Jonathon wanted to make sure that Margaret could not be held as a hostage. If Venetia was prepared to lie about Louisa's death when he lay injured in order to further his relationship with Clarissa, Jonathon knew that she would not hesitate to arrange a marriage that Margaret might not desire. He had a duty towards his sister. Margaret deserved her chance to find love.

What to do about Louisa Sibson and her reappearance in his life? She denied the passion that had existed between them, but it was there, and this time she would stay until the passion burnt out.

Even the last few remaining coals in the fire mocked him, echoing the colour of Louisa's hair. She was here and alive, utterly unrepentant and utterly desirable. How many times had he longed for Louisa's return, if only for a few minutes, if only so he could whisper that he was sorry. He gave a wry smile. His nurse used to say it was never good to get what you wish for.

His mind returned to the early days after the accident when he had asked for Louisa to see if Clarissa's overly pat tale of woe had any substance. Clarissa had been there, competent and efficient, the perfect nurse, alongside Venetia. And each time he had asked, her frown had increased. He clearly remembered the exchange—why is he asking for that governess?—and his correcting shout—*my fiancée*. And his stepmother had patted Clarissa's arm and told her not to worry about the baggage before forcing more of the damned laudanum down his throat.

He reached forwards and gave the fire a stir, making the coals glow bright orange.

Louisa should have trusted him. What more could she have desired from him? What further proof had she wanted? He had asked her to marry him, to run away with him.

He tapped his fingers together. His late great-uncle was fond of quoting Eros's explanation of why he left Psyche—there can be no love without trust, but there can be desire—to say why he had chosen to be a bachelor. Jonathon had never understood the saying until now.

And what of her future plans? Her marriage plans? Did she love this baronet, Francis Walsham, whom she had dangled in front of his nose? Debrett's only listed a solitary name, a man old enough to be Louisa's grandfather, but wealthy. Had she ever kissed Walsham the way she kissed him? The very thought made him want to tear the man limb from limb.

Jonathon took another reflective sip of his port. And why had she returned to England if she intended on marrying? What was there for her here?

'Forgive the late-night interruption, Chesterholm, but you are my only hope.' Furniss burst into the library. 'My need is a matter of life and death.'

'How so?'

'Did you know tonight was the first time that I have seen Miss Sibson flustered? She nearly forgot her reticule in her haste to inform Aunt Daphne of her decision to go. Her reticule goes everywhere with her. Her lifeline, she calls it. Something has unnerved her. She plans to return to Sorrento as soon as she can find passage on a steamship.' Furniss put his hands to his head. 'This is bad, bad, bad. Miss Sibson is notorious for her schedules.'

Leaving. Running. From him or from her desires? But she would fail to escape. This time, he knew she was alive.

'And why should I be able to help you?' He gave a light laugh that sounded hollow to his ears. Furniss fancied himself in love with her. Jonathon ground his teeth. How many bloody admirers did Louisa have? 'I have no power over Miss Sibson's movements.'

'Aunt Daphne is here in the north-east to visit her childhood haunts.' Furniss's ruddy face became alight. 'Then she is returning to Sorrento where Miss Sibson plans to marry Sir Francis Walsham. Previously Miss Sibson promised to stay until Aunt Daphne was ready to go back to Italy.'

'You are making no sense, Furniss.' Jonathon forced his tone to be light as a surge of jealousy cut through him.

'I intend to marry Miss Sibson,' Furniss continued blithely on. 'I will have no chance if she returns to Sorrento and her baronet. Here, in England, I do.'

'You want to marry Miss Sibson? Has she agreed?' Jonathon stared at his friend, furious that Furniss had not bothered to confide in him. Tonight's farce could have been avoided.

'I am certain my late aunt would have approved. Why else would she have left Miss Sibson the money?'

'Why indeed? Perhaps she liked her.' Jonathon shook his head as a primitive urge filled him to proclaim that Louisa was his. Furniss was a far more dangerous rival than the far-off baronet. Furniss had youth and a genial manner on his side.

'You are my last hope.' Furniss settled down into the red armchair opposite and poured himself a glass of port. 'I thought and thought about how I could make them stay.'

'I knew Miss Sibson a long time ago.' Jonathon gave an exaggerated yawn. As if he would provide information to a rival! Furniss was on his own. 'I can provide no insight.'

'Not Miss Sibson. I know all about Louisa. We met months ago in Sorrento.' Furniss gave a little wave of his hand, missing the cut-glass decanter by a hair's breadth. 'I have devoted time to studying her, her ways and how her mind works. She keeps her cards close to her chest, but I think there must be some secret sorrow in her past. She always changes the subject.'

'You did?' Jonathon tightened his fingers about the glass as a white-hot rage shot through him. His friend had known Louisa was alive and had known for months. The time he had wasted. 'Why are you not engaged? You are both free.'

'There was my dear mama to think about.'

'What does your mother have to do with it?'

'Mama would put poison in Miss Sibson's tea if she

could. Mama only went to Sorrento because she was convinced Aunt Mattie was going to leave her fortune to her. In the event, she only received a few pieces of jewellery.' Furniss lowered his voice and glanced over his shoulder. 'Mama feels Miss Sibson exerted an undue influence on my late aunt.'

'Do you?'

'There are reasons why my father prefers to live at his club. Mama should never have made disparaging remarks about Aunt Mattie's cameos. It is her own fault she lost the inheritance. But, regardless, I will get no help from that quarter.'

'What does this have to do with me?'

'Your Uncle Arthur collected cameos. It came to me in the carriage and Aunt Daphne's eyes sparkled when she mentioned him. Perhaps there was a connection.'

'I can't help you, Furniss. I know of little connection between the Misses Elliots and Uncle Arthur. He did not hold women in very high standing.' Jonathon stared at the fire. Furniss was right. There had to be a way of keeping Louisa here, rather than letting her run to ground in Sorrento. 'But if I think of anything…'

'I knew you would help, Chesterholm.'

'I promise nothing.' Jonathon tapped a finger against his mouth. 'But Miss Sibson will not be going to Sorrento.'

# *Chapter Three*

'The concert was a splendid outing. I am so pleased Rupert suggested it. It was just the tonic. I do declare Rupert is far better away from his odious mother, don't you agree?' Miss Daphne said, while Louisa poured the late-night cups of hot chocolate. 'You are going to reconsider going back to Sorrento. Given encouragement, Rupert might… It would do my heart good to see you settled.'

'We have seen everything we came to England to see,' Louisa replied carefully. Tomorrow, she'd go and book their passage back. Marriage to anyone was not in her plans. Tomorrow, she would keep to the strict letter of her rules. Tomorrow she would remember what was important in her life—her future rather than her past. 'We have already spent longer in England than we planned.'

'But why the immense hurry? Only this morning, you appeared content to reside here a bit longer.'

'I have no idea what you are talking about, Miss Daphne.'

'Suddenly you are frightened of staying in England, Louisa. Why the change? There might be things I still wish to see. And my nephew's fascination with you grows. He is not up in Newcastle simply to pass the time of day with his old auntie. I predicted as much in Sorrento last spring.'

'You read too much into his attention.'

'And you read too little, my girl.'

Louisa regarded the chocolate pot for a long moment. One of her favourite Italian rituals was drinking hot chocolate just before bed. Miss Daphne preferred to have heaping spoonfuls of sugar, but Louisa liked it with the barest hint of sweetness. There was a certain something about the way the chocolate tasted—smooth and rich, reminding her to take joy in the small pleasures rather than looking for castles in the air.

Tonight all the hot chocolate did was serve to remind her how easily her present life could be destroyed if she was not very careful. She should never have kissed Jonathon back. She had grown beyond the naïve girl who thought his kisses showed his devotion.

'Nothing about England frightens me,' Louisa said, placing the silver spoon down. 'Sir Francis expects me to return and give him his answer.'

'Poppycock. That man is a puffed-up popinjay. Mattie could not abide him and his airs.'

'She respected his opinion.'

'On cameos.' Miss Daphne leant forwards. 'Sir Francis is closer to my age than yours. You want a young man to warm your bed, Louisa. Trust me on this.'

Louisa took a delicate sip of the chocolate. Miss Daphne seemed to have an uncanny way of knowing if there was an attraction between a couple. This evening's kiss had been about the past, an aberration, and had nothing to do with her present or, more importantly, her future. 'Nevertheless he expects an answer.'

'It was good to see young Jonathon looking so well.' Miss Daphne reached for the sugar bowl. 'Particularly after his accident a few years ago.'

Louisa froze. Until this evening she had not even realised that either of the Misses Elliots knew Jonathon.

'You know about the accident,' she said slowly.

'Mattie liked to keep up with the doings of Arthur Fanshaw and his relations, or at least she used to.' Miss Daphne gave her a sharp look. 'After you arrived, she had a new enthusiasm and rarely spoke of them. I was pleased at the time that she had finally come to terms with her heartache, but now I wonder.'

Louisa swallowed hard. Miss Mattie knew the full story about her past, but had never mentioned it. 'Curious. I…I had left the household before the accident. The first I heard of it was today. Miss Mattie never said anything to me.'

Miss Daphne set her cup down. 'Did Mattie know of your connection to the Ponsby-Smythes?'

Louisa raised her head and met the elderly lady's gaze full on. 'Yes, she did. I explained about my past when the doctor introduced us.'

'She will have had her reasons.' Miss Daphne frowned. 'Old scandals can return when you least expect it. People's memories are long, but I think you are being overly cautious, my dear. There is no need to go back to

Sorrento with your tail between your legs, and accept a proposal that you will regret for the rest of your life. We can keep to our new schedule.'

Louisa reached for the sugar bowl and added another spoon of sugar to her chocolate, before she carefully stirred. The result was far too sweet, but it helped to steady her nerves. 'Perhaps, but I do not want anyone to say that I was wicked.'

'Who would say that?'

'Your niece Honoria. She might say that I exerted undue influence on Miss Mattie before she died. I never knew Miss Mattie intended to leave me the money.' Louisa had never asked for the inheritance. It had come as a complete surprise. Both Miss Mattie and Louisa had shared a common fascination for all things ancient. Under Miss Mattie's tutelage, Louisa had become an expert on cameos and Miss Mattie had considered Louisa the best person to maintain her collection.

'Mattie loved you like a daughter. She also gave Honoria and that solicitor of hers a piece of her mind. You need not fear. You will have no problems from my niece. Mattie made sure of it. Mattie liked to take care of all contingencies and I trusted her.' Miss Daphne reached out her hand. 'But I think I deserve to know what happened with young Jonathon and make my own judgement. You want to run away from me because of it.'

'What happened to me, happened years ago. It is a depressingly old and familiar tale.' Louisa attempted a smile. 'I learnt my lesson. Believing a gentleman who promises the moon leads to disappointment. Miss Mattie agreed with me.'

'I want the story and not the aftermath. The aftermath I know. What passed between you all those years ago?'

Louisa swallowed hard, considering how to tell her tale. She had been an impressionable twenty years old and had thought her fairy tale was coming true—a handsome prince who married for love instead of duty. She should have seen the warning signs—the bored rake home from London, the seduction, and then her giving in and believing him when he had promised to return with a licence to marry her. Mrs Ponsby-Smythe had dismissed her without a character reference when rumours had reached her ears. Then, three months later, she had discovered that she was pregnant and had gone to Mrs Ponsby-Smythe's, searching for Jonathon, and had discovered about the impending marriage between Jonathon and Clarissa. When on the voyage to Naples, she had fallen ill with a high fever and the baby had been born too early—a beautiful little girl with translucent skin and jet-black hair, perfect in every way, except she never breathed. A large part of Louisa had died that day.

'Miss Daphne, he is part of my painful past, not my future.' Louisa put her hand over Miss Daphne's withered one as she finished the story. 'But you can see why I must return to Sorrento. I do not want any rumours to soil your skirts.'

'No, no, that would be giving into the pompous society prigs without a fight. You must stay.' Two pink spots appeared on Miss Daphne's withered cheeks. 'I can fight. I am unafraid and I stick by my true friends.'

'I know.' Louisa smiled back.

She valued Miss Daphne's friendship. It was why she had agreed to this trip and why she knew she would stay until Miss Daphne wanted to leave, but it was unfair to ask Miss Daphne to fight those sorts of battles at her age.

Louisa knew she had made a mistake, and some day she would stop paying for it. She leant forwards and banished tonight's kiss to the further reaches of her mind. Her reaction was an aberration brought on by suddenly seeing him again. Now that she was prepared, nothing like that would ever happen again.

'I am no fool and will not make that mistake again.'

'You are certain of that?' Miss Daphne's eyes took on a knowing gleam. 'I have some knowledge of human nature, Louisa, despite being a spinster. Men seldom look at women like Lord Chesterholm looked at *you* if they are uninterested.'

Louisa concentrated on gathering up the cups and saucers, arranging them neatly on the tray, ready for Jenkins, the butler, to remove it, rather than meeting Miss Daphne's knowing gaze. 'Miss Daphne, you are beginning to speculate. Speculation overheats the blood as Miss Mattie was wont to say. A woman can learn from her mistakes. I learnt from mine.'

'Hmm, but what are his intentions now? I have often found men with fascinating eyes can make a woman forget her lessons. And Lord Chesterholm has some of the most fascinating I have seen in many a long year.'

'Your eyesight must be mistaken.' Louisa focused on the cups and tried not to think about Jonathon's preposterous suggestion that he had a claim over her. She was not an object. Miss Daphne's eyes assessed her for a long moment but Louisa looked back unblinkingly. Finally Miss Daphne turned away.

'I accept you want to believe that, Louisa.'

'Thank you.'

'Please ask Cook to make iced buns for my At Home tomorrow.'

'Iced buns?' Louisa frowned. Miss Daphne never served teacakes at At Homes. The women had a cup of tea or coffee, but never iced buns. The whole procedure was shrouded in tradition, even on the hottest days in Sorrento.

'I am expecting callers, gentlemen callers. You did make an impression, Louisa, even if you wish to deny it.' Miss Daphne tapped the side of her nose. 'And if I am right, tomorrow's At Home will be highly productive. One must fight fire with fire. And then, Louisa, when it is all done, we can go home with our heads held high.'

Miss Daphne swept out of the room.

Louisa stared at the dregs of her hot chocolate, turning the conversation over in her mind. It made a sort of sickening sense. Miss Daphne expected Jonathon to appear alongside Lord Furniss. Louisa reached for the poker and gave the coal fire a final stir, sending an arch of flame into the air.

All she knew was that she could not remain in this drawing room like some scared rabbit, waiting for Jonathon to appear. She had stopped running years ago. Jonathon deserved to learn a lesson in civility and she looked forward to administering it. Miss Mattie would have approved.

'Miss Daphne,' Louisa called on her way to bed, 'the At Home will go splendidly tomorrow. I can feel it in my bones.'

The clock on the mantelpiece was only a few minutes away from twelve. Last night in bed, Louisa had dreaded that Jonathon would arrive bright and early, but now she dreaded that Miss Daphne's premonition was wrong. The sole callers were a Mrs Blandish and her two daughters.

Once the At Home was finished, she would confront Jonathon, corner him and force him to back down. He would cease to threaten her or her good name.

Louisa risked a breath and tried once again to concentrate on the conversation between Miss Daphne and the younger Miss Blandish, a conversation that appeared to have Miss Daphne enthralled beyond the bounds of propriety. The conversation appeared to revolve around Miss Nella Blandish's exploits with a gang of murderous thieves earlier that summer in Gilsland.

'And now my former governess, Miss Milton, is married to Viscount Ravensworth,' Miss Nella Blandish finished with a triumphal clap of her hands. 'I received the letter this very morning. And the entire marriage is thanks to me.'

'That is quite enough, Nella.' The elder Miss Blandish gave a prolonged sniff and toss of her blonde curls. She would be pretty if she did not look so bored with the proceedings. As it was, Miss Blandish reminded Louisa of Clarissa Newton—beautiful, but self-absorbed. 'We all understand that we were not invited to the wedding.'

'Lord Ravensworth procured a special licence, rather

than having a society wedding,' her mother said with a thoughtful expression. 'It is how a governess can come to marry a viscount. Personally I never thought Daisy Milton had it in her, but it turns out she was an heiress all along.'

'Daisy Milton?' Louisa said, sitting bolt upright, all thoughts of ending the visit fled. '*Daisy* Milton, who has a sister Felicity and a young niece?'

'That is correct. Do you have a connection?' Mrs Blandish raised her lorgnette and proceeded to minutely examine Louisa.

'Daisy Milton is an old friend of mine, but I had no idea that she was even engaged. Let alone entangled with jewel thieves.' Louisa put her hands to her mouth. She dreaded to think how Daisy had coped. Daisy had based her entire existence on keeping her reputation spotless. 'I look forward to receiving her latest letter.'

'Indeed,' Mrs Blandish said, settling herself against the sofa's cushions. Her tone implied that Daisy might not have time for such an acquaintance now that she had been elevated to a peerage.

'You do seem to be hearing news about your old acquaintances, Louisa dear,' Miss Daphne said with a twinkle in her eye. 'And here you thought you would not have any connection to Newcastle.'

'Do you know someone else?' Miss Blandish asked, suddenly becoming animated. 'Is it someone we know? Someone in society?'

Louisa inwardly seethed. If only Miss Daphne had had the sense to remain quiet. People had long memories and there was no telling what Mrs Blandish might have heard and how the tale had been twisted. Daisy might even have inadvertently told Louisa's tale. It bothered her that less than twenty-four hours after encountering Jonathon, she was tempted to return to that naïve girl who looked to others to solve her problems.

'I...I...' Louisa began. 'That is to say...'

Miss Elliot rocked back and forth as if she were no older than Miss Nella Blandish. 'The fourth Baron of Chesterholm did Louisa the honour of renewing his acquaintance last evening.'

'And were you good friends with just Lord Chesterholm or his late wife as well?' Miss Blandish asked with a faint curl of her lip. There was a sharp intake of breath from Miss Daphne and Miss Nella Blandish pretended a sudden interest in her glove buttons.

'Susan!' her mother exclaimed. 'Manners are the young lady's greatest asset.'

'I trust you do not think the question impertinent,' Miss Blandish said, her cheeks becoming stained cherry pink. 'You do understand why I ask it? If one is to be a débutante in London, one must be so careful.' She gave Nella Blandish a ferocious look. 'Particularly when one's sister is given to exaggeration. My sister's tongue nearly did for dear Miss Milton's prospects and I must not have the same happen to me.'

'I was a governess to Lord Chesterholm's sister,' Louisa replied with a clenched-jaw smile.

'And you have given up being a governess?' Mrs Blandish asked, leaning forwards, her eyes suddenly alight. 'We are currently between—'

An involuntary shudder went through Louisa. Mrs Blandish with her purple turban and self-righteous airs represented all that was wrong with being a governess.

She pitied anyone who had the misfortune to work for the woman. 'I found it more pleasant to be a companion.'

'But now, Louisa is a dear, dear friend.' Miss Daphne gave a broad smile. 'Louisa is far too modest about her prospects. My sister left her the bulk of her considerable fortune. She has no need to work. I daily expect a good match for her. My nephew…'

'I am sure you choose your friends well, Miss Elliot.' Miss Blandish began to wave her fan about and her eyes took on a hunted expression. 'No harm was intended. Mama is desperate to replace Miss Milton.'

'Miss Daphne and her late sister have never had problems distinguishing between true friends and hangers-on.' Louisa kept her head up. The Blandishes and their kind were the sort of creatures that Louisa despised— only concerned about appearances and quick to judge. Exactly like Clarissa Newton and her parents.

Before Miss Blandish had a chance to reply, Jenkins brought in a silver tray with two cream-coloured calling cards.

Miss Daphne took the cards and her face lit up, becoming twenty years younger. 'Mrs Blandish, my nephew, Viscount Furniss, and Lord Chesterholm have both come to pay their regards as well. What a shame you cannot extend your call.'

'Mama,' Miss Nella Blandish said, 'we ought to depart. Miss Milton always used to say—fifteen minutes and no longer.'

Mrs Blandish made a face like she had swallowed a particularly sour plum. 'Come along, girls. We have other business to attend to. The day is wasting.'

'But, Mama…' Miss Blandish wailed. 'Surely we can stay a moment longer. They are both…eligible.'

Louisa stared at the woman in astonishment.

'Has Susan become utterly devoid of sensibility?' Miss Nella Blandish asked in a stage whisper. 'The Viscountess Ravensworth would be horrified!'

'You will consider staying, Mrs Blandish,' Miss Daphne said, patting the sofa with a conspiratorial expression. 'Some rules were meant to be broken… particularly when faced with an unmarried daughter and two highly eligible titled men.'

Mrs Blandish hesitated, obviously debating the demands of propriety and the demands of matrimony. Matrimony won out and she settled herself back down on the sofa. 'I suppose we can impose on Miss Elliot and Miss Sibson for a few moments longer.'

Miss Daphne gave a beatific smile. Louisa narrowed her gaze. Miss Daphne had some scheme in mind and wanted the Blandish tribe to stay.

'I had hoped you would see reason,' Miss Daphne said. 'Miss Nella tells such *interesting* stories. My nephew loves a good tale.'

Louisa stood up and reached for her beaded reticule. She would find a way to speak to Jonathon in private. The letter was far too damning to be waved under his nose in public, particularly with the Blandishes hanging on every word. But she had cried her last tear over him four years ago.

Jonathon strode in, his frock coat flaring to emphasise the length of his legs. He surveyed the gathered throng, every inch the proud aristocrat from his immaculately tied stock to his butter-yellow gloves and silver-topped cane. Despite all the promises she had given throughout the years, her pulse beat faster as his eyes appeared to linger on her. Louisa turned her gaze to the reticule, going over each damning line of the letter in her mind, reminding her errant heart. He had ruined her life once. Only a fool would allow that to happen a second time and she was no fool.

'Lord Chesterholm, Rupert, what a delightful surprise,' Miss Daphne said, fluttering her fan. 'You must have guessed that Cook baked iced buns today.'

'I tempted him with a promise of your iced buns, Aunt,' Lord Furniss said with smug superiority in his voice. 'You always have iced buns at your At Homes. A shameful extravagance, but a welcome one. My mother would never approve.'

'Just like burning more than one candle?' Louisa asked.

'Precisely, Miss Sibson. You remember my mother's odd quirks.' Furniss flushed slightly and gave a decided nod. 'What my mother remains in ignorance of, she cannot condemn.'

'Dear Rupert,' Miss Daphne said, holding out her hand. 'You must meet the Blandishes. They were involved in the doings at Gilsland Spa. You know… when poor Edward Heritage died.'

'Charmed, I am sure.' Lord Furniss gave the briefest of nods towards the Blandishes, before capturing Louisa's hand and pressing it tightly. Spying Jonathon's glower, she resisted the temptation to pull away and allowed Lord Furniss to hold it for a half-minute more than was strictly proper. 'Now, my dear Miss Sibson, have you missed my company? Did you count the minutes?'

'Rupert!' Miss Daphne exclaimed and Lord Furniss dropped Louisa's hand.

'What is the temptation of the iced buns?' Miss Blandish asked, wrinkling her nose. 'I must confess to never having tried one.'

'You have never tried one! You have not lived until you have eaten iced buns,' Lord Furniss exclaimed. 'Is that not right, Miss Sibson? My aunt's iced buns are known far and wide. The mere memory of them from our days at Eton is why Chesterholm accompanied me here today.'

'And the pleasure of Miss Sibson's company. I found last night's exchange to be most enlightening.' Jonathon's blue-green gaze caught Louisa and held her. Everything else seemed to fade into insignificance.

A small tingle coursed through her. She forced her breath in and out of her lungs. Her reaction was a ghost from ages past. It had nothing to do with the infuriating man standing in front of her and everything to do with her younger, impossibly naïve self. 'Do you not agree, Miss Sibson?'

'Do we agree on anything?' Louisa pasted a smile on her face. 'We spoke of long-ago trifles that had no meaning then and even less now.'

'The value of intriguing conversation is immeasurable,' Jonathon returned smoothly as his eyes taunted her. 'One can learn such fascinating facts through a few moments of idle talk.'

'I think you are correct, Lord Chesterholm,' Mrs Blandish called out from where she sat, making it clear that she for one was following the entire exchange with interest. 'The pursuit of knowledge is always enlightening.'

Jonathon's lips turned upwards and his eyes took on a mischievous expression. 'Particularly when one chances upon old friends one had considered long departed from this world.'

'The way you talk, Lord Chesterholm—' Mrs Blandish's turban quivered with disapproval '—one might think Miss Sibson was dead when she stands before us, breathing and in good health. It would be monstrous to spread a tale like that about anyone.'

Jonathon's gaze travelled slowly down Louisa's form, his eyes lingering on her curves. His smile increased, becoming that special smile, the one which he had always given her just before kissing her. 'No, I agree she is very much alive. I had been wrongly informed.'

'And you are pleased with that,' Miss Daphne said.

'Did I ever say I wasn't?' He lifted an eyebrow. 'Simply surprised to discover the fact. It would appear I put my trust in the wrong people.'

'The notions some people entertain without bothering to check the facts.' Louisa clenched her reticule. She looked forward to seeing Jonathon's arrogant expression replaced with abject begging. And for each barb he sent her way, she'd make him beg a little longer.

'Are we going to discuss cooking utensils now, Miss Sibson?' He gave a slight flourish with his hand, daring her.

'Is that a pile of stones I see beside you, Lord Chesterholm? What is the state of your soul?'

'Utensils, stones and souls? I fear I cannot follow this

conversation,' Miss Blandish declared with a slight pout and shake of her golden curls.

'Honestly, Susan.' Miss Nella rolled her eyes heavenwards. 'A pot calling a kettle black. And from the Bible about someone without sin casting the first stone. Miss Sibson and Lord Chesterholm are having the most interesting quarrel. Now do be quiet and you might learn things.'

'It is a long-standing argument,' Louisa said quickly.

'Miss Sibson and I used to enjoy such arguments,' Jonathon said with a teasing glint in his eye. 'She was quite notorious for her skill with…words.'

'Miss Sibson was renowned for her wit in Sorrento as well,' Lord Furniss said, hooking his thumbs into his waistcoat. 'For my part, I always think of the right words precisely five minutes after I have left a gathering.'

'My poor tongue is feeble compared to the late Matilda Elliot's.' Louisa ducked her head as her insides churned. She had been wrong to give in to that impulse.

'Come, come, Miss Sibson, false modesty does you few favours,' Jonathon said. 'Your remarks were often repeated when you were in my stepmother's employ.'

Louisa fought against a tide of red heat that threatened to engulf her face and banished it. It was up to her whether or not Jonathon discomforted her. Her choice, not his. She gulped a breath of air and met his gaze full on. 'I rarely think about that time. It was far from the happiest period in my life.'

'Indeed.' His eyes became glacial ice. 'It is always pleasant to discover the truth of the situation. I regret that you spent one moment of unhappiness.'

Quietly Louisa consigned Jonathon Fanshaw to the hottest room in Hell. He regretted nothing. He had come here to torment her. He probably intended to make it his mission in life. Well, he'd learn that the new Louisa played by a different set of rules. 'It was a long time ago. I have put it from my mind.'

Jonathon lifted an eyebrow, as if he were inviting the next round. Louisa gave a slight shake of her head and turned her body towards Lord Furniss.

'What do you think of Newcastle, Lord Furniss? Does it meet with your expectations?'

'Very much so.' Lord Furniss made a low bow towards her. 'The day is brighter for having seen you and my aunt.'

Jonathon began to rapidly speak of the latest John Martin exhibition in London to Mrs Blandish, asking Lord Furniss to comment as he had seen it.

'The discussion about John Martin should divert their attention,' Jonathon's low voice rumbled in her ear. 'It is a topic of conversation to keep everyone entertained, but not you, I think. You never did care for painting.'

'You know nothing about me.' Louisa took a sip of her lukewarm coffee. 'I happen to enjoy John Martin's paintings.'

Jonathon pressed his lips together. 'You do?'

'I have changed, Jonathon.'

His eyes searched her face. 'Not that much. You only think you have. And I have only done what your eyes implored me to do—rescue you from Furniss and divert the conversation.'

'I happen to like Lord Furniss's company. Why should

I want attention diverted?' Louisa asked between gritted teeth.

'Our conversation last evening is far from finished,' Jonathan said, looking down at her with hard eyes. 'I wait with baited breath, Louisa. Where is your infamous proof? I had fully expected it to land on my breakfast table while you took the first boat out of Newcastle back into the arms of your aged baronet.'

The words stung far more than they should.

'All things come to those who wait.'

His voice lowered to a seductive and intimate growl, which made her insides curl with warmth. 'I devotedly hope so.'

'You are attempting to disconcert me.'

'Perish the thought.' His eyes deepened. 'My only desire at the moment is for a cup of tea.'

'It is good that your desires are easily satisfied' Louisa said before wincing. Open mouth, insert kid slipper.

'As long as you satisfy them.' The banter was gone from his voice.

Louisa hurriedly looked away and concentrated on pouring the tea. In her haste, she knocked a spoon to the ground and then sent the sugar bowl flying—the actions of a flustered débutante rather than a companion of several years' standing. Miss Daphne gave a mildly disapproving stare from where she sat, but made no move to intervene.

'Are you disturbed about something, Miss Sibson?' Jonathon asked, taking the cup and then placing the sugar bowl back on the little table. 'You appear flustered. But everything is quickly put to rights once one sets one's mind to it.'

'Should anything disturb me, Lord Chesterholm?' Louisa poured another cup of tea. This time, she managed to keep her hand steady.

'Such action could be construed as a guilty conscience.'

'I do have proof, Lord Chesterholm.' Louisa reached for the reticule. 'My conscience is clear.'

'Why didn't you wave the proof under my nose when I walked in the room? The Louisa I knew would have done. Wasn't that what you did with my sister's poem? But then the action was to pique my interest. And this one is…'

The old Louisa. Louisa gritted her teeth. She too remembered that day and what had happened afterwards—their first kiss, a stolen kiss. It was low of Jonathon to bring it up, particularly now. And she had not been flirting with him. He had simply assumed that she did not have anything else to do except answer his impertinent questions about how pretty girls could ever have serious thoughts in their brains. And she had shown him the papers. She had mistaken flirtation for kindness, a silly naïve mistake, and had paid a heavy price.

'I would, but Mrs Blandish is addicted to gossip and her hearing is very acute.' Louisa nodded towards where Lord Furniss was rather grandly informing Miss Blandish that she was completely wrong to consider Turner a better painter than John Martin. 'I would hardly wish to involve you in scandal.'

'It makes a first. As far as I recall you courted it. You were an active participant in our little games.'

'Any scandal that happened was down to your actions and not mine,' Louisa whispered in a furious undertone. 'I behaved impeccably.'

He leant forwards. 'Or are you merely mouthing words without understanding the implications, Louisa? You played your part as much as I did.'

'I grew up.' Louisa batted her eyelashes and made her voice sound as much like treacle as possible. 'Trials and tribulations have a way of doing that to people.'

'We are at an impasse, Louisa. Why not accept that I do have a claim and come away with me?'

'Must you sound like a villain in a penny novel?'

'Why are you casting me as one?' A muscle jumped in his jaw. 'Shall I force you to be alone with me? Or are you scared about what you might discover? When shall it be? This afternoon?'

'Unfortunately, I must decline.' Louisa kept her voice even. 'I must visit the chemist later this afternoon. Miss Daphne finished her tincture this morning. And without Miss Daphne's tincture, the world stops.'

'Ah, our old code.' Jonathon's eyes deepened to a storm-tossed green. 'Shall we meet inside the chemist? What shall I say that I am searching for? A hair restoration tonic?'

Louisa's stomach tightened. She should have remembered about the code and the visit to the chemist for a hair restoration tonic. How they accidentally met to have a proper conversation. And the other times she had pretended to have to get more ink or blotting paper so that she'd get a glimpse or stolen moment with him as he solemnly carried her packages.

She had thought at the time that the code and the

meetings made what they shared more special—keeping it private and between the two of them. But now she saw it for what it was—a means to keep the relationship clandestine until it was far too late for anyone to intervene. And when it had ended, she had been ruined, in the gutter, but he had remained a pillar of society.

'You are misconstruing my words and their meaning.'

'Am I?' He raised his eyebrow higher and she felt the heat begin to gather on her cheeks.

'Yes, I sought to explain why it would be impossible to meet.' Louisa regained control of her body. She refused to be attracted to him. 'I will send you the letter. There will be no need to meet after that. I will return to Sorrento and our lives will go on as before, our paths never crossing.'

'A forlorn hope, Miss Sibson,' Jonathon said. 'You will not get rid of me that easily.'

'Watch me.'

'A challenge.' He put his tea cup down. 'Good. I love it when you issue challenges. Watch and learn, Miss Sibson. Afterwards, and in private, we can discuss how easy I will be to dissuade.'

Louisa shifted slightly on the sofa, feeling that she had played into his hands.

'Miss Elliot,' Jonathon said, giving a loud cough.

The entire room went still. 'Yes, Lord Chesterholm?'

Silently Louisa prayed that Jonathon was not going to do anything untoward, not with Mrs Blandish in the room.

'I understand that you spent some time in the Kingdom of Two Sicilies. Did you manage to collect any

Roman cameos? My late great-uncle had a collection and, since his death, I have developed an interest and I am eager to learn more.'

Louisa stared at Jonathon. Since when had he become interested in cameos? He had been far more interested in racing and placing bets, living the life of an overly indulged son. She doubted if he could even name any of the Roman emperors.

'My sister was a keen collector. It was how we first met Arthur Fanshaw.' Miss Daphne waved an arm. 'I am afraid I did not have the head for it. All Latin and Greek. Louisa is the woman to speak to about such things. In her last years, my late sister relied on Louisa's eye.'

'Miss Mattie and I travelled to inspect the diggings at Pompeii and Herculaneum.' Louisa's shoulders relaxed slightly. Jonathon had miscalculated. She could easily turn the talk to her travels. The days she and Miss Mattie had spent in Pompeii with Mount Vesuvius gently billowing smoke in the background had been some of the most pleasant of her life.

'Are the ruins as good as they say?' Miss Nella Blandish asked, sticking her face between Louisa and Jonathon. 'Miss Milton told me all about them. How you can walk the streets. And how they have put the skeletons that they found in various places just as they would have been.'

'With Herculaneum, you have to descend stairs and go underground,' Louisa said, expounding on the theme. A few more minutes and the allotted time for a visit would be up. Jonathon would be forced to make his excuses and leave. 'The guides carry torches. But Pompeii is exactly like walking a deserted street. They say that there's over a hundred years of digging to be done. Miss Mattie found several pieces for her collection there, including a very lovely Psyche.'

'And are they here?' Jonathon asked, breaking into the conversation. 'Or have they remained in Sorrento? I have heard rumours about certain Roman cameos that she might have had in her possession. I believe she outbid my late uncle on one or two pieces.'

'Oh, yes, my sister did enjoy besting your late uncle!' Miss Daphne clapped her hands. 'And you are clever to guess that Louisa brought a few pieces with her, including the Herculaneum ones. Not the whole collection, just a few to show honoured guests.'

'And Miss Sibson is now the expert.' Jonathon wore a superior expression. 'She knows the ins and outs…of the cameos.'

Louisa's next remark about the delights of Pompeii died on her lips as Miss Daphne started frantically gesturing to her. 'I will show the collection to Lord Chesterholm, Miss Daphne.'

'That would be a good idea,' Miss Daphne murmured with an approving glint in her eye.

'May I come as well?' Miss Nella Blandish asked. 'I am going to be a lady explorer. Some day I am going to find a lost city. It will be much more interesting than being in society and marrying some stupid titled peer as Susan wants to.'

Mrs Blandish blanched. 'No, Nella, you can stay here with me. You have done quite enough exploring for one summer. We had best be going. Susan will be attending the Assembly Rooms ball this evening and must make her preparations. Are you going, Miss Sibson?'

'I am otherwise engaged…with the study of the cameos,' Louisa said, banishing all thoughts of how Jonathon had once taught her to waltz.

'Some other time. And the gentlemen?'

'A pity that I am otherwise engaged,' Lord Furniss said with a bow.

'I shall be returning to Chesterholm in the morning and wish to make an early start.' Jonathon looked directly at her. 'Provided nothing detains me.'

'I once went to Chesterholm as a young girl. It is a magical place with a Cedar of Lebanon in the centre of a maze,' Miss Daphne proclaimed after the Blandishes had departed.

'I was unaware you had a direct connection to Chesterholm, Miss Elliot,' Jonathon said with an astonished look.

'The cameos. You wished to see the collection,' Louisa said quickly as she spotted a deepening gleam in Miss Daphne's eye.

'Louisa, be quick about showing Lord Chesterholm the cameos. Rupert, I want to speak to you about your mother's letters.' Miss Daphne made an irritated sound. 'Honoria has written to me again about candles! I am not a blushing school miss to be reprimanded. I was once though, years ago when we went to Chesterholm. I suppose I shall never see Chesterholm again.'

Louisa sucked in her breath at the blatant attempt at securing an invitation. What was Miss Daphne doing? Not cause scandal, but matchmake. Miss Daphne had always proclaimed she was a dab hand at it. Louisa concentrated on the pug figurine. Any matchmaking tendencies had to be nipped in the bud. But she would redirect Miss Daphne's attention later, after Jonathon had departed, chagrined and chastened.

'This way, if you please, Lord Chesterholm.' Louisa made a flourish with her hand. 'The cameos I brought with me are in the library. It is reckoned to be as fine as any collection of cameos in Sorrento, if not the Kingdom of Two Sicilies.'

'I await the collection with eagerness. My uncle felt the loss of a "Psyche undergoing her trials" cameo to Miss Mattie with particular keenness.'

'I hadn't realised you were interested in Roman remains, Lord Chesterholm,' Louisa said as they started down the passage towards the library.

'Chesterholm lies beside a Roman fort. Unfortunately, my late uncle had the remains of the Roman village swept away. He wanted an uninterrupted view down to the Tyne.'

'And you disapprove.'

'I have an interest in preserving the ancient. I am hoping to prove that the wall was indeed built by Hadrian.'

Louisa stared at him. The Jonathon she remembered had been interested in having a good time, drinking and pretty women. He had had little time for history, declaring it to be dull fodder for growing minds. And now he wanted to prove that the wall had been built by Hadrian.

'Miss Mattie liked cameos—both the Roman paste type and the ones carved from shells. Sorrento has many cameo makers. Did you know that you can tell a real cameo by holding it up to the light?'

'And how can you tell an errant fiancée?' Jonathon murmured. 'One who prefers to jump to conclusions, rather than waiting for answers? One who seeks to deny certain things even when the truth is obvious to everyone else?'

Louisa gritted her teeth and revised her opinion. Jonathon had not changed. He remained the same single-minded man that he had always been. He was seeking to put her off balance. But he was going to be the one to learn and to suffer. 'I will let you know when I meet one.'

# Chapter Four

Jonathon watched with grim amusement as Louisa marched down the hall towards the library, her shoulder blades twitching in mock indignation. She expected seduction. Good. She needed the anticipation. But it would be she who seduced him, and not here but at Chesterholm. Miss Elliot had neatly solved his problem. Louisa would be going to Chesterholm. It would give him the perfect opportunity.

In the intervening years, Louisa's beauty had grown and matured rather than diminished. Her clothes and hair might not be precisely up to the minute, but there was a certain sensuousness about the way she moved and the way the light lit the red fire in her hair. His body stirred with anticipation.

He could remember what she'd looked like—her glorious titian hair spread across his pillow and body, long white limbs and rosy mouth whispering how their love was eternal, how he was the only man for her. Right before she'd disappeared. Now she was back and her beauty, instead of fading, had deepened and ripened.

On how many other men had she practised her schemes? How many other men had run their fingers through her hair, enjoying its silky smoothness as it covered their bodies like a protective cloak? Had she kissed the baronet? Furniss?

A surge of jealous anger went through him. He refused to think about any other man touching her. The current of desire ran between them, unabated after all these years. Jonathon clenched his fist around the head of his silver-topped cane and regained control of his body. The important thing was ensuring Louisa did precisely what he wanted her to, rather than thinking about his rivals.

She walked quickly to the library and with practised movements began to pull out the various drawers where the cameos were stored, talking very quickly and loudly about the merits and where the collection was from.

Jonathon wondered how many times she had played this little game, keeping the door open just wide enough so as not to excite the servants' curiosity. Once he had thought innocence and purity had shone from her face. An uneasy thought whispered in the back of his mind that she had been pure until he had introduced her to the arts of love and subterfuge. He silenced the thought. He had to get her out of her environment and into his. They would start playing by his rules. Now.

Jonathon closed the door with a decisive click, half-expecting an immediate protest at the impropriety. Louisa stopped for a moment and their gazes held. Her lips parted as if she was about to protest, but then she gave a slight shrug and concentrated on straightening the cameos.

'You will want to see the best. It took me a moment to find them and here they are.'

She pushed a drawer forwards. The deft movement emphasised the length of her fingers, slender and tapering but with a certain resilient strength.

He had always admired her hands and how they moved. When he was recovering from the accident, he had lain awake, imagining what it would be like to have his brow stroked. He could remember her innocent hesitant touch becoming more assured as she had gained in confidence until she'd touched his body with the skill of a courtesan, playing it like a musician plays a fine instrument. But it had been that underlying innocence that had heated his blood to fever pitch.

He wrenched his thoughts away from the past.

Her lips curved up into a secret smile, challenging him to make his move. 'This is the cream of the collection. Miss Mattie used to show all her visitors these cameos. The fact that others coveted them only increased their value.'

'Where is Eros? Psyche is alone in each of these cameos.'

'You know the myth!' Her eyes widened in astonishment.

'Going to Eton did give me a classical education, Louisa. The myth serves as the basis for *Beauty and the Beast* and several other fairy tales.' Jonathon leant forwards and dared her to say the truth.

'Eros abandoned Psyche. He flew away and left her to

her fate. Miss Mattie and I prefer the ones with Psyche alone and surviving. They are more honest.'

The words cut through him, but he pushed the thought away. He had not abandoned her. He drew a steadying breath and kept his gaze on her. Louisa had obviously forgotten the entirety of the story. Eros had won in the end. He had made Psyche into a goddess.

'Or could it be that Miss Mattie was shocked?' He allowed his eyes to dance. 'Some in my late uncle's collection are very *risqué*. Eros and Psyche intertwined. Hardly the subject for an unmarried spinster.'

'This one might be to your taste.' Her eyes flashed fire. 'You do, I believe, have a healthy appreciation of the female form.'

'On occasion.'

He held out his hand. She dropped the cameo into his palm, being careful not to touch him. Psyche about to enter the underworld stared up at him, her figure much as he remembered Louisa's.

'What else does the *collection* offer? Which ones are *your* favourites? Do you have a healthy appreciation of the masculine form?'

Louisa's tongue flicked out and moistened her lips. Her hands pressed harder against the table and her pupils flared slightly. Her breath emerged as a hiss before she seemed to regain control and reached for the drawer again. 'That is a personal question. Are we now moving to the personal, Lord Chesterholm?'

'Everything between us is personal, Louisa. But I can answer the question. You once watched me bathe.'

'You have no interest in the cameos.' She gripped the drawer so tightly that her knuckles shone white. 'Why lie? Why not tell the truth? You intend to seduce me, but you will fail, sir.'

Her tongue flicked over her lips and he knew she remembered. It was enough for now. Soon, they would repeat the performance. Slowly. With candlelight flickering, red rose petals shimmering on the water and the soap sliding over her naked back as she sighed. Jonathon forced his mind from the image.

'You have no idea what I am interested in,' Jonathon said, crossing his arms. 'You make assumptions without bothering to discover the facts. I inherited my uncle's collection. I know the difference between the modern and the ancient. Between the German paste and the carved shells from Naples. But I want to learn more.'

'Why?'

'Because Chesterholm was robbed recently and they jumbled up the cameos. My uncle never trusted the so-called experts. So I am not entirely sure what there is and what is missing. Teach me, Louisa. Everything.'

He watched as her fingers fiddled with the cameos.

'Come with me to Chesterholm,' he purred and waited.

Instantly her backbone straightened. 'No.'

Jonathon blinked. He had misjudged the situation. 'What do you mean, "no"?'

'You closed the door. You seek to use this collection for your own purposes.' Louisa ticked each point off her fingers. 'Deny that if you will. There is another purpose to you.'

'The light is better with the door closed.' He smiled, daring her to deny it. 'I want you to come to Chesterholm and help.'

'Why would you ever think that I would agree to help you? After all you did to me?' Her treacle-heavy voice taunted him as her eyes became more catlike. Jonathon tried to see the girl he had loved so desperately all those years ago, but all he could see was the harridan in the making who cared more for objects than people.

'Does Miss Elliot even know what happened between us?'

'She knows that you ruined me. I drew a veil over the details.'

'You failed to inform Miss Elliot that we were engaged. Or that you left without speaking to me.' Jonathon stared at Louisa in astonishment. 'It is a wonder that Miss Elliot continues to receive me. Perhaps she thinks there is more to it than your story.'

'Do not seek to judge me, Jonathon.' Her cat eyes narrowed and spat fury, but her breath was far too quick and her lips glistened from where her tongue flicked. Jonathon took a steadying breath as he felt his control begin to slip. He concentrated on the cameos and regained his purpose.

'Some day, you will learn, Louisa. When you are playing games, decide in advance the sort of reaction you are hoping to provoke.'

'What sort of response would that be?' She tossed her head back slightly. 'Why do you think I seek anything from you?'

The very air crackled between them. Reaching into the depths of his will-power, Jonathon forced his hands to stay at his sides. If he reached for her now, he would be the one punishing her with a kiss. When they next kissed, it would come from her. She would be the one to shatter.

'Anything at all.' An uncertain pucker appeared between her perfectly arched brows.

'Are you seeking to be kissed?' he said in a lazy voice. 'I thought last evening would have shown you how dangerous that is.'

Her rosebud mouth became a perfect O and colour flamed on her cheeks. Deep within him, Jonathon was relieved that she could blush, that not all of her innocence was gone. He reached for her. Fury came into her eyes and she twisted out of his grasp.

'Not much for pleasant conversation or small talk, are you, Jonathon? Always seeking to dominate with the physical. You did not get my immediate agreement to go with you, so you are going to attempt to seduce me into it. The answer will remain no, no for all eternity.'

'I have never felt the need to dominate or use force.' He took a step closer, touched her arm with a featherlight brush of his hand. She did not move. 'You came to my bed willing. Stop pretending otherwise.'

'I have never pretended.' Louisa retreated and bumped against a drawer with a small thud. 'No doubt in time, you will find someone else to answer your questions about cameos. We would not suit. And in any case, I am wanted elsewhere.'

'When do you depart England?'

Her eyes darted everywhere but on his face. His blood boiled as Furniss's intelligence from last night was confirmed. She was going to leave, thinking that he would not follow and that she could live in relative obscurity abroad. A miscalculation on her part.

'We only came for a visit. That visit is now over.' She snapped her fingers. 'We are in the waning days.'

'You are planning to abandon Miss Daphne without asking if she wants to visit Chesterholm.'

'Why would she want to do that? She has never mentioned going there before.' Her voice sounded suddenly less certain. She bit her lip. 'But you distract me. Read this. Then tell me that I lie.'

She reached into her reticule and withdrew a heavily creased piece of paper. The ink was blotched in a few places as if she had cried over it. His heart twisted and he knew the image of her crying would haunt his dreams.

He took the stained piece of paper in silence and rapidly perused it. Four months on from his accident, he had been recovering at the Newtons', practising his first steps with Clarissa hovering at his elbow. His stepmother had paid for Louisa's passage out to Italy and had asked Louisa to contact her when she arrived. She had also informed her to be careful as fallen women never fully recovered. At the end Venetia had wished her a happy twenty-first birthday. Spiteful and cruel words.

He folded the letter and put it in his pocket, refusing to think how they had planned to spend that birthday compared to how she must have actually spent it. 'I believe you, Louisa, but this changes nothing between us.'

Unshed tears shimmered in her eyes. 'Do you know what it is like, Jonathon, to be made to feel like you are a piece of dirt on the bottom of a shoe? To have everyone see the shame on your cheek?'

'You exaggerate.' He touched her soft cheek, but she turned her face away.

'It is in my past.' Louisa's knuckles shone white against the blackness of her reticule. 'I have another future, far different from the one your stepmother had planned for me. Nightly I go on my knees and thank God for Miss Mattie and her offer when I was at my lowest ebb. Trust me, Jonathon, the girl I once was has long since vanished.'

A cold fury filled Jonathon. He had promised to protect Louisa and she had not even believed in him enough to demand to hear the words from his lips. She had believed Venetia. His late uncle had been right when he'd said that there could be no love without trust. Louisa had not trusted him. She had not loved him. It changed nothing, but it still hurt. 'Why did you believe my stepmother rather than my promises to you?'

Louisa's face became mutinous as her tawny eyes darkened to rich amber. 'You accepted her story without questioning.'

Jonathon winced as the barb hit home. He had accepted the story of Louisa's death, because who would be wicked enough to lie about such a thing? He had made his feelings about Louisa quite clear. He had wept for days after he had been told, wept in a way that he had never done before or since. Venetia had made noises, but she had known the depth of his feeling for Louisa.

'I will be interested to hear the explanation.' Jonathon inclined his head.

'Our business is satisfactorily concluded.' Louisa began to close the various drawers. 'That particular episode may now be once again consigned to the past and

youthful folly. We may both continue with our lives.'
She gave a perfunctory nod. 'Good day to you, Lord
Chesterholm. May your future be a pleasant one. For
me, Sorrento beckons.'

Anger surged through Jonathon. If she thought she
would be rid of him this easily, Louisa had another
think coming. He would confront his stepmother.
Venetia would never be able to play that sort of trick
again, but that had nothing to do with his relationship
with Louisa.

Love might have fled, but passion and desire
remained. They were not finished until he said so. He
hated to think of another man looking at Louisa, let
alone touching her. Somewhere beneath that bravado
and polished veneer lurked his Louisa, the woman he
had dreamt about spending the rest of his life with, the
one whom he had sworn to protect. She would go to
Chesterholm and she would confess her untruths.

'You remain intent on marrying your baronet.' Jonathon's muscles tensed.

'As much as I ever was.' Louisa's laugh rang out, high
and shrill. 'My future is none of your concern, Lord
Chesterholm. Our connection is over, severed. You have
no claim.'

'I looked his name up in Debrett's. It was most
enlightening.'

'You obviously have more time than I do.' Her smile
wavered slightly. 'Did you find it interesting?'

'He is twice your age. Is that why he wants you,
Louisa—to add to his collection of pretty things? Has
he ever kissed you?'

Louisa's hand plucked at her skirt and she pressed

her lips together and slowly, almost imperceptibly, she shook her head. 'Such matters are none of your concern. But know that he has great admiration for me.'

'Admiration,' Jonathon scoffed as the white-hot rage in his soul eased. 'Is that the same as love?'

'It is a form of love.'

'Is it a passionate love match, then?'

'Yes, yes, if you insist. It is…what I want.' She shook her head. 'Not that you would understand such simple concepts as restraint and forbearance.'

'Why isn't he here with you?' Jonathon brushed her cheek. 'If this man was dying of love for you, why did he allow you to go back to England alone? Any man should know the folly of that. If you were my fiancée, I would make certain no other man had a chance of going near you.'

'I don't believe in love, not that sort,' she whispered, not meeting his eyes. 'I seek the comfort of companionship.'

'You did once.' He trailed a finger down the side of her face. 'You were the most passionate creature I had ever met. You wanted to grab life with both hands. And now, you only want a companion. You might lie to yourself, Louisa, but do not lie to me. Sir Francis and his bloodless offer is not what you desire.'

'That is all in the past, Jonathon. Finished and ended. It was never love, simply desire. Desire that flared out of control, but burnt out quickly.'

'It is something you should worry about. Do you think Sir Francis will want to marry you once he discovers your youthful indiscretion?'

Louisa stared at him in astonishment. She had given

him the letter that proved her point and he still appeared intent on destroying her and her reputation. Surely he had to let her go. Last night proved nothing except that she was a fool. 'What do you mean?'

'What a man asks from a mistress is different from what he demands from a wife.' A faint smile appeared on his lips. 'Have you told him about what passed between us? Surely a husband deserves to know about his wife's lovers.'

'There is no us, Jonathon. That particular folly ended years ago.' She tilted her head and dared him to say otherwise. The sudden image of Jonathon vital and determined in Sorrento flashed through her brain—Jonathon loudly declaiming to Sir Francis and everyone else who gathered on the Hotel Trasemeno terrace for their afternoon tea about her past, or, worse, Jonathon gathering her in his arms and kissing her in front of everyone. The thought unnerved her. She glanced at him under her lashes. He would never do it, would he?

'Then he has no idea why you left England. Interesting. Perhaps he should be enlightened.' Jonathon cupped his fingers under her chin and forced it upwards so he gazed directly into her soul. The shifting colours in his eyes mesmerised her. 'What hurts most, Louisa, is that you think so little of the people you profess to care about. You were the one who said that those closest to you should share your innermost secrets.'

'Are you threatening me?' She wrenched her chin away. 'Threats are only effective if the person is prepared to carry them through. Venetia Ponsby-Smythe taught me that.'

'Threats or promises, Lou?' he asked, using his old

pet name for her. He ran his hands lightly down her arms and saw the pulse at the base of her throat quicken. 'What will Sir Francis do when I appear in Sorrento to give this demonstration?'

Jonathon traced the outline of her lips with the back of his thumb. They shifted and moved under the subtle pressure, sending pulses of warmth throughout her body, making an ache grow within her.

Louisa inhaled and caught his citrus scent. Heat infused her body as her breast strained against her stays. It would be so easy to give into him, so easy to become the person that she swore she would never be again. With her last ounce of self-preservation, Louisa straightened her shoulders and moved out of his grasp.

'What do you want from me, Jonathon?' she asked, hating the faint sardonic smile on his face as if he knew of her inner turmoil. 'How can I get you out of my life?'

The creak of the door gave her a split-second warning and she jumped away, aware her colour was far too high.

Miss Daphne entered the room, with Lord Furniss nearly tripping on her heels. Miss Daphne wore a concerned expression, but Lord Furniss's was a cross between concern and outrage.

'Chesterholm, what do you think you are doing?' Lord Furniss thundered, shaking his fist at Jonathon. 'Miss Sibson is not some piece of Haymarketware to be trifled with. Miss Sibson, your reputation... I demand the satisfaction of an explanation, Chesterholm.'

'Miss Sibson's reputation is in no danger from me.' Jonathon made a bow. 'I hold Miss Sibson's reputation in very high esteem, Furniss. There will be no need for seconds. It was a matter of the light and the cameos. Nothing has happened here that was intended to dishonour Miss Sibson.'

'Humph.' Lord Furniss's brow wrinkled as he digested Jonathon's statement. 'With any other man, Chesterholm, I might wonder, but I know you to be a sound fellow.'

Silently Louisa cursed her stupidity in not insisting that Jonathon open the door. A few more heartbeats and she would have been properly in his arms, surrendering her mouth and body.

Louisa pressed a hand to her forehead. He was not the one making piecrust promises. She was. And she had to get him out of her life or risk losing all the respectability that she had worked so hard to regain.

'Ah, I see Louisa has worked her usual magic with the cameos. Personally I can never see the attraction, but my late sister was enthralled, particularly with the Psyche ones.' Miss Daphne frowned slightly. 'But the door…'

'Miss Sibson protested and I overruled her. I needed less light.' Jonathon carefully placed the last remaining cameo in its resting place and shut the drawer. 'Sometimes there are delicate shades in cameos that need bringing out, or so my late uncle said. Subtlety is all.'

'My sister taught her well.' Miss Daphne beamed benevolently. 'My sister was readily acknowledged to be an expert in the field, and Louisa proved to be an apt pupil. We were so lucky to find her.'

'I am certain she would be an apt *pupil*. Miss Sibson shows an aptitude for any number of areas.'

Louisa forced a smile until her jaw ached. She refused to give Jonathon the satisfaction of knowing how he disturbed her with his little innuendos and *double entendres.*

'Lord Chesterholm has seen all that he requires. He will be leaving.'

'Next time, Louisa, I trust you will remember that you are no longer in Italy, but in England,' Miss Daphne said, shaking her head. 'Servants will talk if you close doors. Appearance, my dear, appearance is all important in English society.'

'Appearances can be deceptive,' Jonathon remarked.

'It is unbelievable how quickly scandal can travel, Aunt.' Lord Furniss dropped his voice. 'A whisper here and a word there and suddenly one can find oneself embroiled in a full-blown scandal that is reported in all the scandal sheets. Miss Sibson must be careful. Cameos or not.'

'I trust you will remember your words, Rupert… should you become embroiled. Your dear mama would be mortified.' Miss Daphne bowed her head, but not before Louisa detected a faint gleam in the old woman's eye. 'Louisa is guilty of no more than being accustomed to Italian manners.'

'I will endeavour to remember the point for the next time.' Louisa kept her voice even and avoided Miss Daphne's glance. Less than a day after meeting again Jonathon and she had forgotten all the lessons she had learnt. There would be no next time. She was not going to be alone with Jonathon again. 'As Lord Chesterholm said—the light was not conducive to viewing the cameos. The delicate shading was hidden by the bright light. The fault was all mine. I did not think that it could be misconstrued.'

'Miss Sibson has proved most enlightening on the subject.' The colour of Jonathon's eyes deepened and shifted. 'I am hoping you and Miss Sibson might be persuaded to visit me at Chesterholm, Miss Elliot. I would like to get some expert advice on several cameos in my collection.'

'You can bring them to Newcastle,' Louisa said quickly as Miss Daphne's ribbons twitched. 'Perhaps there will be time before the packet leaves.'

'Mattie and I enjoyed a prolonged stay at Chesterholm Grange in our youth.' There was a wistful look in Miss Daphne's eyes. Louisa groaned, remembering where she had seen Miss Daphne's look before—last autumn in Sorrento when Miss Daphne had attempted to play cupid with Miss Henderson and Colonel Prism. Only Miss Mattie's quick thinking had saved the situation and the pair was now happily married but it had been a close-run thing. 'It lives as a happy memory. I never thought I would return...not after what passed between them. But now my entire being longs to see it one more time.'

'I had not realised it was such a happy time in your life,' Jonathon said, giving Louisa a significant look. Louisa glared back at him. He had known. It was underhanded using Miss Daphne in this way. 'Furniss explained you were visiting your old girlish haunts. It would be remiss of you not to come to Chesterholm, particularly now that we have made our acquaintance again.'

Miss Daphne's eyes shone like two beacons. 'I would love that.'

'Perhaps you can explain a mystery about my uncle,' Jonathon said smoothly. 'He kept himself to himself in later years, but I understand he had heartache as a youth.'

'Mattie and he had an understanding, but then they quarrelled. Over the Romans, of all things. Poor Mama took to her bed for weeks. Neither married.' Miss Daphne clapped her hands and the years fell away. For the briefest of instances Louisa glimpsed the beauty that Miss Daphne must have been in her youth. 'Yes, it would be very fitting to return there before I depart for Sorrento. Very fitting indeed. I accept your invitation with pleasure.'

'And Miss Sibson?' Jonathon turned his hard gaze on Louisa, daring her to refuse. 'Will you accept? Or is there somewhere you need to run away to?'

'Louisa promised to look after me on my journey,' Miss Daphne said, giving her a wistful look like a child about to be denied a longed-for treat.

'And she never breaks her promises.'

'Miss Daphne knows that I will stay until she is ready to go back to Sorrento.' Louisa clenched her fists. Very well, he was determined that she would visit Chester-holm. She would, but on her terms. He would discover that it took more than an indulgent smile and a purring voice to seduce her. And when she had finished with him, he would learn never to involve himself in her life again.

A slow appraising smile crossed Jonathon's face. 'Then I will take it as a yes.'

'If you must.' Louisa pressed her palms into her eyes and regained control of her temper.

'Miss Sibson is angry with me for suggesting the visit.' He hung his head in a show of mock remorse. 'And my intentions are pure.'

'Should I be angry?' Louisa gave him her most guileless smile as inwardly she longed to throw the box of cameos at his head. 'For you have done nothing wrong. The only thing you are guilty of is wishing to know the truth…about your cameos.'

Jonathon made a small bow towards Miss Daphne. 'Then I will be delighted to show off how the estate has changed and improved since my great-uncle's time. Were you there before or after he demolished the Roman settlement?'

'Before.' Miss Daphne's eyes twinkled with a mischievous light. Louisa frowned. Had Miss Daphne expected the invitation? 'And I would look on it as a great personal favour if you invited my nephew to join this house party of yours.'

'Furniss? Will you join us?'

'Of course, my dear chap.' Furniss touched his fingers to his hat. 'I would be honoured. The last time I visited was when you had just inherited the house. I look forward to seeing the changes.'

'And the Blandish family.' Miss Daphne's eyes took on a distinct gleam. 'I am taken with Miss Nella. She bears cultivating, that young lady. And Miss Blandish will be making her début this Season. It must be about time for your half-sister, Margaret, to make her début.'

'Miss Blandish is to have a Season?' Lord Furniss asked.

'New money, Rupert,' Miss Daphne said. 'Your mother would never approve, even if Miss Blandish does have a well-trimmed ankle.'

'Am I a slave to my mother? And upon my soul, I never said anything about Miss Blandish's ankle! I remain loyal to Miss Sibson.' Lord Furniss clasped his hand to his heart. 'Miss Sibson, you must—'

Louisa concentrated on the Psyche cameos. 'Lord Furniss, this is not the time or place, but know you have my lasting friendship.'

'Thank you.' Lord Furniss bowed his head. 'I always treasure your friendship.'

Louisa simply looked at Jonathon and dared him to say something untoward. He arched his brow as if the exchange amused him.

'Your wish is my command, Miss Daphne. The Blandishes will be invited,' Jonathon said. 'I, too, found Miss Nella a charming conversationalist. The Grange has not seen a house party for a long time.'

Louisa crossed her arms and longed to wipe the self-satisfied expression from his face. A house party indeed! He would be on his knees, begging her forgiveness before the party was finished.

She looked forward to being the one to administer the lesson in humility. She was never going to go back to the girl she once was, yet she found it impossible to silence the little voice inside that whispered perhaps she was wrong. Perhaps, Jonathon Fanshaw was a different man to the one she had known all those years ago. Ruthlessly Louisa silenced it.

# *Chapter Five*

*You are a different person. You are. You have changed. You will not have feelings for Jonathon. You will survive this ordeal. You survived before.*

Her boots pounded out the message as Louisa strode towards the Chemist. When she'd been in Sorrento amongst the lemon groves and watching the sparkling water with Mount Vesuvius towering over the Bay of Naples, it had been easy to think about what might happen if they ever met again and how she'd show him that she had changed. But now she was not sure. Jonathon seemed insistent that she was the same.

After her encounter with Jonathon, the walls pressed in and Louisa knew she had to leave the house in Charlotte Square and clear her head. She always thought better whilst walking rather than whilst sitting still.

With Jonathon Fanshaw, she needed her head even clearer than she had when he was Jonathon Ponsby-Smythe. That Jonathon she had understood with his boyish enthusiasms and impulses. This Jonathon was new, thoughtful and considering. Somehow she suspected he had known about Miss Daphne and Chesterholm and had intended to invite them both all along.

It bothered *her* that she even cared what he thought and that thinking about him was taking up more and more of her time.

A great mass of humanity seethed around her—shawl-clad factory girls, flat-capped boys pushing barrows and harassed mothers with children hanging off their skirts. All about her the lilting accent of the northeast, so very different from the sounds of her native Warwickshire, but they were speaking English instead of Italian and somehow it was comforting. Her throat closed. It was a small thing, but she had missed the background chatter in her native language.

A man barged into her, causing her to stumble. 'You should watch what you are on about. Dreaming your life away.'

Louisa clutched her reticule tighter and hurried on. Dreaming. Once she had spent her life with her head in the clouds. She had sworn never again.

Beside the chemist stood a booking office with various notices in the window advertising excursions and destinations home and abroad. It would be so easy to book a steamer back to Sorrento. Louisa's throat closed. Jonathon would not follow.

Louisa shook her head. In many ways, she remained the naïve girl of four years ago. Jonathon would follow and would make her life a misery.

She turned her back on the booking office. It was time to slay her demons. She was through with paying for her mistake. This time she was going to fight for the life she had worked so hard to regain.

Louisa turned and spied a woman carrying a valise. Her clothes were neat, but there was a wild look about her face and hair. Louisa's heart squeezed as she recognised the look. Not so very long ago she had stood on the quayside in Naples with the exact same expression of utter hopelessness and then people had turned their backs. She had always vowed if ever given the chance, she would assist rather than condemn.

'Is something wrong?' Louisa asked in a quiet voice.

The woman fumbled for a handkerchief. Silently Louisa handed her one from her reticule. 'I made a mistake. I...'

She dissolved into great noisy tears.

'It is a man and now he has left you,' Louisa said with sudden certainty.

'How did you guess?' The woman stopped mid-sob. 'Is it that obvious? Does my wickedness show? My grandma always said that it would.'

'It is generally a man who causes those sorts of tears. They promise you the moon and stars, but leave you before the sun rises.'

'He said that he'd take me to Gretna Green, but we went to Newcastle instead and I discovered he already has a wife, plus three bairns.' The woman looked at her with tear-stained eyes and reddened nose.

*A wife and children.* Louisa swallowed hard. How simply dreadful for this woman. Jonathon had only been promised to another.

'Do you have somewhere to go?'

Louisa's mind raced. She could hardly ask Miss Daphne to help. They had more than enough staff. Leaving the woman stranded on the street corner where she'd be prey for all the various ne'er-do-wells was unthinkable.

The woman shook her head and her blonde ringlets bobbed about her plump face. 'I can't stay in Newcastle. I keep thinking that somehow they will know about what I have done and they will whisper about me. They say that it clings to your skirts. I am willing to work, but who will hire a wicked woman for honest work? I have no references.'

Louisa closed her eyes, remembering the feeling of hopelessness.

'They won't. They are more interested in selling tickets. Think about how many hundreds of people go through that booking office.' She paused, trying to get her thoughts in order. 'Is it the expense you are worried about it?'

'I have money. Me mam guessed what I was on about and she slipped me some money when me da wasn't looking. One of my aunts—well, she was in difficulties when she was young. Left high and dry, like.' The woman twisted her handkerchief. 'Me da warned me that I would come to a bad end, just like she did, and on no account to come back if I left. He will turn his back on me and cast me out, if I go back.'

'Have you ever thought about going back? Perhaps they will have a change of heart. Blood counts for something.'

The woman wiped the tears from her eyes and appeared to consider the request. 'No, I can't do it. Not with me da. He uses his fists and asks questions later. I met a woman a while back and she said if I was to get in trouble that I could go to her. She might find me a job. She used to work at the castle and looks after pretty doves. She appeared to be a kind sort.'

Louisa pressed her lips together. The young woman was naïve. She knew exactly the sort of job that kind elderly woman had in mind—selling the young woman's body.

'Shall I go in with you?' Louisa offered. She could not do much, but a little advice could go a long way. 'You know, I discovered that it is best to actually see where you are to work before you do. Sometimes people try to trick you and you end up having to do things that you did not bargain for.'

'They do?' The woman's nose wrinkled, but her eyes grew wide with astonishment. 'I never thought of such a thing. She seemed such a nice person, but now that I think on it, she kept touching my cheek.'

'Do you have enough to purchase a return ticket?' Louisa continued. 'Just in case the job is not what you think it is. They might take your money, but a ticket is easier to conceal.'

'That's a bonny idea. I wish I were clever enough to have thought of that.'

Helping the woman to purchase her ticket took no more than a few moments, but it brought back so many memories. Louisa gritted her teeth. How she wished someone had taken the time to help her. But she had survived on her own and she would do so again. This time, though, she refused to run. She would fight for her life and her future.

'Ah, here I find you. You were true to your word about the chemist.'

Louisa controlled the sudden race of her pulse. Jonathon. And it was not a coincidence. She pasted a smile on her face. He might have bested her in the first round, but she would refuse to give in.

'Miss Daphne needs her tincture. After this morning's excitement, Miss Daphne requires rest. I lost Miss Mattie earlier this year and I do not intend to lose Miss Daphne.'

'You care about her.'

'Of course I do. It is the only reason I returned to England. Miss Daphne is family.' Louisa brushed Jonathon's hand from her elbow. 'Now, if you will excuse me, you must find someone else to spy on. I have a tincture to purchase.'

'I was not spying on you. I was visiting a pawnbroker.' He nodded towards the shop where a trio of gold balls hung. A variety of items were displayed in the window.

'Are you let in the pockets?' Louisa gaped at Jonathon. There was nothing about him to indicate that he was short of money—quite the opposite. His expensively cut frockcoat, silver-topped cane and the intricately tied neckcloth screamed discreet wealth.

'Hardly.' The faintest hint of a smile touched his lips. 'Chesterholm has suffered a series of thefts in recent months. Several of the items turned up in Newcastle. I have been visiting other pawnbrokers in the area to put the word out.'

'Have you caught the thief?'

'He and his accomplice have escaped so far.' He

frowned. 'I will catch the thief in time. Whoever it was will regret tangling with me.'

A small shiver went down Louisa's spine at the determination in his face. 'I have no time for those who steal. Even when I was starving and could find no work, I never stole.'

'How did you survive?'

'I sold my hair.'

'You did what!' The colour drained from his face. 'Your hair... You considered it to be your crowning glory. You were determined to have it as long as possible. Cutting your hair would weaken you.'

'Foolish notions vanish when faced with reality,' Louisa said quickly before she lost her nerve. Jonathon had to understand what she had gone through and how she would never have voluntarily cut her hair. 'Selling my hair was preferable to selling my body. Without references people were not willing to take a chance on a governess.'

'But you went back to my stepmother. She paid for your passage to Italy. Did you sell your hair there?'

'In England. It was only after the money was gone that I went back seeking your whereabouts and your stepmother paid my passage to get rid of me. She did not want me disrupting your impending nuptials.' Louisa hugged her arms about her waist. It was as much of an explanation as he deserved.

Jonathon stared at her in astonishment. 'You are joking. Your hair is long now. You have it done up in a crown of plaits.'

'I would never joke about the matter.' She gave a mental sigh. Jonathon probably did not even remember how proud she had been of her hair. 'You should have seen me with short curls. It was quite fetching, very Roman in a way. The summer is so hot in Italy that short hair helped a great deal.'

There was no answering smile from Jonathon. If anything, his face became more creased and concerned. 'Did it hurt you very much?'

Louisa blinked rapidly. He did remember. He was not supposed to remember the little details. She clutched her reticule tighter to her bosom. 'Having your hair cut does not hurt, Lord Chesterholm.'

'Once you thought otherwise.' A smile tugged at the corner of his mouth. 'When I cut a lock of your hair for a keepsake, you yelped.'

'And then you kissed me to ease the pain,' Louisa whispered. The corners of her mouth tingled with anticipation.

'Yes, that's right.' He looked down at her. His eyes softened and deepened, glowing with a warm light. The crowds faded to background noise until it was the two of them standing there, just looking at each other.

Louisa blinked and dragged her mind back from that moment, forced herself to remember the afterwards part rather than the spun-glass bubble dream.

'It was that kiss that gave us away. Or so your step-mother claimed. Her maid, Lily, spotted us.' A bitter laugh escaped her throat. 'Even if I had not gone with you that day, she had planned to dismiss me. We were living on borrowed time. But your stepmother was correct—I had betrayed her trust.'

'That was never its intention,' he said quietly.

'I weathered the storm.' Louisa kept her head up and

ignored the great hole opening up inside of her. She was not going to cry. It was somehow worse having Jonathon being kind. 'My hair grew far quicker than I could have imagined. They would have cut it anyway when I had the fever in Naples.'

'You were ill?'

'For a while. It was how Miss Mattie discovered me and took me under her wing.'

'Kindness itself.'

'Yes, she was. I need to get Miss Daphne's tincture.' Louisa drew her shawl tighter about her body, aware suddenly of how close he was and how comforting his arms could be. And how she'd vowed over her daughter's body that she'd never need him again. 'She will worry if I am gone too long. She depends on me.'

He put his hand on her shoulder and the warmth radiated outwards, but it also held her in place. 'What were you doing in the booking office? It seems a strange place to purchase a tincture.'

'Doing my good deed for the day.' Louisa pointed towards where the young woman stood patiently waiting for the coach. 'Helping that woman purchase a ticket to safety.'

Jonathon's entire body tensed as he turned his head.

'Thompson! Thompson!' Jonathon called and a heavy-set man appeared at his side. He gestured towards the woman. 'I believe we have found Sims's missing daughter. You know her better than I, but she reminds me of the girl.'

'Yes, master. It is the young person.'

'Then she is alive and well and not at the bottom of

the Tyne as you predicted. Her parents will be relieved to see her again.' Jonathon pointed to the woman. 'Whatever you do Thompson, keep her from getting on that mail coach. We want her to go home voluntarily.'

The man hurried off towards the woman and spoke to her, gesturing towards where Louisa and Jonathon stood.

'What are you doing, Jonathon?' Louisa caught his sleeve. 'You have no right to prevent that woman from getting on that coach. I will not allow your man to abduct that woman.'

'Annie…Annie Sims!' Jonathon called out and the woman turned. Her ruddy complexion burned scarlet, but she quickly dropped a curtsy. Louisa sucked in her breath. Perhaps she was wrong. Perhaps Jonathon did know her. 'Stay there! Wait for Thompson.'

The woman obediently moved out of the queue. Louisa let Jonathon go, but to her surprise, he stood there watching as Thompson moved in between the carriages. 'What with one thing and another that woman has caused me a great deal of trouble over the past few weeks. Hopefully now Sims will begin to shoe horses properly again.'

'You know her?' Louisa stared at Jonathon in surprise as the burly Thompson caught up with the woman and began an animated conversation. After a few words, Thompson handed her a handkerchief and Annie burst into noisy sobs. He then led her away. 'Where he is taking her? It is against the law to abduct a woman.'

'I am doing what is best.'

'If a hair on that woman's head is harmed… I

should call a parish constable! You are not in Chester-holm now!'

'Thompson is my valet. He is trustworthy. You need not worry. Annie is safe. She will be amongst friends. She does not belong with this filth of humanity.'

'But what is your connection with Annie Sims?' Louisa crossed her arms. Jonathon might be able to act in that high-handed fashion on his estate and with his employees, but not with her. 'What right does your man have to take her anywhere?'

'Annie is the only daughter of my farrier, Matthew Sims. Home is Chesterholm village.' Jonathon stared down at her, his eyes serious. 'Her parents are sick with worry about her, so much so that her father has been unable to shoe horses properly and I have three lame race horses as a result. I promised them if I should dis-cover her in Newcastle that I would bring her home.'

'When did she leave?'

'Annie vanished in the night several weeks ago, about the time of the latest thefts. Her father swears she was not involved, but—'

'She left because of a man,' Louisa interrupted. 'It is an old story.'

'Yes? Where is this man of hers?'

'He is married with children, so she left. A depress-ingly familiar tale. It will be just a coincidence about the theft happening at the same time.'

'But she has money to take a mail coach.' His face showed his scepticism. 'Or did you give that to her?'

'Her mother slipped her some…in case. But she does not want to return home. She is afraid of her father's fists,' Louisa explained slowly.

'Matthew Sims would not harm a hair on his daughter's head. He worships the ground she walks on. She…' He sighed. 'Come with me and speak to her if you don't believe me.'

Jonathon led her over to the inn and a small private room where Annie and his valet sat in close conversation.

'Got her, my lord!' Thompson called out. 'She's going home! We will have runners in the Hexham Plate after all.'

'I suppose you are pleased. Horses must come before what a woman wants,' Louisa said as a self-satisfied smile crossed Jonathon's face and the tension appeared to flow out of his shoulders.

'A thoroughly satisfactory outcome.' He straightened his hat and sobered. 'It is one item off my list. I promised her father that if I encountered Annie in Newcastle that I would bring her back. I would have done this even if my horses were not involved.'

'Are you ready to go then, Mr Thompson? I'd like see my mam as soon as possible, now that his lordship has said it is fine.' Annie pushed her glass away from her and then gave a quick gasp of pain. 'Oh, no, someone left a splinter of glass on the table. I cut my wrist. Stupid, really. It shows what my day is like.'

Louisa watched in horror as several dark red spots appeared on Annie's wrist.

'Here.' Jonathon withdrew a snow-white handkerchief from his pocket. 'Bind it up with that.'

'I couldn't possibly.' Annie protested. 'It belongs to your lordship. I could never—'

'Do it!' Jonathon ordered.

Annie bound her wrist up. 'Your lordship is very kind. I hadn't expected—'

'I look after my own, Annie. Remember that.' Jonathon patted the woman's shoulder. 'Go with Thompson. He will see you right.'

Louisa stared after the pair.

'She trusts you? She was adamant before…that she'd never go back.'

'Some people do, Louisa, as surprising as it seems to you.'

'And when she gets back to the village. Will you keep her safe then?'

'Sims knows what will happen if he crosses me. The entire village knows it. I once beat a man who tried to steal one of Sims's horses.'

'You beat someone.' Louisa stared at Jonathon. She had always considered him more of a lover than a fighter, someone who avoided unpleasantness.

'All those pugilist lessons came in use that night. I developed a mean upper cut. The man deserved it.'

'And do you really think she had something to do with the missing cameos? She did not even want to take your handkerchief.'

Jonathon shrugged. 'Whoever took the cameos had a great deal more knowledge about the security in the house than Annie. They knew the combination for the safe and where they were stored.'

'Could her lover have been involved without Annie's knowledge?'

'I will obtain a description of the man she ran away with and see if any of the servants were seen with him.'

Louisa listened with growing surprise. The old Jonathon had never known anything about the servants, let alone servants' gossip. But he appeared to know about this woman, what she did and who she associated with. 'It is good that Annie has someone looking out for her.'

A muscle jumped in his jaw. 'You have nothing to fear when you and Miss Daphne are guests in my house. Once you trusted me…'

'And if I have grown beyond needing your protection?' Louisa asked and forced a warm curl from her insides. Jonathon had not changed, not really. He remained the same sort of man that he had always been—self-absorbed and concerned only about those things that affected him. He was speaking about her surrendering her independence and she had no intention of becoming a clinging vine, running to him for every little thing as she had done before.

'It is still offered.' He reached out and tightened the shawl about her shoulders. 'The rain is starting. You do not want to catch a chill.'

'I know what to do.' Louisa kept her body stiff and away from his touch. 'I learnt my lesson a long time ago.'

'Louisa, I look forward to welcoming you to Chester-holm, to my home.' He tilted. 'Will Furniss be travelling with you?'

'He is Miss Daphne's nephew.' Louisa gave her brightest smile. Here finally was a chance to show Jonathon that she did have other beaux. 'He is very attentive to his great aunt. It has been most refreshing to see.'

She strode purposefully away, resisting the temptation to see his reaction.

* * *

'You returned.'

'You seem surprised.' Louisa carefully retrieved the tincture from her reticule and set it on the table in front of Miss Daphne. She shook the raindrops from her shawl.

'It did cross my mind that you would book your passage to Sorrento and go. You were flustered when you left. You forgot your umbrella.' Miss Daphne's eyes narrowed. 'First time ever.'

'It was not raining when I left.'

'This is Northumberland, rather than Sorrento. It rains.'

'I know where I am,' Louisa replied carefully as she poured a scant measure of the liquid and handed it to Miss Daphne. 'Why are you asking me?'

'Because you have returned with bright cheeks and sparkling eyes and the wrong sort of tincture. That is the one I used to take, the one Mattie complained always made me too merry in the evening. It has gin in it. Lots of gin.'

Louisa stared down at the label and gritted her teeth. She had been positive that she had chosen the correct tincture. But in her haste and confusion, she must have asked for the wrong one.

'You met Lord Chesterholm while you were out.' She leant forwards and her smile widened. 'Deny it at your peril, Louisa.'

Louisa pretended to take an interest in replacing the stopper on the tincture bottle. Carefully she explained the incident. 'It was the purest chance. He thought I might be running away as well, but, Miss Daphne, I stopped running years ago. Miss Mattie taught me that problems were to be faced. Everything is possible if one holds true to one's ideals.'

'Mattie was always liberal with her advice, but rather less inclined to take it in her own life.' Miss Daphne waved her hand, dismissing the reference. 'Did you run the first time?'

'I had no choice. Mrs Ponsby-Smythe—'

'Piffle, you always have a choice. You simply chose not to use it. You were young. You were pushed.' Miss Daphne put down the book of poetry that she had been reading. 'You have a second chance.'

'A second chance for what? I will not make a fool of myself again.'

'You sound exactly like Mattie there and where did it get her? A lonely bed on a foreign shore, dedicating her life to bits of rocks and shell.'

'She was happy. She had a fulfilling life. An exciting one. She travelled far and wide.'

'Have you been living or merely existing?' Miss Daphne tapped her finger against her mouth. 'You have seemed a different person since we encountered Lord Chesterholm. Far more alive. There is a glow about you. Rupert remarked on it as well. My nephew would make an excellent catch.'

'I have no intentions in that direction and your nephew has not said a word.' Louisa gave Miss Daphne's hand a pat.

'That is only because you cleverly turn the conversation.' Miss Daphne gave a sigh. 'I suppose I shall have to discover someone else for him.'

'Isn't it better to let things take their course? Lord Furniss might have his views on the subject. Miss Daphne, you must call a halt to this matchmaking. You could get yourself in trouble, or cause serious damage to innocent people's reputations.'

Miss Daphne wrinkled her nose. 'It is far more amusing my way. I am merely giving Eros a helpful push, so he can aim his arrows of love straight. It is up to the couple if they get married or not.'

'I am old enough to make up my own mind without any assistance—divine or otherwise,' Louisa said firmly. 'I don't plan to be dependent on any man, even Sir Francis.'

Miss Daphne tapped her fingers against her mouth. 'All in all today has presented me with a solution to a most perplexing problem. I am looking forward to the Chesterholm house party more than ever.'

A warning prickle went down Louisa's back. 'Miss Mattie is not here to pick up the pieces.'

'Mattie would agree with me wholeheartedly…this time. I believe she might even have had it in her mind.' Miss Daphne rocked back and forth like a young girl. 'Mattie would completely agree with my assessment of the situation. I wonder that I did not see it before. It was she who suggested that I revisit old haunts.'

'And you are not going to tell me?' Louisa leant forwards. 'I could assist you.'

'When the time is right, Louisa, my dear. Please trust my instinct.' Miss Daphne reached for the bell and summoned the maid for tea, ending the conversation.

Louisa forced her expression to stay bland. Miss Daphne might be confident about her matchmaking skills, but Louisa knew that there was no love in her future. Love was something that happened to other people.

A house party, a bloody house party, something he had sworn never to endure again after Clarissa had died—but Louisa had left him little choice.

He stared at the scrawled note. And now he had the added complication of Venetia arriving in the midst. Louisa would be protected from her, but he refused to allow the problem to fester. Venetia was even likely to take Margaret away if she heard about Louisa's reappearance.

Jonathon strode back into Chesterholm Grange, his boot heels ringing on the polished marble floor as he advanced towards his study. There was something uplifting about returning to this estate. Despite the austerity of the Palladian façade, he loved the warmth and comfort of its interior. It was safe and it was home.

When he had left here a week ago, his future had appeared certain and, if he had been honest, a bit staid. And now everything he held dear had been turned upside down and his life, rather than being straightforward, had become a tangled web of half-truths.

He walked over to his desk and picked up the crude pen-and-ink drawing he had framed four years ago. Silently he took the black ribbon from around the frame and tossed it on the fire. He eased the picture out of the frame, intending to toss that as well. Louisa's long-ago face stared up at him with its secret smile, daring him. Jonathon's heart squeezed. Despite everything Louisa had said, he found it impossible to believe that the Louisa he had known was gone and in her place a doppelgänger. No, the Louisa he knew was somewhere buried beneath the layers of smooth sophistication and quick-witted banter.

He put the drawing in a drawer. Then he opened the back of the frame and took out the licence, a special one, and the lock of hair. By rights they should go, but he couldn't. He slid the licence into a drawer. Some day the proof of his intentions might be needed, but only if there was no other way of reaching the woman buried deep inside Louisa.

'Lord Chesterholm?' The nurse came into the study, carrying his son. 'Arthur thought he heard the carriage. He went to the window and stood there, pointing.'

Jonathon slammed the drawer shut. Louisa would have to wait. His son needed him.

The dark-haired boy peeked at him shyly for a minute. Jonathon squatted down and held open his arms. The toddler rushed into them and Jonathon swung him up into the air before bringing the boy close to his chest amidst the shrieks of laughter. Jonathon breathed deeply, savouring his little boy's smell of soap and soft skin. Standing there with this scrap of humanity, his boy, in his arms, Jonathon knew that he would not wish the sands of time back. Of all the things he had done, Arthur was the crowning glory. He made life worth living again and had taught Jonathon to take joy in simple things.

When Clarissa had died, her family and Venetia had strongly hinted that it would be for the best if Arthur came to live with them, but Jonathon had refused. Arthur was his son. He fought them all. His son would be brought up in the way he wanted.

Louisa had wanted a large family, children tumbling about everywhere. Because she had been an only child and then an orphan, she had been determined to have a large family. And now she was on the verge of becoming engaged to Sir Francis.

'Has he spoken properly yet? He was nearly there before I left.' Jonathon ruffled Arthur's brown hair. 'Have you been practising? Has the cat got your tongue?'

Arthur giggled and snuggled closer to Jonathon.

'He will speak soon, won't you, poppet?' Nanny Hawks gave him a beatific smile. 'He's quiet-like around you. You're his father. There's naught to be worried about. He will speak when he is good and ready.'

'I wish I had your confidence, Nanny Hawks. I want my son to speak beautifully. He will have a position in society.'

'He is young, my lord.' The nurse bobbed a curtsy. 'Is there anything else?'

'We will be having visitors, a house party.'

'You wish me to keep Arthur out of the way? He has hated strangers ever since the Newtons tried to seize him that time.'

'They will not try that again.'

'We can go to my sister's if you like. She has expressed a wish to see this gentleman ever since he was proven partial to her buttered toast, and Elizabeth is missing her daughter. Ever so.'

'No, I have spent far too much time away from my son recently. Soon I fear he will scream and hide his face when he sees me.'

'There is no fear of that, my lord. He adores his papa.'

Her face crumpled slightly. 'Any word of our Annie? I fear the worst, truly I do.'

'Your niece has returned, Nanny Hawks. I, or rather a Miss Sibson, discovered her in Newcastle. Your sister will have her house full again and no need to miss anyone.'

'Oh, praise the Lord.' The woman fell down on her knees and lifted her arms to heaven.

'Nanny Hawks!' Jonathon stared at the woman, shocked at the emotional outburst.

'I have gone down on my knees every night begging for forgiveness and asking for Annie to come back to the family.' The woman wiped her eyes with a corner of her apron. 'It is so very hard to lose a child. I consider Annie to be my own.'

Jonathon put Arthur down. For the life of him, he could not imagine why Nanny Hawks would need to ask for forgiveness. Arthur's nanny was one of the kindest women he had met. 'I wish to be kept informed of all nursery doings, particularly if any of the women happen on the nursery.'

'I understand, my lord.' The woman hesitated. 'And what do I do if this *lady* should come in to the nursery?'

'Inform me immediately. Allow me to handle it.'

Jonathon reached out and touched Arthur's silky brown hair. Arthur gave him a sudden smile that reminded him of Clarissa.

Jonathon's stomach churned. Had Clarissa known when they had married that Louisa was alive? Certainly as she lay dying after Arthur's birth, she had begged him to look at their son and to always remember that she had

had his best interests at heart. At the time, it had struck him as strange, but now he wondered. How much had she known? Had guilt racked her? Did that explain her distance?

Their marriage might have lacked passion and he knew that he had not been the husband Clarissa had wished for, but he had thought they were friends. It had surprised him, though, how much emphasis Clarissa had put on outward appearance and how cold she was.

Jonathon buried his face in Arthur's hair, savouring the clean, little-boy smell. The past could not be undone. Whoever's fault it was, it most definitely was not Arthur's.

'And this lady who will be visiting, is she kind?' the nurse asked.

Louisa's intent features as she had pleaded for Annie Sims swam in front of him. The old Louisa existed. All he could do was hope that he never had to make a choice between her and his son.

'I have reason to hope so.'

## Chapter Six

Chesterholm Grange was far too grand and austere to ever be called home. Louisa knew that the instant she saw it from the carriage window. Palladian architecture with its mock-Grecian columns and unadorned frontage shouted power and prestige rather than cosy warmth and welcome. A mansion, a hall, or perhaps even a seat, but never a home.

Louisa alighted from the carriage and stared up at the rose-grey edifice. Venetia Ponsby-Smythe's mocking voice echoed in her brain. *And you aspire to be the chatelaine of a great house? My stepson has expectations and will require a wife who is worthy of the Chesterholm heritage. You, my dear, are not even fit to wipe its doorstep.*

Seeing Chesterholm Grange for the first time on a sunlit summer's day with its many-paned windows sparkling and lawns rolling down to the water, Louisa knew what Mrs Ponsby-Smythe had meant. This sort of house demanded someone trained from birth in how to run and organise a complex estate. The mistress of such a house had duties and responsibilities as well as prestige. Louisa knew her upbringing had not prepared her for such a task. However, Mrs Ponsby-Smythe had been wrong in her assessment. She might not have been the world's best governess, but she was fit for more than washing doorsteps. And she was certainly about to walk through the front door as a guest rather than a glorified servant.

Nobody was ever going to intimidate her again.

Louisa twitched her skirt so the folds fell in a regiment of straight lines. She gave Miss Daphne a quick smile and offered her arm as the elderly woman stubbornly refused to use a cane despite having trouble walking any long distance.

'You are wearing your pensive face, Louisa,' Miss Daphne said, waving Louisa's arm away. 'Stop troubling trouble. All will be well, I can feel it in my bones.'

'Are your bones trustworthy? I think they must be very tired after the amount of time we have spent in the carriage.' Louisa put her hands on the small of her back and stretched, loosening the kinks. 'A pity Lord Furniss could not join us.'

'Rupert always enjoys travelling slowly. He wants to stop at every inn for a glass of something refreshing. It was much better that we came on our own,' Miss Daphne said with a decisive nod.

At Miss Daphne's insistence, they had barely stopped on the journey, only taking a short break each time the horses were changed. With each bump of the road, Louisa's bottom had met the hard seat until she was certain she had obtained a first-rate collection of bruises.

Miss Daphne had appeared not to notice, simply settling against the cushions and resting her eyes.

'They may be old, but they are reliable.' Her lips curved upwards. 'I am an excellent traveller, Louisa. You should know that by now.'

Louisa rolled her shoulders. 'All I know is that my back aches from sitting in the coach for hours.'

Miss Daphne gave Louisa a pat on her shoulder. 'It is a time for girding your lions as my dear mother would have said.'

'You mean loins.'

'My mother considered loins to be vulgar.' Miss Daphne gave an infectious laugh that sounded like it belonged to a twelve-year-old rather than an elderly lady. 'And I have loved the mental picture of fastening a belt around a lion. Ah, even the air smells the way it used to—all old oak and the sweet tang of autumn approaching.'

Louisa shook her head. Miss Daphne and her sayings. It was one of the reasons she adored her. But Miss Daphne was wrong this time.

'There is no need for any special preparations or concerns.' Louisa waved an airy hand. 'There is nothing between Lord Chesterholm and me except an old worn-out acquaintance. I promise you that.'

'Some promises are made to be broken,' Miss Daphne reminded her. 'It is you that he wanted here, not this old bag of bones. Inviting me to revisit a place of girlish memory was the threadbare excuse. He is having a house party for you.'

'I plan on spending as little time in Lord Chesterholm's company as possible and you are far from a bag of bones.'

'You are sounding more like Mattie every day.'

'And this is a bad thing?' Louisa gave a laugh. All the way over she had kept thinking of how Miss Mattie would have approached the problem. She suspected the woman would have had no difficulty in dealing with Jonathon and the growing attraction.

'Vinegar tongues only serve spinsters with enough money not to mind what others think of them.' Miss Daphne sighed. 'Mattie once cared too much, but she allowed her pride to stand between her and her love. Will you?'

Louisa gazed at the battlements. Miss Daphne appeared to think Miss Mattie had had regrets about her chosen path in life. Louisa had never seen them. 'What was between Lord Chesterholm and me was a young man's fancy, nothing more.'

'There is always a second chance for love while both remain living. Mattie refused to acknowledge that. She preferred to be alone in her righteousness. To quarrel over a silly story.'

Louisa concentrated on keeping her step steady as the gravel crunched under her feet. A second chance for love—that was the last thing she wanted. Love was something that happened to other people. What had been between Jonathon and herself had been passion, pure and simple…and it had burnt out. She had been ready to pour all the love she'd had to give into their child, but the baby had rejected her as well and died. It was then that she'd decided to stand alone.

'I have always felt sad about Mattie and the late Lord

Chesterholm, what might have been had each been a little less stubborn. Each one had had to be right and neither was prepared to make the first move towards reconciliation,' Miss Daphne continued blithely on. 'I do find it unfathomable why she never told me of your connection to Chesterholm. But, Louisa, Mattie loved you for you, not because you once kept time with young Jonathon.'

Louisa bowed her head. Once again Miss Daphne had seen to the heart of the matter. 'I miss her and her counsel.'

Miss Daphne gave Louisa's hand a squeeze. 'I always have considered "what might have been" to be the saddest words in the English language. Remember that.'

Before Louisa could answer, she caught sight of Jonathon striding from the house. His dress was far more casual than when Louisa had last encountered him and his black riding boots were splattered with mud. Two black-and-white sheepdogs raced along at his feet, pausing every so often to give him a look of adoration before running off to find the next stick of interest. He seemed far more approachable, far more like the Jonathon who haunted her dreams. It also made him far more dangerous.

'Miss Elliot and Miss Sibson, it is good of you to arrive so promptly. Welcome to my humble home.' He grasped Miss Elliot's hand and raised it to his lips. 'You are the first.'

'The first?' Louisa said, concentrating on the sheepdog who came up to her and dropped a stick. She had rather hoped that the others would have arrived before them so she could become lost in the crowd. The only thing she could be thankful for was that Jonathon could not have overheard their conversation.

'Somebody has to be,' Miss Daphne said with maddening complacency. 'I am always delighted when it is me.'

'Well said, Miss Elliot. I was rather hoping it would be.'

Miss Daphne's cheeks grew rosy under the warmth of his smile. Quickly Louisa concentrated on the ground, rather than on him. He had hoped for them to be the first. She hated that her pulse leapt. He wanted to see her and spend time with her, rather than concentrating on the other guests. She tried to think clearly. 'As long as I am not a fly to be trapped in your web.'

'Perish the thought.' A smile tugged at his mouth. 'But it will give us some time to get the business of comparing my uncle's catalogue with the remaining cameos completed. Mixing business with pleasure is a dreadful notion to my mind.'

Louisa tilted her head as goose bumps ran down her arms. Her entire strategy for getting through this house party had been to fade in to the background and to be ignored. Now between Miss Daphne and Jonathon, she would have to come up with another scheme, something that did not involve rekindling her attraction to him. Rekindling?

Louisa started.

The physical attraction had never gone away. It had been there lurking in her mind, waiting to strike. And if Jonathon knew, he'd use it against her as he had done before.

'Business?' she squeaked.

'You are here to give advice on my late uncle's cameos.' He lifted an eyebrow as if to dare her to say differently. 'What other sort of business would there be? Everything else is for your enjoyment. Pleasure is the order of the day at Chesterholm. Was that not always the case, Miss Daphne?'

Miss Daphne murmured her assent.

Louisa pressed her lips together and held back the swift retort. Whatever this party was about, it was not for her enjoyment. 'Do we know when the Blandishes will arrive?'

'I wish I had considered sending Rupert with the Blandishes. He could have done with the company.' Miss Daphne gave an exaggerated yawn. 'Travelling from Newcastle exhausts aged bones.'

'In a few weeks' time when the railway line opens, it will be much quicker. You can drive your carriage down to the train and take it back to Newcastle. It will take no more than three hours.'

'Three hours.' Miss Daphne shook her head. 'We truly live in an age of miracles. I can remember the wagon-ways of my youth. And the steam engines at the pit heads—great rattling things that belched smoke. It is a wonder that they ever were able to move. You will never get me behind one of those monsters.'

'You should rest, Miss Daphne,' Louisa said firmly, preparing to offer the old lady her arm. 'Supper on a tray might be good. I could sit with you to give you company.'

The dimple flashed in the corner of Jonathon's mouth as if he knew what she had planned and refused to let her win that easily. 'Miss Daphne should be the judge, but I assure you that tonight's entertainment will be quiet.'

'And you should take a turn about the garden. It clears the young mind after a carriage journey,' Miss Daphne said. The wrinkles on her face seemed more pronounced than ever but a calculating gleam appeared in her eyes. 'I have a memory of a great cedar tree in the centre of a maze.'

'The cedar still exists, but the maze is gone,' Jonathon informed her. 'My uncle must have done away with it in his youth…when he changed the garden. I think there might be some sketches.'

'The maze was near a stream, before you came upon the Roman ruins,' Miss Daphne replied. 'Mattie adored it.'

'Ah, I know where you must mean.' Jonathon's brow cleared. 'I can take you there on the way to the house.'

'Louisa, you may give me a report of the tree. My old bones need to rest.' Miss Daphne looked at her with a stern expression. 'I am certain Lord Chesterholm's servants can show me to my room.'

Miss Daphne swept away as Louisa stared after her in astonishment. Miss Daphne had not complained of feeling tired before. She glanced up at Jonathon, who stood so the shadow from the yew hedge obscured his expression.

Jonathon snapped his fingers and the dogs came to him immediately, sitting by him with expectant faces. Louisa was impressed at how he was able to command such obedience.

'Miss Elliot appears determined to leave us together.

Do we oblige her or not?' Jonathon murmured, putting his gloved hand under her elbow.

'Miss Daphne is starting to show her age. It is why she wanted to return to England and say goodbye to the places she loved as a girl while she could. Of course, she also hates it if one reminds her of the fact.' Louisa tightened her grip on her reticule and attempted to breathe steadily. The last thing she wanted to explain was Miss Daphne's misguided and utterly obvious attempts at matchmaking. Or the fact that Miss Daphne had guessed that Louisa wanted to build castles in the air.

Just because Jonathon was standing next to her did not mean that her body had to be aware of his every move. She fought the temptation to lean into his light touch and moved her arm. Instantly he released her.

'How ill is she, Louisa?'

'Not ill, old. There is a difference. The journey must have tired her out more than I imagined. Oh!' Louisa cried as a bramble wrapped around her boot and held her fast.

'Allow me.' Jonathon bent down. 'Save getting your fingers dirty.'

'I can do it myself,' Louisa replied firmly and she tugged at the bramble, overbalanced and fell to the ground, sending her skirts flying up. The dogs thought it was a great game and began to lick her face, putting their muddy paws all over her travelling dress. She looked up at Jonathon. The corners of his mouth twitched. 'Don't you say a word!'

'I would not dream of it.' His face instantly became serious.

Louisa's shoulders shook as she failed to suppress a

laugh. Then Jonathon joined in the laughter as she shook her head. 'I must have looked a sight with my petticoats all in the air.'

'I was a gentleman and looked away.' His eyes danced as their laughter mingled. 'After a brief glimpse to make sure you were uninjured.'

'My gloves remained clean at any rate. And the mud will sponge off.'

'Next time, remember—accepting help can be beneficial to one's dignity.' He held out an arm. 'Do you wish to go to the house?'

'A bit of mud will not hurt me.' Louisa ignored his hand. 'I am capable of walking without assistance.'

'That's the old Louisa spirit! I had wondered where it had gone.'

Louisa allowed him to stride off a few paces. She shook her head. It was no good. The old Louisa kept threatening to appear. She had to do it. She had to be honest with him. They had to get the rules and boundaries clear or she'd be tempted to fall into old habits again. 'I…I refused your help as I had no desire to pay the price.'

'What price would that be?' He stopped and turned. His face was a cipher.

'A kiss. I know you of old, Jonathon.'

He raised his eyebrow. 'What is this in aid of? You keep saying you have changed. Am I not allowed the same courtesy?'

'Your past actions speak louder than words,' Louisa said quickly before she lost her nerve. Things needed to be said. Rules drawn up and adhered to by both of them. It was the only way she'd survive this house party. She should have seen that earlier. 'Will you give me your promise that there will be no attempts at seduction while I am Chesterholm?'

'Who don't you trust—me or yourself?' He crossed the distance between them in a few short strides.

'It is important we have the rules clear and precise. It makes for an easier life.'

'Does it? Why?'

'Your actions…what we shared before…things are different now…' Louisa twisted the handle of her reticule about her fingers. He was going to understand the boundaries before she went into his house if she had to write them in blood and pin them to his forehead.

'Which actions? When haven't I behaved like a gentleman?' Jonathon's eyes shone with fire.

'You think that kissing me at the Assembly Rooms was the act of an honourable man?'

'There were two people involved in that kiss, Louisa. Stop trying to twist the facts. Or are you saying only gentlemen should refrain from acting on their desires?'

Louisa examined the pearl button on her gloves. He was seeking to twist things. Had he not kissed her, she would have withstood the attraction, but right now her body hummed with awareness. 'A lady should expect protection from a gentleman. You initiated the kiss. Deny that at your peril.'

'You recently refused my protection. Does this mean you wish to be kissed?' There was a steely determination in his features that had not been there the last time they had met. Louisa's stomach tightened. 'Do you ever wonder what happened to the girl you used to be?'

'She and all her dreams vanished, buried under the weight of reality.'

'It is a pity, as I rather liked her.' He leant forwards so his hot breath caressed her cheek. 'And rescuing her.'

'She made far too many mistakes.' Louisa stared down at the dogs. 'She was overly inclined to believe in her dreams and to act before she had considered the consequences. I am far happier being independent and taking the time to consider what is best for me.'

'Independent? Relying on no one? You were never a naïve fool, Louisa. You had admirable qualities. You grabbed life with both hands. Now you want to run away from it.'

'I stopped searching for a white knight, Jonathon. I no longer need rescuing, especially from myself.' Louisa breathed deeply and tried to regain control of her tongue. The conversation had strayed beyond the bounds of politeness and it was all her fault. But she also knew that she could not stay, worrying about this. 'Will you give me your promise, Jonathon? You will stay within the bounds of propriety for my visit here.'

'Do you truly expect me to answer?' He regarded her for a long moment. Then his face cleared, and tiny sparkles came into his eyes. 'Be careful what you wish for, Louisa. I agree to your rules. However, if you should break them, I will consider the agreement null and void. Do we have a deal?'

'Yes, we do.' Louisa held out her gloved hand.

He took it for a moment longer than was strictly proper. 'I look forward to seeing you keep your rules.'

'I must freshen up after the journey, particularly after falling. The tree can wait until Miss Daphne feels strong enough to accompany me.' Louisa gave the dogs another pat. The simple action helped distract her. How hard would it be? 'It is amazing how soiled one can get, travelling.'

She started to sweep away, deliberately turning her back on him. She could keep to her rules.

'I never meant to hurt you, Louisa.'

Something in his voice curled around her insides like an invisible thread and held her there. When she had been on the boat steaming towards Italy, all she had wanted to do was to die. Then she had discovered that one never did die of a broken heart, one simply existed until one day her heart had stopped aching so much. Hurt! He did not even know the meaning of the word. And whatever happened between them here, she would not let him in her heart again. She refused to give him a third chance.

'It is in the past.' Her voice sounded thick to her ears as something deep within her flickered and then flared to life. And she knew she lied. The hurt was with her. And what was worse, she wanted to forgive him. 'In the past, Jonathon. Where it stays.'

'And the past is to be forgotten and never referred to.' Jonathon's words were a statement, rather than a question. She longed to know if it was what he believed, or what he wanted to believe. The past for her could never be forgotten.

Louisa turned around and saw him standing there with the two dogs sitting at his feet. A faint breeze ruffled his golden-brown hair. He was the very picture of masculine temptation. And she knew if he made one gesture towards her that she would be lost. And it was pointless as whatever should have been said between them needed to have been said years ago. He made it sound like she should forget everything that had happened and start again. It was not that easy…not for her.

'I find it best to keep the past in the past,' she said. 'I turned my face towards the future years ago.'

'Have you, indeed? Then why are you so afraid of it?'

Jonathon took a step closer, watching the way Louisa worried her bottom lip. An errant curl of red hair skimmed her cheek and her bonnet was askew. He was very tempted to forget his resolutions and kiss her. His mouth longed to taste her. But he was greedy. He wanted to possess more than just her body.

'Why does your past frighten you if it means nothing?'

'I am not frightened of anything,' Louisa said quickly, far too quickly. 'You know about Sir Francis. I want to be able to look him in the eye when I return to Sorrento.'

'Tempted, are we, Louisa?' he asked in a low murmur, forcing the jealous rage back down his throat. 'You are making paper-thin excuses. You have no intention of marrying Sir Francis. You value your independence too highly. His name is a shield, nothing more. He does not make your blood sing or your body thrum with desire. But every time you want to kiss me, you mention him. Are you going to marry him, Louisa, or are you going to be true to your ideals?'

His entire being tensed as he waited. The last time he'd been this tense, Arthur was being born and he was waiting to hear if he might live. Louisa had to tell the truth or the temptation to seduce her and claim her as his own would grow too great. And if he did that, he'd lose her. She had to come to him. Their desire had to be a mutually acknowledged thing.

Louisa crossed her arms, glared at him. Suddenly a broad smile broke out across her face. 'Yes, you are right. I will never marry him. I have no plans to marry anyone. I have decided to follow Miss Mattie's example and remain a spinster. Satisfied?'

Jonathon ground his teeth. She had relinquished the myth of Sir Francis, but had raised a formidable shield in its place and he had allowed it to happen. Spinster? Louisa was far too alive to become a dried-up old maid. 'Did Miss Elliot desire you to become an ape leader?'

Louisa wrinkled her nose. 'Miss Mattie was a shining example of why spinsters should not be pitied, but admired.'

'Which is why you want to create rules to keep your independence.'

'I want to make sure that we both *understand* the rules before this house party of yours begins. Too much is unsettled between us.'

'Some rules are meant to be broken.' He lowered his voice to a purr.

'And others need to be kept. Rules keep people safe.'

'The enjoyment is in deciding which is which. Taking a risk.' He paused. How far could he push her? He had to time her shattering. Too soon and she'd slip through his fingers. 'Do you know how to take risks in this new life of yours, Louisa? I can remember when you caught that horse, the one that shied with Margaret on it. When everyone shouted at you to stay away. You broke the rules then.'

'That was a long time ago and I acted on pure instinct.' Louisa spoke quickly, blotting out the memory. Instinct was not something to be proud of. Instinct led to trouble. 'I thought everyone would understand that I acted out of the purest of motives. It was not to attract attention, like some accused me of.'

'Perception is all.'

'It is indeed and it is important that Miss Daphne does not get any ideas in her head.' Louisa attempted a sophisticated laugh, but it came out like a strangled cat. 'I doubt she is very tired. She is normally an excellent traveller with far more stamina than I, but generally very little interest in cedar trees.'

'Why would she want to do that?' He reached out and adjusted her bonnet so it sat squarely on her head. 'Why would she possibly think that we had any interest in each other? Particularly after you told her the truth about what happened four years ago.'

Louisa scuffed her kid boot in the dirt and ignored the way his finger happened to lightly brush across her temple. 'Perhaps she thinks a relationship with you will make me stay in England. She seeks to fan embers where there are none.'

'How can she meddle when we both know what she is on about? And if you say there is no attraction…she will believe you as you never change your mind.' Jonathon's eyes danced.

'I suppose you are right. After this conversation, we both know where we stand.' Louisa wrinkled her nose. Jonathon appeared amused rather than annoyed by the situation. Perhaps she was unduly worried. Perhaps he felt none of this insistent attraction when they were together.

'I know I am right. You are worrying over nothing.' His eyes crinkled. 'I am anxious to show you the comforts of Chesterholm Grange. It has become my home and I could wish for no finer place to live.'

'It seems very austere and grand from the outside.'

'It is what is on the inside that counts, its heart. It is my creed. You said it to me when I despaired of my carriage not being up to the minute.'

'I may have done. I used to be impertinent.'

'You were perfection that day.'

'Only the memory is perfection.'

He was silent for a long moment. And she knew he remembered the incident as well as she did. It was after he had returned a victor from the race that he had asked her to marry him, declaring that she was the best thing to ever happen to him, his personal lucky charm. 'It was a long time ago. We agreed. The past stays in the past.'

'I have written out a schedule.' Louisa dug into her reticule. 'It came to me during one of our all-too-brief stops. I trust you will find it adequate.'

He barely glanced at it before tearing it into four pieces. 'That won't be necessary. Not today. Possibly not ever.'

'But...but...'

'The walk to the cedar tree can wait for another day. Be sure to schedule it,' he said, lifting his chin and becoming every inch the disdainful aristocrat whose smile only showed pity for a lesser mortal. 'I have no wish to quarrel with you, Louisa.'

'Then this conversation is over as we are quarrelling.' Louisa forced her lips to smile as sweetly as possible. Once such a display of arrogance would have sent her blood boiling but she had learnt the value of keeping a cool head and sticking rigidly to the rules of politeness. 'I think in future, Jonathon, it would be best if we kept Miss Daphne with us and the topics safe.'

'Do you have a list of safe topics? Or am I to guess?' His lips quirked upwards. 'And I thought you were immune to my charms.'

'I am, but this goes beyond charm. It is provocation.' Louisa tapped her foot on the ground. 'I will not be held responsible if I am driven beyond all civility.'

The colour in his eyes deepened to a storm-tossed green. He moved closer—so close that if she breathed deeply her chest would brush his frock coat. 'You have no idea how provoking I can be.'

'I know exactly how provoking you are right now.' Louisa straightened her shoulders and gave him a quelling look. She could ignore her racing pulse and the way her breath came a little quicker. 'I have no time for such things. Our rules.'

He looked down at her. His face betrayed little emotion as his gaze travelled slowly down her form and then back up again, lingering on her curves. 'Some day, Louisa, you will not feel the need for shields with their rules and regulations. Schedules and lists chain you and keep you prisoner rather than free you.'

'And I devotedly pray that day will never come

as then I will cease to be me,' she said, looking him directly in the eye.

'When that day comes, you will prefer the person you have become.' He tilted his head and silently assessed her. 'Or maybe it will be the old impulsive you. I find I miss her.'

'No, that person is dead,' Louisa said as firmly as she could and hoped he believed her. She wished she believed it.

# *Chapter Seven*

L<small>OUISA</small> clutched her fan tightly, and straightened the skirts of her evening gown as she stopped in the middle of an unfamiliar corridor. She had been far too busy reviewing her rules on the proper way to behave in Jonathon's presence to pay attention to the many twists and turns of Chesterholm Grange's passageways. The way had seemed so straightforward when the underhousemaid had showed her yesterday that there had been no need to ring for an escort.

Louisa attempted to retrace her steps but found herself in another corridor. There was no escaping the obvious: the pictures on the walls were far from familiar; the carpet was far more faded, but there was a certain well-worn comfort about this hallway that the more formal rooms lacked.

The urge to explore nearly overwhelmed her sensibility. But her common sense reasserted itself when she regarded the hastily written schedule she kept in her reticule. Lord Furniss and the Blandishes had arrived earlier in the day. Separate carriages, but within an hour of each other. Jonathon had been true to his word—it was a proper house party. And it would never do to be whispered about as being tardy to supper.

She turned around and started to retrace her steps.

A door crashed open. Louisa jumped and dropped her fan and reticule. As she bent down to pick them up, a naked little boy rushed out of the open door, closely followed by a plump middle-aged woman dressed in a dark gown, enveloping apron and cap.

'You scamp, come back. You were supposed to stay still!'

The little boy gave a merry peal of laughter and wriggled past the nurse's skirts.

'Somebody help me catch him afore he catches his death or worse.'

Louisa bent down and blocked the toddler's way just before he dashed down the stairs. His skin smelt of soap and young child and his hands and feet created damp patches on the white silk of her evening dress.

'What a little angel,' Louisa said and the boy beamed up at her. When she had first arrived at the Ponsby-Smythes, a portrait of Jonathon with angelic dark curls and a white dress leaning against his mother's knee had hung in the hallway near the schoolroom. This little boy was the near mirror image. 'Who do you belong to?'

The boy put his thumb in his mouth and stared up at her with solemn grey eyes.

'Thank you, miss, for rescuing him.' The rather large nurse puffed up and attempted to take the boy from Louisa. The boy gave a determined shake of his head and clung tighter to Louisa.

'Perhaps it might be easier if I took him back to the nursery for you,' Louisa said. It was far too late to worry about the damp patches.

'It is kind of you, miss.' The nurse gave a small curtsy. 'He has a right mind of his own, this one. He decided that he was not going to wash and wear his fine clothes for company.'

'What happened?' Louisa asked as she deposited the little boy in the well-equipped nursery. The nurse quickly gathered him up and towelled him, before pulling on his clothes.

'I turned my back for the barest second to get the soap, and he was gone. The master will have my hide if this rascal appears at less than his best. Can't have him shaming the family.'

'Whose child is he?' Louisa asked as her heart began to thump in her ears.

'This here is Arthur Fanshaw, the master's son and heir,' the nurse said.

Louisa sucked in her breath. Jonathon had a son. Clarissa was dead. She had died hours after giving birth. He had said that when they'd met, and she had not thought to ask about a child, a living child. Tears pricked the back of her eyelids. For nearly four years, she had actively avoided children, and now she was confronted with Jonathon's little boy. All her promises of no regrets and no thinking about what might have been seemed hollow. She had lost her baby to a fever and the doctor had said that she would never bear another child. But another of her rules was broken.

She gave an inward smile. Somehow, her heart failed

to ache as much as she thought it might. Maybe the rule had been unnecessary.

'Are you all right, miss? You look as if you want to cry.' The nurse's voice came from a long ways away.

'I am fine.' Louisa put her hand over her mouth. Jonathon must never know. Thankfully he had not guessed why she had gone to Venetia Ponsby-Smythe. And now, she did not want him to. The future was important. She could adapt her rules. 'Perfectly fine.'

'Are you certain?'

Louisa swallowed hard and looked again at the little upturned face as he clung to her skirt. This little boy, this Arthur, knew nothing of the past. He only wanted to be her friend. She could do this. It was a test of her resolve.

She bent down and held out her hand. 'It is good to meet you, Arthur. I'm Louisa Sibson.'

'Excuse me, miss, did you say Sibson? The one who found our Annie?'

'Annie? Annie Sims?'

'She's…my…niece and I wanted to say thank you for returning her. Safe like.'

'It was my pleasure.'

Arthur gave an infectious laugh and launched himself into Louisa's arms.

'Would you look at that!' the nurse exclaimed. 'He is normally shy with strangers, but you, you he has taken to.'

Louisa stroked his fine hair, which curled about his cherub-like face in dark brown ringlets. 'He's a beautiful boy. His eyes remind me of his mother.'

'Most comment how like his father he is,' the nurse said with a hint of ice in her voice.

'That, too,' Louisa said carefully, wondering what she had said, 'but I met his mother several times and she had the most remarkable grey eyes.'

Arthur put his thumb in his mouth as his other hand curled tightly in her hair.

The nurse's face broke out into a wide smile. 'Well, I'll be!'

'I suspect he is a friend of my heart.' Louisa inhaled his fresh baby scent. 'It is what a dear friend of mine used to say when you met someone and felt an instant connection.'

'That is a good way of putting it. A friend of your heart. Yes, I like that.' The nurse gave a nod. 'I can understand it, like. I shall have to tell the master, mind. He wants to know everything that happens to Arthur. He will be interested to hear about Arthur's new friend of the heart.'

'But I have not been properly introduced. I did not even know...Lord Chesterholm had a son.'

'The master will not mind. He gave orders this morning that Arthur was to be dressed and presented before supper. Arthur hates wearing fine clothes, particularly the ones Mrs Ponsby-Smythe gave him, but they make him look like an angel. And I wanted such fine a company to have a good impression of him.'

'I am certain we will.'

'I will cry when Arthur's curls are cut and he is put into long trousers.'

Dressed and presented. Louisa used to cringe when the orders were given, generally by parents who never saw their children at any other time. She had always found her charges were excited the whole day and invariably acted badly. Mrs Ponsby-Smythe had been a great one for treating Margaret like an object, rather than like the lively girl she was. And Louisa was always blamed if things went wrong.

'Does Lord Chesterholm often come to the nursery?'

'When his duties permit, Miss Sibson. His lordship is a busy man. My poppet understands that about his papa.'

'Papa, Papa,' the little boy sang out. 'Lady, lady.'

She gave Arthur a hug as he nestled his head into the crook of her neck with a contented sigh.

'You have a magic touch with Arthur. He normally screams when a stranger comes near, and don't speak neither, just makes little grunting noises.'

'I suspect that Arthur will speak in time.'

The nurse pressed her lips together before beginning to clean up the spilt puddles of water. 'Lord Chesterholm worries about Arthur's speech.'

'Perhaps he has not been listening carefully enough. Children often bill and coo, but they are really trying to talk.'

The nurse gave a laugh. 'You try telling his lordship anything.'

'I shall be delighted to tell him.' Louisa handed the little boy back to the nurse. Her heart panged slightly. Jonathon's child was a handsome boy who cried out for proper love. 'He is not so old. Lord Chesterholm is worrying for nothing.'

The nurse sighed. 'I keep telling Lord Chesterholm

about some of my other babies. Lord Coltonby's youngest took an age but now he is all grown up, you cannot keep him quiet.'

'Have you been with the family long?'

'Since a few days after Arthur's birth, miss.' The nurse gave a small curtsy. 'The mistress had died and the master wanted someone experienced to look after his son. Not the woman his in-laws suggested either!' She stopped and her eyes narrowed. 'Are you related to the Newtons? Is that why you said about Arthur's eyes?'

'I was acquainted with them once—before Lord and Lady Chesterholm married.'

'I should have thought.' The nurse nodded. 'His lordship is unlikely to have any Newton relation in the house. Not after he threw them out. They tried to take Arthur.'

Louisa frowned, surprised at the nurse's presumption and indiscretion. The woman did not even know anything about her. But the intelligence did not surprise her. Clarissa's mother had very decided opinions and did not hesitate to voice them in private and sometimes even in public. And Jonathon hated being told what to do.

At the look, the nurse's cheeks coloured slightly. 'I fear my tongue is worse than a babbling brook these days. I didn't mean no harm. His lordship operates by his own rules, he does. He is determined to protect those who are dependent on him.'

'Yes, he always was.' Louisa closed her eyes, remembering how she loved it once. Jonathon had promised to remake the world for her and protect her from life's storms. In those long-ago days, she would have been content to be a clinging vine, but now she was glad for the opportunity to fight her battles and to find her own solutions, rather than accepting misguided advice.

'Then he hasn't changed,' the nurse said with a laugh. 'The master does what he thinks is right and he is a good master. Not like some of the others, mind.'

Louisa swallowed hard. Was Jonathon really that good or was the nurse proclaiming far too loudly? He had not brought Arthur down to meet the guests, nor had he really mentioned Arthur's existence. And having met the boy, Louisa was convinced the fault lay with Jonathon.

Louisa gave Arthur's hair one last stroke. She could not risk coming again. Arthur was Clarissa's child, not hers. Getting attached to any child, particularly one of Jonathon's, would only lead to heartache.

'Is this what you called dressed for company, Nanny Hawks?' Jonathon's rich voice boomed from the doorway. 'Did I not say—promptly?'

'Promptness is a virtue that Master Arthur does not possess,' the nurse said. 'He was born late and has stayed late ever since.'

'Hung by my own words, Nanny,' Jonathon said with a laugh. 'But I have no wish to scandalise the guests with him appearing without a stitch on.'

'And whose fault was that, sir? I like to have my lads well turned out…'

'Guilty as charged.'

Immediately Arthur gave a squeal of delight and started to run towards his father, but the nurse held him back exclaiming about wet hands on immaculate dinner clothes.

'It is my fault, your lordship.' Louisa stepped in front of the pair. 'I became lost and Arthur rescued me. I am certain though I can find my way now.'

'You are willing to take the help of an eighteen-month-old toddler, Miss Sibson, but not me.' His eyes crinkled with amusement as if they were sharing a private joke. 'I do hope this was in your famous schedule.'

'I fail to see the humour. You should have told me you had a son,' Louisa said, lowering her voice.

'You should have asked.' He reached out and captured the wriggling boy. 'Arthur here is more than a son; he is a whirlwind of mischief.'

Arthur gave a shriek of delight as Jonathon swung him into the air. Both faces were alight with the joy of being with each other.

Louisa bit her lip. For years she had told herself that Jonathon would have made a terrible father, but here he was enjoying his son and he had obviously fought to keep him.

Jonathon put Arthur down. 'Now, my lad, if you let Nanny Hawks comb your hair and tidy you up, you may come down and see the pretty ladies.'

'La,' Arthur said pointing at Louisa.

'Yes, I can see you have an excellent eye, son. Miss Sibson will be there.' Jonathon held out his arm. 'Shall we go and leave Arthur to his ablutions, Louisa? Nanny's charges must be well turned out.'

'I became lost,' Louisa said once they were clear of the nursery. 'It was purely unintentional. It won't happen again. It would have been helpful if someone had provided a plan of the house.'

'If you say so. None of the other guests have mentioned the problem.'

'I know how nurses like to think of the nursery as their private kingdom,' Louisa said to forestall the lecture she was certain was coming. 'You needn't worry. I will not lose my way again.'

'It is well I found you. The company is beginning to assemble for dinner. I have invited a few people from the neighbourhood and would hate to send a search party.'

'More guests?'

'If one is to have a dinner party, one might as well do it properly.'

'No one said.' Louisa stared at him in astonishment. It all made sense now why Arthur was being made ready. Jonathon wanted to exhibit his son. No doubt the company would be the great, the good and the very worthy. And the poor boy disliked strangers. She could remember hating it when she brought down Margaret Ponsby-Smythe. Her evening dress had always seemed plain against the brilliant silks and satins. And everyone seemed to think her manners were awkward and gauche.

'I am saying so now. You will like them.'

Louisa straightened her spine. She was no longer a twenty-year-old orphan, but twenty-four with independent means. 'It is well that I wore one of my better evening dresses.'

His gaze travelled down her neckline to where it skimmed the tops of her breasts. Louisa wished that she had used lace, but it was not as daring as some of the dresses in Naples. 'It will do. You used to wear simpler dresses. And your hair was not quite as elaborate.'

'My style has changed.' She gulped in a breath of air and regained control of her nerves. 'I have changed. Become a woman of substance.'

'You have said, but underneath there is a small bit of you who remains the wide-eyed governess I found cowering in the study.'

'I was not cowering. I was waiting.'

'There is no need to wait now.'

He tucked her arm under his. A warm insidious curl went around her stomach and it took all of her will-power not to lean against him. She pulled away from his arm and made a pretence of straightening the ruffles on her gown.

'What did you think of my son? You can be frank, Louisa.'

'He is a darling and very like you except for his eyes.'

Jonathon nodded, his face giving nothing away. Louisa wanted to scream with frustration. She wanted to know what he was thinking and how he felt about her discovery. But he was impossible to read.

'And now you are ready to give me a lecture about seeing my son more often,' he said. 'Or, in some way, implying that I am an unfit father, that Arthur would be better off somewhere else.'

'How did you know what I was thinking?' Louisa narrowly missed stepping on the hem of her dress.

'You have an expressive face, and you were ready to do battle when I came into the nursery.'

'You never said anything about having a son. I

did not even know he was here. Why are you hiding him?' Louisa crossed her arms. 'There, I have said it, Jonathon.'

'Was it any of your business? What lies between us, Louisa, is confined to you and me.'

'You like to keep your life in compartments.'

'It can be useful.' There was an arrogant tilt to his chin. 'Isn't that what you try to do with your past? People in glass houses, Louisa, and right now, yours is made of thin crystal.'

'You should have said something.'

'Would it have made a difference?'

Louisa kept her gaze on his impeccably tied stock rather than on his eyes. 'Yes, it would have.'

'Are you always this arrogant, Louisa—assuming you know everything? I cannot undo the past.'

'We are not talking about my past. I am speaking of the now and the fact you had a son with Clarissa!'

'Is this about my son or the fact I married Clarissa?'

'How am I supposed to answer that?' Louisa drew a deep breath. 'I simply know it is wrong to bring children out and exhibit them like a prized artwork.'

'My son is the bright star of my life. I am determined to be a far better parent than either of mine were. I spend as much time as possible with Arthur. It is why he is with me, rather than with the Newtons. And if I wish him to meet people, he will. It is none of your business, Louisa.'

'You are right. It is none of my business and thankfully it never will be.'

'Arthur gives me a reason to hope for old age. Something I lacked until he came along.'

Louisa stared at her hands. She had misjudged Jonathon. Again. 'I understand.'

'Do you?' His eyes assessed her. 'I wonder.'

'Young Arthur Fanshaw is a perfect darling,' Miss Blandish confided as they processed back to the drawing room after supper. 'I knew Lord Chesterholm was a widower, but he is so good with his son. The little boy adores his papa.'

'A man who is good with children is a prize beyond rubies, Miss Blandish,' Miss Daphne said. 'They are very rare. Don't you agree, Louisa?'

'Lord Chesterholm does appear to be devoted.' Louisa ignored the tightening of her stomach. What was Miss Daphne up to, pointing out Jonathon's virtues to Miss Blandish? Miss Blandish and he would be bored within five minutes. Louisa gritted her teeth. Or was it more subtle—a misguided attempt to provoke her to jealousy? Unfortunately, it nearly worked.

'Are you feeling quite the thing, Louisa dear?' Miss Daphne asked, laying her hand on Louisa's arm. 'Rupert and I had a discussion about it this afternoon. You have an admirer in my nephew.'

Louisa squeezed Miss Daphne's hand. Life would be much simpler if she had been attracted to Lord Furniss, but she was not. 'What shall the evening's entertainment be?'

'Dancing,' Miss Daphne declared. 'I have a dislike of parlour games.'

'Dancing?' Louisa stared at Miss Daphne. She had expected something far more sedate. 'But you gave up dancing after the last Christmas ball at Hotel Trasemeno. You were laid up for a week with aching joints.'

'Oh, you will know all the sophisticated dances, rather than us countrified folk, having been on the Continent,' the vicar's wife said with a clap of her hands. 'I have been simply longing to learn some new dances.'

'Miss Sibson does,' Miss Daphne declared. 'You must ask her. She rarely dances, but when she does it is with great skill.'

'I would be willing to teach you one or two if you wished,' Louisa said, seeing the woman's eager face. 'They are very simple to learn.'

'You know, I was simply terrified when Lord Chesterholm invited us,' the vicar's wife confided in an undertone to Louisa. 'And then when I saw you, Miss Sibson, in all your glory and sophistication, I thought what could we possibly have in common, but you have put my mind quite at ease.'

'Sophisticated, me?' Louisa stared at the vicar's wife. 'I have never considered myself particularly sophisticated.'

'But you have travelled the world and I have never been out of Northumberland.' The vicar's wife gave a sigh. 'I do so love dancing. About these new steps…'

'Yes, please, Miss Sibson. I am so pleased Mrs Merrick worked up the courage to ask,' Miss Blandish said. 'I am always longing to learn more steps.'

'I would be delighted to show you a few before the gentlemen return,' Louisa said with a smile. 'Country dancing it is.'

'I shall play the spinet and Nella Blandish may turn the pages of the music. I dare say these old fingers recall more country dances and quadrilles than you consider possible.'

Nella Blandish stood up a little straighter, beaming while everyone else made approving noises. Louisa fought the urge not to laugh. Here she had been terrified of them and they were thinking that she was terrifyingly sophisticated.

'The servants had best move the furniture, then.'

By the time the gentlemen entered the room, the sofas and chairs had been moved against the wall and the Turkey carpet rolled up. Louisa had shown the ladies a few of the dances that were all the rage in Sorrento, and they had agreed on a programme.

'It appears tonight's entertainment is settled,' Jonathon said, coming into the room. 'Did you have a hand in it, Miss Sibson?'

'Miss Sibson objected most vigorously, but my sister and Mrs Merrick insisted as Miss Sibson has lived abroad. And then Miss Sibson relented and has been teaching everyone to dance.' Miss Nella made a little curtsy to the gentlemen. The corner of Jonathon's mouth twitched and his eyes seemed to say—I told you so. 'And I am to stay up and turn the pages.'

'As long as you are quiet and lady-like,' Mrs Blandish said with a resigned shudder. 'I shall have to discover a new governess when we return to London.'

Nella gave a theatrical sigh and clapped her hands over her mouth. Louisa hid her smile behind her hand, but she caught Jonathon's eye. Then the laugh bubbled up inside her and escaped. The entire company followed suit. A feeling of belonging swamped Louisa.

'Miss Sibson, you will do me the honour of being my partner for the first dance,' Lord Furniss said, as the laughter subsided. 'The memory of dancing with you in Sorrento has sustained me for many months.'

'With words like that, how could I refuse?' Louisa put her hand in his.

As the first figure started and they linked hands, Lord Furniss cleared his throat. 'Miss Sibson, I hope you do not consider me impertinent but you have no one to guide you.'

'I am used to making my own way in the world.'

'You should be able to lean on someone. It is not right for a lady such as yourself—'

Louisa stepped heavily. Lord Furniss gave a muffled yelp. Her shoulder relaxed slightly. Crisis adverted. 'Do excuse me, Lord Furniss. I missed a step.'

'Do you understand what I wish to ask?' he said in a low urgent tone.

'You do me great honour, but this is hardly the time or place for such a conversation.'

'When shall we speak elsewhere?'

'The dance, Lord Furniss. We need to change partners. See, Miss Blandish waits.'

He went scarlet. 'Yes, yes, of course. I am always getting my figures mixed.'

Louisa heaved a sigh of relief and turned towards her new partner.

'What were you and Furniss discussing so intently?' Jonathon's hand closed about hers. Strong and masculine. A small pulse of energy jolted her.

'We weren't discussing anything of import.'

'You missed a step.' His eyes blazed green and his

hand tightened about hers as if he was determined to keep her by his side.

'I was concentrating on the conversation. He wished to go out in the garden.'

'And you refused?'

'I arranged the dancing. How could I leave?' She willed him to believe her explanation. The last thing she wanted to confess to Jonathon was how she had been avoiding Lord Furniss's proposal for the last few weeks.

A muscle jumped in his cheek and he entirely missed a turn in the dance. 'Arranging assignations on a dance floor must be breaking a number of your rules, Louisa.'

'Jealous?'

He gave a heart-melting smile. 'Utterly.'

'Jealousy is not a becoming trait, Lord Chesterholm, and I do know my rules.'

His hand tightened on hers and pulled her close. Their breath mingled. 'Will you keep your much-vaunted independence? Will you accept his proposal? He intends to marry you.'

'Why should I want to become the property of some man even if he has a title? Why should I change my course?'

'Because he is The Man for you, rather than some abstract notion. And I do speak in the abstract, Miss Sibson.' He inclined his head and one lock of hair flopped over his forehead. 'Your servant, Miss Sibson. I believe your next partner awaits.'

He turned away and left her in front of the vicar. Louisa rapidly attempted to compose herself. The Man indeed.

* * *

'I have finished cataloguing and cross-referencing the cameos,' Louisa said going into Jonathon's study with a sheaf of papers the next morning.

'So quickly? I thought the jumbled mess would take you into next week.' Jonathon stood up and came over to her, taking the papers from her outstretched hand and rapidly examining her notation. 'You are tremendously efficient.'

'It became easy once I understood your uncle's system. It was remarkably similar to Miss Mattie's.' Louisa hid a yawn. There was the little point that she had not slept, but had used the cameos to keep her mind from wandering back to Jonathon and the way his hand had felt against her back.

'That is curious.'

'Perhaps they were too alike and stubborn. Never backing down and admitting they were wrong.'

'Like someone else I could mention?'

Louisa took a deep breath. She had to seize the opportunity, admit her mistake and demonstrate she could. 'I wish to apologise for saying those things about Arthur and Clarissa before supper last night. It was wrong of me to criticise without knowing the full truth.'

'I accept your apology. You underestimated me, Louisa.' Jonathon put his hands behind his back and his face offered no comfort. 'You expect me to trust you, but offer nothing in return. Not even the scrap of thinking that I might want what is best for my son.'

'Should I trust you?'

'When I met you, I was determined for once in my miserable life to do everything properly, I even obtained this.' He went over to his desk and handed her a piece of paper. 'Read and learn what your distrust cost you.'

Louisa took the paper, being careful not to touch his hand. The words Special Licence and the date leapt out at her. He had done it. He had obtained one, even after their quarrel. And she had been positive that he had lied about his intention.

Louisa closed her eyes. The ticking of the mantel-piece clock sounded throughout the room. Her life could have been so different…if only…she had believed. 'Why are you showing this to me now?'

'Because you persist in believing in your self-righteous indignation, rather than accepting some of the blame.'

'We both made mistakes. I was certain you went to London. They were the last words you shouted at me.'

Jonathon's face became grim. 'That year I never made it to London. I was seriously injured, Louisa, in an acci-dent, the same accident I thought you had died in. You do not look for someone who has died. You might want to die, but if you can't, you have to live.'

Louisa hugged her waist and her head began to pound.

How right Miss Daphne had been when she'd said that the saddest words were *what might have been*. But she could not deal with the ifs and onlys. Her past was unchanging. There was only her future spreading out bleakly in front of her.

She had once dreamed of a marriage to Jonathon, but he was right: she had never fully trusted him. Right now all she wanted to do was to curl up in a ball and cry.

'You never answered my letters. Ever.' The ribs of

her fan dug into her tightly clenched fist. Didn't he know how she had waited, hoping against hope that she was wrong and that he'd come for her? She remembered his grim face when he'd set off that morning, and how she had called out to him to write. His only answer had been a wave of his hand and it had nearly broken her heart.

'You asked me why I didn't come after you. I have told you. Now I ask you—why were you so ready to accept the lies? Why didn't you demand to see me? Put your accusations to my face? They could not have stopped you.'

'Because,' she whispered, looking at her hands for a long time before glancing up at his intent face, 'I was certain they were the truth. I was always worried that what we had would pass. The time we had together seemed too good to be true. And I could not bear to see indifference on your face.'

'How little you thought of me then.' His mouth held a bitter twist.

She longed to scream at him—yes, yes, his accusation was true. He had never given her cause to think otherwise—charming, but liable to give in to impulse before thought. In that respect, Mrs Ponsby-Smythe with her little helpful hints and comments about Louisa's lack of standing and ability had been right—a marriage between them would never have worked. Louisa had thought the sun rose and set with him and could not cope when her hero showed his feet of clay.

Louisa moved swiftly, not giving herself time to think. She took the licence, intending to toss it on the fire. Jonathon's hand clamped about her wrist, preventing her from moving. She twisted her arm, but he simply pulled her against his chest. Her body collided with his unyielding frame, hard, solid. The collision stunned her into inaction. All she could do was to stand there and breathe in his crisp masculine scent.

He twitched the paper from her nerveless fingers and slid it back into his pocket. The action released Louisa from her stupor.

'Let me go.' Louisa struggled against his grip. Each time she moved, each time her body collided with the hard planes of his, she became more aware of Jonathon as a man: how he breathed, the warmth of his body and the nearness of him. She spun slightly and regained a small measure of sanity.

'Why?'

'The best place for that licence is the fire. The people we were are dead. We can never go back to those people. We have both changed beyond recognition.' Louisa tried to focus on the piece of paper rather than on the nearness of him.

'No, it simply serves as a reminder of what could have been.' He slid his fingers along her arm, tucked slightly on the sleeve of her gown, probing and sliding over her soft flesh. The nature of his touch changed and created ripples of warmth that cascaded through her body, weakening her resolve. 'And we have not changed all that much. Trust me on this, Louisa, if nothing else.'

'Trust you?'

'Yes…' his words were an enticing whisper '…trust me. Look at me, Louisa. Tell me what you see.'

Louisa glanced up into his sea-green eyes, eyes that

reminded her of the sea around Sorrento on an autumn day. They stared at each other, chests heaving, close enough to touch, but not touching.

Louisa became aware of the way his fingers held her wrist, stroking its vulnerable underside, gentle but firm. A simple touch, but one that she wanted to continue, needed to continue. A desperate hunger consumed her being. She needed more. She had been alone for so long. Surely she could take one step closer without giving into the desire.

'Jonathon,' she whispered, not knowing if it was a plea or a cry. She raised her face and swayed towards him, putting her hands out, encountering his chest. 'You must…we must…'

He lowered his head and his mouth captured her lower lip and suckled. Her hand curled about his neck, holding him there, and she knew it was what she needed. It was the safe harbour of her dreams. A soft sigh emerged from her throat.

His arms came about and moulded her to his body; her curves met his hardened muscle. Heat surged through her, blocking out all coherent thought as she sank down into the maelstrom of his kiss.

'Not here,' Jonathon murmured, his breath tickling her ear and sending little tongues of fire throughout her body. 'We need to go somewhere else. Staying here risks exposure, something I believe you wish to avoid.'

The words cut through the sensuous web he had spun and she pushed against the circle of his arms, stumbling backwards. He knew exactly what he was doing and she had fallen into his trap again. He was an expert seducer.

That had not changed. She had come within a breath of becoming that wanton clinging creature again.

'It stops now.' Louisa concentrated on the swirling patterns of the carpet and tried to marshal her thoughts. Jonathon was in far more control than she was. What was worse, she wanted it to continue. She wanted to be in his arms and feel safe. 'It may be that I have not changed that much, but I have learnt from my mistakes. I have finished paying for them.'

'Have you?'

Louisa fought the rising tide of panic. She had made a huge mistake giving into the temptation of Jonathon's touch. With the merest brush of a finger, he had transported her back four years, but she was not going to stay there or revisit that place.

'I am more concerned about living in the now than trying to repair past mistakes,' she said, putting finality in her voice.

'Are you?' His gaze assessed her and Louisa feared that he could see the longing in her soul. She rapidly transferred her gaze to the Turkey carpet. 'Or are you simply afraid of living? Is that why you have your rules, because secretly you want to break them?'

Louisa balled her fist. Afraid of living? Her? How dare he! Simply because she chose not to give into temptation and desire! Because she chose the wise path rather than the risky one! 'This concludes our business, Lord Chesterholm,' Louisa said through clenched teeth. 'We will not be alone again.'

'You will find a reason, Louisa. It is merely a matter of time and my door is open to you.'

'You know nothing about me.'

'Teach me. I want to learn...everything about this new Louisa.'

Louisa drew a deep breath. 'I stopped teaching when I ceased to be a governess, Lord Chesterholm.'

# Chapter Eight

'It is good of you to call, Lord Chesterholm.'

'I came as soon as I heard,' Jonathon said, ducking his head to avoid hitting the top of the doorway as he went from where Matthew Sims shoed horses into the main part of the cottage. Thompson's message that Annie Sims was desperate to speak to him and only him had arrived at precisely the right time. Kissing Louisa this morning had been a false step. No matter that she had fit into his arms exactly, it had been the wrong moment and she had had time to remember her blasted rules.

He had been about to go after her and haul her into bed, but then came this summons. Normally he'd send for Annie, but getting out of Chesterholm would give him a chance to regain control and perspective. The next time, he would not make the same mistake.

'Thank you for coming so quickly, your lordship.' Mrs Sims made a low curtsy as behind the kettle simmered on the open fire. 'It is a great honour to have you here.'

'I understand Annie wishes to say something.'

'She didn't mean no harm, your lordship,' Mrs Sims began, twisting her apron. 'She thought the man would marry her. He promised her everything.'

'Hush, woman.' Sims put a beefy hand on his wife's arm. 'His lordship knows that. Our Annie were led astray, like. I told you his lordship would call if Thompson delivered the message. His lordship is like that.'

'Aye, you did, Mr Sims, that you did.' The wife nodded.

'Annie should have gone to the big house straight away like, once we realised but she was frightened. Doesn't want anyone to think bad of her.'

'She is back amongst her family. She is safe now.' Jonathon frowned. What had Annie neglected to tell Thompson when he had interviewed her in Newcastle? Somehow he was missing a vital clue as to what had happened. 'I gave you my word and I did what I could to bring her home unharmed.'

'That's the point. He was a bad 'un, her fellow. A right slubberdegullion if ever I saw one. Mrs Sims's sister might have had her head turned, but not me. I knew he was a wrong 'un the moment I clapped eyes on him.' The large man twisted his cap. 'Annie! Annie! Come show his lordship what you showed your mam. Tell the truth and shame the devil!'

Annie reluctantly came out of the back kitchen. Lines of worry were etched on her round face, but she appeared far happier and content than she had in

Newcastle. Had it not been for Louisa, he might have missed her.

'Miss Sims, what has happened? What do you have to show me?' Jonathon spoke in an even voice, one that he might use to gentle a horse or when he had to deal with Arthur's screaming night terrors.

'I should've told Mr Thompson afore now. It were wrong of me but I wanted to be away from that awful place. And I weren't sure if he would be as kind as that lady.'

'Which lady?'

'You know, Miss Sibson.' Annie drew designs in the dust with the toe of her boot. 'She is a right canny lass. I was scared I was going to turn out like…well…like some folk.'

'Miss Sibson is a friend,' Jonathon said gravely.

There was a distinct whine of self-pity to the woman's voice. 'Me da said that straight away when I told him, like. Annie, me girl, he said—you tell his lordship and all will be made right.'

'Tell me what?'

Annie burst out into fresh sobs, but, giving a glance at her father, she straightened her back and reached into the pocket of her voluminous apron.

'I think Trevor had something to do with the missing things up at the big house. He boasted something fierce about how he kept happening on things. Before I left, I found one of them snuffbox things.' Annie brought out a little gold box. 'Me da says it must belong to you as it has the Chesterholm crest on it.'

'There is a substantial reward for this box.'

'You see, my girl, it pays to be honest.' Sims puffed out his chest.

Annie placed it in his hand and gave a small curtsy.

'Did your man have a name?'

'He called himself Trevor, Trevor James. Said he were a horse trader, but he weren't a very good one. Too clever by half for a start, if you get my meaning,' Sims said, tapping his nose. 'Kept saying he knew this peer or that one. Boasting with a manner far too fine for his britches.'

Annie wiped her eyes with a corner of her apron. 'It weren't his real name, Da. It were Trevor Brown. I found a letter from his wife. It's why I left. A wife and three children. That man lied to me.'

'His lordship understands, dear.' Her mother put a comforting arm about the girl. 'You ain't done nothing wrong. Just followed your heart a bit too much, a bit like our Mary. Men are like that sometimes. It is why I say to get that ring on your finger afore anything.'

Jonathon closed his hand around the snuffbox. Had Louisa received the same sort of well-meaning advice in her hour of need?

'Did he say who he met at the Grange?' Jonathon asked before Annie could begin a litany of self-pity.

Slowly Annie shook her head. 'I was crazy in love. He promised me all sorts of fine things and then I found myself in a tiny room in Newcastle where all I could see was the privy. It weren't what I thought it was, see.'

Didn't think? Or did not want to know? Annie was Nanny Hawks's niece, but… Jonathon tapped his riding crop against his thigh. How much did she know? It was clear that she was unwilling to confide in him.

'Shall I bring Miss Sibson to see you?'

Annie's cheeks grew bright pink. 'Would you? I should like to thank her.'

'We all would. Without Miss Sibson, I doubt our Annie would have come home,' Mrs Sims said.

'I will see what I can do,' Jonathon said, a plan beginning to form in his brain. Two things at once. Louisa could discover the secret Annie was hiding and Louisa and he would have time alone, uninterrupted.

Louisa held the ball in her hand and eyed the bowling green and the distance to the jack. Several hours later and her mouth still gently ached from Jonathon's kiss. Nothing seemed to distract her mind from those few moments in his study and, what was worse, the woman she was now appeared no less immune to Jonathon's attractions than the girl she once had been. It was just as well that he had departed on business as it had allowed her time to recover.

'Is this an easy shot, Miss Sibson?' Miss Blandish called out from where she stood on the edge of the bowling green as Louisa went up on her toes, getting ready to roll her bowl.

'Shh, Miss Blandish, Miss Sibson is trying to concentrate. Don't you know anything about bowls?' Lord Furniss remonstrated. He turned towards the rest of the group. 'Everyone, quiet, please! Miss Sibson is about to bowl her final ball of the match.'

'Miss Sibson plays ever so much better than I do,' Miss Blandish cried.

Louisa watched as the bowl, rather than heading

straight for the jack, veered off to the left, missing it altogether.

Miss Blandish gave a pleased twirl of her pink parasol. 'You have won, Lord Furniss. Miss Sibson has missed.'

'Bad luck, Miss Sibson,' Lord Furniss shouted, giving Miss Blandish a hard look. 'You must try again…in silence. I have no wish to win in this manner. It is terribly unsporting. Perhaps I could show you how to turn the bowl more to your advantage.'

'I would not dream of it, sir. You won.' Louisa dropped a small curtsy. 'It was an honour to play against such a worthy opponent.' Lord Furniss turned scarlet.

'Really, Miss Sibson, you are quite the expert.' Miss Blandish's tone dripped honey-laced jealousy as she handed Louisa a cup of tea. 'And you in that dress. Quite up to the minute, isn't it?'

'I used to be quite the expert at bowls. Margaret Ponsby-Smythe and I played quite frequently, but my eye is not what it used to be and bowls is a sedate occupation,' Louisa said smoothly as a plan began to form in her mind. Miss Blandish was developing a tendre for Lord Furniss, something that was definitely to be encouraged. 'We should have the next match.'

'I am not good enough. I can't spin the ball like Lord Furniss does.' Miss Blandish gave another twirl of her parasol. 'I rarely play these days.'

'Playing bowls is one of life's great pleasures,' Lord Furniss proclaimed. 'How could anyone give it up? I play whenever I can.'

Miss Blandish shook her head. 'I am not sure I even remember all the rules.'

'Susan prefers to practise her singing,' Mrs Blandish said, taking an overly refined sip of tea. 'It is such a worthy pursuit for an accomplished young lady.'

'But she makes everyone's ears ache.' Miss Nella put her hands over her ears in a dramatic pose. 'Scales morning, noon and night as if that will make some aristocrat fall in love with her!'

'Nella!'

'I could teach you like I taught Margaret Ponsby-Smythe, Miss Blandish,' Louisa offered as Miss Blandish's cheeks flamed scarlet. If she could get Miss Blandish playing bowls, perhaps Lord Furniss would transfer his affections. She hated playing matchmaker, but Miss Daphne would be disappointed if she actually refused Lord Furniss outright. Redirecting his attention was by far the best course. 'It is very easy to learn, Miss Blandish. The rules are far from complex. Within a few hours you will prove a formidable opponent to Lord Furniss.'

'I would like that,' Miss Blandish whispered, ducking her head. 'Thank you.'

'I keep forgetting you were a governess to Lord Chesterholm's family,' Lord Furniss said, wiping his forehead with a handkerchief. 'I must say that playing bowls brings up a tremendous thirst.'

'Miss Milton also plays well,' Nella said in a singsong voice. 'It is something governesses do… It used to be the highlight of my day. We played and played, rather than learning boring things like deportment and the proper conversation one has with an eligible man, like Mama was lecturing about in the carriage all the way here. Boring!'

'Nella!' Her mother said. 'That is quite enough of that particular conversation.'

'Why?' Nella put her hands on her hips and faced her mother. 'Why are the interesting topics of conversation never proper? If Susan wants to make herself a ninny over a man, I am sure that it is no concern of mine. Even if she chooses the right man to be a ninny over and, knowing Susan, she won't.'

'Nella!' Her mother's cap shook as Miss Elliot began to speak very loudly about the weather to Lord Furniss.

Louisa's lips twitched upwards at Nella's intelligence and she studiously avoid catching either Miss Daphne's or Lord Furniss's eye.

'I understand that Margaret Ponsby-Smythe is quite the bowls player,' Mrs Blandish remarked into the silence. 'Did you teach her, Miss Sibson? Or was her brother involved?'

'Lord Chesterholm is quite a keen player,' Lord Furniss remarked. 'We often play.'

Louisa suddenly wished that she had not had her corset tightened this morning. She used to take her charges out for a bit of fresh air and peace and quiet. And with Margaret, there was always the chance that Jonathon would happen along and put his arm about her waist under the guise of correcting her shot. Louisa forced her mind away from that memory. She refused to remember his touch and yet everything she did, even a simple game of bowls, brought it back.

'Do you know the answer?' Mrs Blandish rattled her tea cup with an imperious air. 'From whom should my daughter seek instruction?'

'I am really not sure who taught Margaret,' Louisa confessed as everyone turned towards her. Silently she cursed. She had made the situation worse. Everyone was looking at her with expectant expressions as if she was hiding something.

'I wonder where Lord Chesterholm is. He would know the answer to the question,' Mrs Blandish said, finishing her drink and standing up.

'What question should I answer?' Jonathon's rich voice floated out over the bowling green. 'You must forgive my absence, but duty called.'

Louisa turned her head and saw him striding towards the group with his dogs at his heels. His hat was pushed back slightly and his brown cutaway coat was cut to highlight his shoulders. His tan-striped Cossack trousers were moulded to his legs. Heat curled about her insides. He had no right to look that good.

'We understand entirely, Lord Chesterholm. It takes a great deal of knowledge to run an estate like this one,' Mrs Blandish simpered like a frumenty kettle. 'Perhaps you would be so good as to settle the dispute. Who should my daughter Susan have as a bowls teacher?'

Jonathon's eyes turned a sparkling green. 'Furniss should teach Miss Blandish. His ability to spin the ball is second to none.'

'You are far too kind.' Lord Furniss made a bow and he gave Miss Blandish a speculative glance. 'But I am not certain.'

'Would you please, Lord Furniss?' Louisa said quickly. 'It was your skill that won the game.'

'If you insist, dear Miss Sibson, I will do it for you,' Lord Furniss said.

'Then it is all settled,' Jonathon said with a bow. 'Lord Furniss will undertake to instruct Miss Blandish in the finer points of bowls.'

Louisa sucked in her breath, but no one else appeared to notice the innuendo. She saw with relief as Miss Blandish accepted the idea with enthusiasm. Why was it that Jonathon possessed the ability to make something as innocent as bowls sound like a seduction in a harem?

'Are your skills becoming rusty, Miss Sibson?' Jonathon asked. 'Do you need to obtain some instruction from a master?'

'My skills are just fine, Lord Chesterholm,' Louisa replied with crushing firmness.

'And yet you lost this match. You should be careful or you may find your reputation slipping through your fingers.'

'My reputation remains as it has been—spotless.'

'Or are you simply afraid to risk your reputation with me?' Jonathon tossed the jack ball in the air and expertly caught it. 'Surely you can play a simple game without fear of compromise.'

'I believe Lord Furniss wishes to instruct Miss Blandish on the finer points of bowls now.' Louisa gave Jonathon a severe look.

The corners of Jonathon's mouth twitched. 'I will yield the green then.'

'And I will get the bowls set up while Lord Furniss explains the rules to Miss Blandish.'

Louisa began to carefully set up the bowls again, taking time to place each ball precisely as she tried to marshal her thoughts. Every time she glanced over, Jonathon was watching with a sardonic expression. By the time she had finished, she knew that she had to do more than stand there and make polite conversation while Jonathon played increasingly intricate word games whose sole purpose was to set her off balance.

'Miss Daphne, are you certain that the black shawl is the correct thing? I may have made a mistake when I packed the basket,' Louisa said, thinking quickly. The excuse was paper thin, but hopefully Miss Daphne would understand the unspoken message. 'Perhaps your white one would have been better for an excursion like this one, considering the weather.'

Miss Daphne gave her a significant look. 'My white shawl is one of my favourites and you are quite right, the black would be far too heavy for this sort of weather.'

'It is utterly my fault.' Louisa heaved a sigh of relief. Miss Daphne had guessed her purpose and with any luck would detain Jonathon with questions about bowls.

'Then you should rectify it immediately. And dear Nella may keep me company.'

'It would be my pleasure.' Louisa set off at a quick walk. When she was out of sight of the group, she ran.

Jonathon waited at the bottom of the stairs. It was only a matter of time before Louisa appeared. Her little act of having to fetch Miss Daphne's shawl fooled no one, least of all him. However, it did show that his plans were progressing. If she was entirely indifferent, Louisa would have stayed and flirted with Furniss to prove her point.

'My lord, this arrived for you.' Reynolds held out a piece of thick cream paper.

Jonathon broke the seal and frowned. Venetia was on

the move. Finally. She and Margaret planned on arriving tomorrow. Jonathon tore the note into pieces as light footsteps sounded on the stairs.

'Jonathon?'

'Miss Daphne sent a message—her black shawl will do admirably. You must not hurry on her account as Nella is keeping her entertained.' Jonathon concentrated on Louisa rather than the note.

'Something has happened, Jonathon. Do not bother denying it. I recognise the look,' she said. 'Has something happened to Arthur? What are you worried about? You did not come back in just to give me the message.'

'Arthur is fine.' Jonathon caught her arm and led her towards the terrace. 'Or at least he was this morning when we breakfasted together. He asked after you. You made quite a conquest there.'

'I will go to see him soon.' Her hands twisted the lacy shawl. 'I had no wish to disrupt the nursery routine.'

'He would like to see you.' Jonathon frowned. Something was making Louisa hesitate. She used to love children. He shook his head. 'I will let Nanny Hawks know to expect you.'

'Then what is it?'

'You could always tell when something was wrong. Have the others been making comments as well?'

'No one has said anything.' She drew a deep breath, making her chest fill out agreeably. 'Your face was thunderous when you arrived at the bowls and even blacker when I came down the stairs. I recognised the expression. It was precisely the same as when you had Bee's Wing put down.'

'I am flattered you remembered,' Jonathon replied. 'But nothing was bothering me at the bowling green. You are reading too much into my expression. A lesser man would think you cared.'

'And he'd be right. I hate to think of anyone in distress.'

When he had arranged the house party, he'd thought it would be simple. Louisa would tumble into his bed, and he would be able to banish Venetia without Louisa being unduly disturbed. And he would be free to spend time with Arthur. Keep the parts of his life separate, just as he had always done. Now he discovered Louisa had guessed something was wrong and he wanted to share, but he also wanted to keep her from getting hurt. And that was an unforeseen problem.

'Louisa, is my heart supposed to be touched?' Jonathon hardened his voice. It was far better for her to be slightly hurt now than to face the worry and fear of his stepmother. After Margaret was safely in his custody and his stepmother gone, he'd confess, but for right now, he had to keep Louisa in ignorance. 'Why did you leave the bowls if you were so concerned about me?'

Louisa concentrated on the summer house at the end of the terrace.

'Miss Daphne helpfully sent me for her shawl.' She paused and her cheeks coloured. 'There was little need for me to stay.'

'You always could think on your feet.' He gave a little shake of his head. 'Would you care to share the true reason that you decided to leave, or shall I guess? You might wish to forget the past, Louisa, but you can't help remembering it and what we shared.'

'I...' She took a deep steadying breath. 'We can bandy words about if it will make you feel better, but it will solve nothing. Yes, I remember, and, yes, I kissed you this morning.'

'That is hardly my fault.' He put out his hand and touched her cheek. 'Nothing happens unless you wish it too.'

'Where were you?'

'I went to see Annie Sims. It proved to be an interesting visit.'

'Was Annie well received when she returned home?' Louisa asked.

'Well enough.' He gave a slight shrug.

'Are you trying to say that I should never have brought her to your attention? You promised me, Jonathon.' Louisa put her hand on his sleeve. 'No harm would come to her.'

'Why should you care about what happens to that woman?' Jonathon stared at her. 'A woman you have spoken no more than ten words to?'

'I have been in the same situation. I know what the reception can be like.' Her eyes became haunted and she bit her lip as if she was afraid to say more. 'I am not devoid of human feeling. Annie was scared to return home; knowing how people can behave, I do not blame her. Did her father beat her?'

Jonathon looked down at her face and saw the shadow of pain.

'Were you hurt? Did your cousin lay a finger on you after you were dismissed?' Even now, Jonathon knew he would go and hunt her relations out, make them pay for what they had done, if they had dared to hurt Louisa.

Louisa's lips twisted up in a bitter smile. 'They turned me out and refused to have anything to do with me. I was dead to them. But, no, they never beat me.'

With effort Jonathon regained control of his temper. Later, he would discover them and make them pay. He had not cared for the cousin with his pompous swagger the one time they had met. 'And this is supposed to be a good thing?'

'I survived.' She put a hand on his arm. 'I could either be consumed with bitterness or I could get on with my life. A life well lived is the best revenge. And I must admit to being amused when my cousin and his wife heard of my good fortune from a mutual acquaintance.'

'Why?'

'Instantly they wrote, asking for money and saying how clever I was.'

'And did you give it?' Jonathon asked.

'No, I did not. I thanked them for the good wishes and left it at that.' She shook her head. Jonathon was impressed. The old Louisa had always been concerned that she was not worthy enough. She had desired a family. 'I do know who my true friends are and true friends are worth more than blood.'

'If I have time tomorrow, shall I take you to see Annie? To put your mind to rest.' Jonathon smiled. The solution to the problem was suddenly clear in his mind. He could keep the parts of his life separate.

'I would like that. Yes, I would like that very much.' Louisa bit her lip. 'Have you discovered if she has anything to do with the theft? You said that several things went missing about the time she left with her lover. Were either involved?'

Jonathon stared at her, impressed. He had not expected her to remember. 'Yes, I believe so. She has given me her lover's name as well as one of the missing snuffboxes, but I want to find out how the theft occurred. How did he get into the house? Annie says she has no idea but I think she does.'

'Shall I ask her about it? She might be willing to confide in me.'

'I forbid it, Louisa. It is far too risky. Do not even attempt to discover who helped her lover.'

'It is not as if I am going to put myself in any danger,' Louisa said, suddenly annoyed with Jonathon. He was acting like she should be wrapped in cotton wool. 'What could possibly happen to me at her house? It will give me something to do. Something to occupy my time while I am here. Miss Daphne will come along with us, I am certain about that. She will want to see how the neighbourhood has changed.'

'You need a chaperon? Why?' The words were said so softly that Louisa wondered if she had only imagined them.

She stared at him for a long moment. 'Are you asking me to risk my reputation by being alone with you?'

'Nothing will happen. You have your rules as your shield.'

'We have an agreement, Jonathon. After this party Miss Daphne and I are going back to Sorrento. We are only here because of Miss Daphne's desire to revisit old haunts.'

His hand reached out and touched her elbow, holding

her in place. 'Is it just being with me that frightens you, Louisa? I have given you my word. Why can't you trust that? Or is it your desire that you do not trust?'

Louisa straightened her shoulders and stared directly at him, knowing she had to lie to save her soul. He must never guess that she cared or that the temptation was growing inside her to confide everything that had happened to her and how she had lost her baby, their baby. Right now, she dreaded to think how his eyes would change. 'I find caution is the better part of valour. Once I took risks, but never again. It is remaining within the accepted limits that keeps me safe.'

# Chapter Nine

'Here you are. I had been scouring the house for you.'

At the sound of Jonathon's voice, Louisa glanced up from the game of wooden blocks she was playing with Arthur and her heart skipped a beat.

'Yes, I found a source of alternative entertainment— your son. He takes delight in knocking my towers down.'

Jonathon laughed. 'I can hardly blame him.'

Why did Jonathon have to appear now when she was busy playing with Arthur? Louisa sighed. She had taken pains over her dress and had sat doing her needlework this morning before taking coffee with Miss Daphne and the Blandishes. The conversation had revolved around London and its forthcoming exhibitions. And as the morning wore on, Louisa had become convinced that Jonathon had forgotten all about his promise to take her to see Annie. So she had given into her impulse and gone to the nursery where Arthur had welcomed her with a joyful whoop.

She should have guessed that Jonathon would remember. Instead of unapproachable perfection, he saw with her hair pins askew, crouched down on the nursery floor, rebuilding the fort that hid Arthur's toy soldiers.

'I promised to visit when I had time and suddenly there was time.' Louisa scrambled to her feet. 'Do you wish to postpone the journey?'

'This morning has been far more hectic than I first imagined.' He ran his hand through his hair, making it stand on end. Louisa remembered the nervous gesture from years ago. He was keeping something from her.

'Will the visit have to be postponed?' she asked, pushing her hair behind her ear. Disappointment coursed through her. She had been looking forward to the trip.

'I managed to sort the difficulty out.' Again a shadow went over his eyes.

Louisa struggled against the impulse to ask him about it. He had to want to confide in her. She could not make him.

'Miss Elliot has declared she will remain here, though,' he said. 'Something about listening to Miss Blandish practise her singing. Do you think you can risk travelling with just me? I give you my word as a gentleman that your reputation will not be put at risk. Miss Elliot considered it permissible as we are in the country.'

Louisa concentrated on rebuilding the tower for Arthur. Miss Daphne was being utterly transparent in her matchmaking. She should refuse, but she had looked forward to pitting her wits against him, the gentle teasing and to putting her mind to rest about Annie. She put the final block on the tower. It swayed slightly, but remained upright.

'It would be my pleasure. I am looking forward to meeting Annie again and getting to the bottom of the mystery.'

His gaze travelled down her costume and Louisa was acutely aware of the grubby handprints and ink stains. He reached over and straightened a brick. 'You need to strengthen your walls.'

'Do you think so? My walls are built to withstand any onslaught.' Louisa wet her lips and prayed he was speaking about the wooden walls of the fort, not the ones surrounding her heart.

'Most definitely. They are in danger of crumbling. Arthur here has found a way.'

Arthur pushed the tower down. The crash resounded around the nursery. He picked up the toy soldier that Louisa had hidden at the centre and gave a cry of triumph.

'I shall have to take lessons from my son, then,' Jonathon said quietly and Louisa knew he did not mean the wooden-brick towers.

Arthur held up his hands, begging to be picked up. Louisa knelt down and gave him a quick hug. 'I need to go, Arthur.'

'La-Lou. Boo. Boo.' He waved his hand.

'Bye-bye to you too.'

'My son is enchanted with you. He rarely speaks.'

'It is the age,' Louisa said with a smile as she gave Arthur's head a pat. Even in the short time they had spent together, Arthur had wound his fingers around her heart. 'He is quite the charmer. I can't remember when I laughed so much.'

'He is my tonic, but I can never quite make out what he is saying.'

'You need to listen harder. Hear what he is trying to say.'

She put her fingers to her lips and Arthur began to shout *pa pa pla pla*.

'He wants you to pick him up and play. Build him one last tower before we go.'

'You are right, Louisa.' Jonathon's deep green gaze caught hers and held it. 'Perhaps I have not been listening hard enough.'

He swung Arthur up into the air. The little boy responded by clapping his hands and shouting, 'Pa. Pa.' Their shared laughter rang out. Jonathon looked at her and held out his hand.

'Shall we have Miss Sibson join in the fun?'

Louisa backed up and quickly shook her head. 'I am grubby enough all ready.'

His eyes narrowed for an instant, piercing her to her soul. 'Very well. I shan't insist…this time.'

Louisa knew she was making a bittersweet memory for when she returned to Sorrento.

'I will be ready to go to the Sims within the hour.'

He looked over his son's head and mouthed *thank you*.

Louisa hurried away before her heart demanded that she stay for ever.

Jonathon reached over and closed the carriage door with click. At his signal, the carriage began to roll away from the Sims's cottage.

Louisa, he noted with an inward smile, was not hugging the opposite wall as she had done on the trip to the cottage, but sitting in the centre of the seat. Her ribbon-trimmed bonnet shaded her face and her hands were primly folded on her lap. The very model of outward respectability.

With each turn of the carriage wheel, they went closer to Chesterholm and Jonathon knew his best chance would vanish. He had given his word that the first sign had to come from her and all she needed was a slight push.

As the carriage turned a corner on to the longer way home, Jonathon switched his place so he was sitting next to her.

'There is plenty of space on the other side.'

'I find going backwards makes me feel ill, particularly when there are bumps in the road.'

'The journey out was smooth.'

'We are going a slightly different way home. I wanted to stop at one of my farms. The farmer has a new foal that I want to inspect,' Jonathon said smoothly and waited for the objection. The matter was far from pressing, but it served to prolong the time they would be together and away from Chesterholm. With any luck, by this evening, Margaret would be under his roof, safe from his stepmother, and Louisa would be in his bed. 'Will you indulge me?'

She nodded and gathered her skirts in her hand, moving them slightly so they did not touch his leg. 'This is the first I have heard of you being ill from carriages.'

'Why do you think I used to drive?'

'I thought you enjoyed the challenge.' She inched slightly towards the carriage door.

He raised an eyebrow and her cheeks coloured slightly. Her tongue wet her lips, turning them cherry red. His instinct was correct. She was fighting the same temptation that he was. All she needed was a push in the right direction and the walls that hid her inner self would come tumbling down.

'And what did you think of your meeting with Annie?' he asked, allowing his leg to brush hers. 'Are you satisfied that her father has not beaten her or fed her on gruel? You spent a long time speaking with her. Sims had gone through his entire collection of horse brasses before you finished and that has not happened before.'

'It was an exercise in futility,' Louisa said, pulling her bonnet so that it sat more squarely on her head, shading her expression. 'Annie Sims keeps her secrets close. Despite listening to my tale about Miss Mattie, she refuses to say much about her experience. She claims not to remember much about the night she left.'

'Why do you think she is hiding something?'

Louisa gave him a quick glance. 'She kept holding up the handkerchief to her eyes, giving great noisy sobs without her nose going red or a single tear shimmering in her eyes. Later when I contrived to touch the handkerchief, it was dry.'

'She says very little, but what she does say is intended to tug at the heartstrings. She was blinded by love, but the scales have fallen from her eyes. She hates him now, but she can remember nothing about the night she left.' Jonathon leant back against the seat and stretched his arms along the back, not exactly embracing Louisa, but resting against her shoulders. He noted with satisfaction that she neither twitched nor moved away. By the end of the journey she would beg for his kiss and one more wall would be gone.

'Yes, that's exactly what she said. How did you know?'

'She said much the same to me. She might genuinely forget a few details, but that night should be branded on her memory.'

'It is possible that she is determined to rewrite history.' Louisa frowned. 'Is Annie the Sims's only child?'

'I believe so.' Jonathon frowned, trying to remember. 'I will confess to not having paid much attention.'

'I just wondered where Nanny Hawks fits in. Annie is her niece and I wondered if there were other children in the family.'

'Nanny Hawks?' Jonathon adjusted the way he held his arm so that he neatly cupped her shoulder, moving her ever so slowly closer to his body. 'Nanny Hawks rarely speaks of her niece. I doubt they are close. And Nanny Hawks's first loyalty is to Arthur and me. She will not have had anything to do with it.'

'Annie strikes me as someone who has a lot of pride and she should be more vocal about her hatred. He betrayed her,' Louisa said, dipping her head so that her eyes were hidden by the brim of her straw bonnet.

A pang of remorse sliced through him. He had sworn to protect her. He removed his arm from behind her and studied the outline of her bonnet. 'Did you hate me?'

'Yes, I thought I did.'

'Do you hate me still?'

'We were speaking of Annie and her lover,' Louisa said, turning her head towards him. 'But I have stopped hating you.'

'A start.'

She smiled back. 'More than a start. But we are speaking of Annie and not me.'

'Her sentiment was perhaps too perfect?' he asked quietly and ran an exploratory finger down the length of her arm. The pulse at the base of her throat quickened slightly from the light touch.

'Yes, that's right.' Louisa developed an interest in her gloves. 'You have it exactly. It is almost as if the speech has been rehearsed time and time again until she had it letter perfect. Why would this Trevor want her to return here? There could be nothing for him here, particularly when she returned the snuffbox. He will know that he is a wanted man.'

'Do you think Annie is in danger, then?'

'How could she be with her father there to protect her interests?' Louisa said. 'Annie might be hiding something else entirely. If only she had trusted me enough to say. She should have seen that I wanted to be her friend.'

'Trust is important—particularly between friends.'

Jonathon allowed his hand to hover and her body slowly moved away from it until she rested snugly against him. She jumped slightly and hurriedly moved back towards his hand.

'Shall I visit her again without you? It is not as if there is any danger and she might be more forthcoming if Lord Chesterholm is not within earshot,' she said, relaxing back against his arm. 'She refuses to say who at the Grange handed him the artefacts.'

'Refuses?' Jonathon removed his arm and stared down at her in astonishment. 'You spoke to her about this? You promised, Louisa!'

'There was little point in not asking. We have both experienced heartache. She was quite willing to tell me the tale, but she deliberately skimmed over certain details.'

'Indeed.'

'I think she has a shrewd idea of who the insider is.' Her clear amber gaze tumbled into his before she glanced away. 'And I think she is protecting them. I wish I knew why.'

'She should trust us to do the right thing. She should want to bring the culprit to justice.'

'Perhaps her loyalties are at war. She grew up around here, but she still has feelings for this man. Love is not an emotion that you can just turn off at will, as much as one might desire it.' She gave a tiny shrug.

'Thank you for trying to help, Louisa.' He twisted his fingers about hers and brought them to his lips. Her fingers trembled under his touch and her indrawn breath echoed around the carriage. 'I will handle it from here. If he did send Annie, then he is dangerous and I cannot put you in danger. Promise me you will not contact Annie again.'

'I am hardly a fainting violet.'

'Allow me to worry about you. We are friends.'

'If she contacts me, I will let you know. Does that satisfy you, Jonathon?'

'It will have to do, but, by God, Louisa, you are far too independent for your own safety.'

Louisa allowed her hand to rest in his for a few heartbeats, luxuriating in his touch before giving in to propriety and withdrawing it. It would be so easy to give in and turn her head the barest bit and brush his lips with hers.

The invitation was there. It would be easy to let the last of her defences tumble.

A soft sigh escaped her throat.

Already she was coming to care for him and his son. It was wrong to hope. She knew precisely where that had led the last time and she had changed.

Perhaps his intentions had been honourable, but that did not mean they would have remained together in the way she wanted. Less than twenty-four hours after being with her and he had been travelling to see Clarissa to apologise. It was the only explanation for why he had had the accident where it had happened. She had always vowed that she'd never do such a thing again and yet here she was in a carriage with him.

She wanted to believe his words about what had happened before. He certainly had done everything he had promised so far. The grown-up Jonathon was proving a good deal more responsible than the man she had known before.

The temptation to go back to that lovestruck creature she once was washed over her. It was would be foolish to deny her growing attraction to Jonathon, but equally foolish to act on it. She knew the difference between what one should do, and acting on one's impulses.

'Why did you come with me today, Louisa?' he asked in a lazy voice that sent ripples down her spine. 'Why were you so eager to join me on this journey? Only yesterday you used the excuse of Miss Daphne's shawl to avoid playing bowls.'

'Why should I worry about being alone with you in a carriage?' Louisa forced her voice to sound even and unperturbed but she was intensely aware of his nearness.

All she had to do was to lean a few inches closer and their lips would touch. Even his hand slipped from its resting place to further down her shoulders, urging her to snuggle closer. 'You have protested that you are a gentleman. You have given me your word that I will be safe in carriages. I decided to trust you. And…'

He gave her a smouldering look.

Louisa forgot to breathe. Tiny bubbles of warmth fizzed through her veins. The kisses yesterday morning should never have happened. What was worse was that she kept replaying the entire scene in her mind and knew that she wanted to feel his mouth against hers again. She wanted his arms to hold her and to hear the thump of his heart against her ear. She wanted to believe in second chances and that, like Eros and Psyche, some people were destined for each other. There could be true meeting of heart and soul.

Here in the darkened carriage where they would not be interrupted, the urge to meet his lips and to turn her face towards his was growing with each beat of her heart. All the promises and protestations were just shields to keep her heart safe and her heart was whispering to take that last step and to take a risk, just as she had four years ago.

'And…' she began again, wetting her lips. 'I enjoy pitting my wits against you. You make me think.'

'What do you dream about?'

Louisa pressed her hands together. Unlike four years ago, she had grown and knew the difference between love and desire. It was simply a natural reaction to a highly attractive man. This time she was in control and she understood there was a limit to the affair. This was not about love, but mutual attraction. It was about finishing what they had started all those years ago. She wanted him out of her blood. Maybe this was finally her opportunity to move on. 'I no longer dream.'

'Louisa, sometimes you have to take a chance,' his voice rumbled in her ear, doing strange things to her insides. 'Give me a chance to make your dreams come true.'

'What if I am afraid?' she whispered with her lips nearly touching his. 'Following my dreams has not always brought happiness.'

'You have to trust your instinct,' he mouthed the words against her skin.

A sudden jolting of the carriage sent her sprawling towards the floor and then threw her back against the backboard. Everything slowed down and took an age. She saw the colour drain from Jonathon's face as he reached towards her. Then suddenly the world sped up again and her head connected with the side of the carriage and the thump reverberated throughout the carriage.

His hand grabbed her waist and hauled her back against him. His face was white and tense.

'What happened? An accident? Has your coachmen hit something?'

'All will be well, Louisa, I promise,' he breathed against her hair. 'More than likely the carriage hit a pot hole. The sooner they get John McAdam and his miracle road surface out here the better. We will move on soon.'

'Yes, roads are terrible wherever you go unless they have been macadamized.' Louisa gave a little laugh to show she was not frightened or unduly disturbed by the slight accident. Having Jonathon near her was far more disturbing. 'Wise travellers always prepare for such things, or so Miss Mattie used to say. The problem is not hitting a rut, but staying in one.'

The carriage jerked forwards and then lurched to one side. Louisa grabbed on to his arm in an effort to steady herself. Her breasts skimmed his chest; if she leant a little further, her lips would meet his throat. She breathed in and savoured the scent of crisp linen and Jonathon before forcing her body to move away from his protective embrace.

'What's going on up there, Dexter?' Jonathon rapped on the roof. 'I pay you good money to drive this carriage safely and not put people in danger.'

'Clipped a rut with the left side, but the carriage wheel should be fine. It don't look too bad from here.' The coachman let out a long curse.

'Dexter, there is a lady present.'

'Begging your pardon, ma'am. The right side has become stuck in the mud I was attempting to avoid in the first place.'

'Do you need to inspect it? See if the shaft is broken?'

'Shouldn't think so, my lord. It doesn't look too deep and the horses are strong.'

'See if it can continue, but if you need assistance, ask,' Jonathon said, sitting bolt upright. 'Miss Sibson would like to return to the Grange as soon as possible.'

Louisa opened her mouth to protest, but then realised it was providence. She should be on her knees, grateful for the accident, rather than wishing it had never happened. 'That's right. We need to return to Chester-holm with all speed. Miss Daphne will become concerned if I am gone too long.'

'But in safety.' Jonathon's face was remote and Louisa knew the moment of intimacy had passed. A pang ran through her. Her insides ached for him. 'We must go at a slow speed. Trust me on this, Louisa. Slow but steady and we will arrive.'

'It is better than not arriving at all.'

'Precisely.' He ran an exploratory hand down her arm. 'Are you certain you are uninjured?'

'I might have a bruise or two, but nothing untoward. It was the merest bump.' Louisa concentrated on her gloves. She had to remember her rules and principles. Nothing would happen that she did not desire. There was the rub. She did desire his touch and his kiss, but she needed more than her desire. 'I am a good traveller. You need not be concerned about me.'

'If you are sure…' He touched the brim of her bonnet with his forefinger. 'You are a guest in my house.'

Louisa moved over to the other seat so she sat facing him. She had to look on this as an act of providence. She had been in the process of forgetting her rules. Another few heartbeats and they would have gone so far beyond the bounds of propriety that she would never be able to find her way back. Only, propriety seemed suddenly to be a very lonely place. 'I am sure.'

The carriage limped on for a few more turns of the wheel before juddering to a stop. Louisa stared at Jonathon, who closed his eyes and swore under his breath.

'It is no good,' she said. 'Even I can feel that the carriage is broken. It will never make Chesterholm unless a new wheel is found.'

She began to gather up her things from where they had tumbled to the floor. She tightened the ribbons of her bonnet and tried not to think how it would be ruined if the rain began to pelt down. Luckily she had worn her stout boots rather than the kid slippers she'd had on earlier and they had to be about halfway back to Chesterholm. If she walked quickly, it might not take her longer than a half-hour, forty-five minutes at most.

Practical things rather than thinking about being out here alone with Jonathon where anything could happen.

'Where are you going?' He grabbed her arm as her hand jerked the door open.

She stared at him in surprise. Surely he didn't think they could stay here in this intimate darkness, waiting for another carriage.

'We are going to have to walk. That's all that there is to it.' She glanced down at her boots.

'It is pelting down, Louisa.' He spoke as if she was no more than a child. 'We are a long way from Chesterholm. Three or four miles.'

'I will get wet. I often used to go walking in the rain in Sorrento.' Louisa kept her voice even. She went walking in the rain when there was no risk of thunder showers. 'Miss Mattie proclaimed it was good for her blood and she wanted a companion for the walks. One of her doctors recommended it.'

'It is a wonder she lived as long as she did,' Jonathon remarked drily.

'A constitutional in all weathers was her motto.'

'The rain in Northumberland is different from that in Sorrento. You will be chilled to the bone in that dress. I have no wish to have you develop lung fever.'

He moved the brim of her bonnet so it set more squarely on her head. 'Allow me to look after you, Louisa. I want to.'

'Why?' She blinked up at him as her entire being trembled. She was poised at a crossroads and she had to make an irrevocable decision. 'The time has long gone since I looked to you or anyone else for assistance. I gave up being a clinging vine years ago.'

'Who called you that?'

Louisa clamped her mouth and refused to let Clarissa's name escape. 'It does not matter.'

'You are a guest in my house. You get my protection whether you want it or not.'

'I deserve a choice.'

'Not this time.'

Louisa peered out of the small window at the rain. What had begun as a gentle drizzle was now falling as a curtain of silver. Mentally she said goodbye to her straw bonnet, but it could not be helped. It wasn't so bad—not as if it were a thunderstorm. And Jonathon could stop worrying about her. She was not some clinging vine. She was capable of standing on her feet. 'Even if I wish to make my own way?'

'It is for your own good, Louisa. Do you really want to risk lung fever? Who would look after Miss Daphne then? Who would look after you?'

Louisa collapsed against the carriage seat. 'What do you propose?'

'Another carriage will be sent. We wait here in the

dry. If nothing else, it will save your bonnet. Wait here.'

Jonathon went out and spoke to the driver. The voices rose and fell. He came back. His face was stern and unyielding.

'You will have to get out. There is a shepherding hut a few hundred yards from here. You can rest there.'

'Why?' Louisa asked. 'What is wrong with the carriage?'

*A hut? Alone with Jonathon?*

Her mind raced ahead to the scene. It would be far too easy to see what he planned on next—a prolonged seduction and then sex. And she would be powerless to resist temptation. She was not even certain that she wanted to resist it now.

The thought of their joining sent a warm curl around her insides. Did his skin taste like summer rain still? Were his muscles as well defined?

Louisa wrenched her thoughts away from that destructive path. She was not going to go down it. She refused to take the risk.

'I thought I could wait here. In the carriage.'

'We are going to move the carriage off the road. It's market day and this track is fairly busy. The last thing we want is an accident.'

An accident? There was something in his voice that made her blood chill. He had never spoken of the accident. She should have demanded the details, rather than letting it be unremarked on in the past. Sometimes her rules were wrong.

'Your curricle hit another vehicle, a vehicle that someone had abandoned to a mud pool,' she said with sudden certainty. 'Is that why the accident was so bad?'

'Someone had abandoned a farm wagon half-on and half-off the road. The reason was never clear.' He closed his eyes, pained.

'Can you remember much?'

'Barely anything. The Newtons' steward explained… weeks later.' His brow furrowed. 'I took the corner far too fast for the conditions and careened in the wagon. You were right to chastise me for my driving earlier that day. Arrogance always pays a price.'

'But it wasn't your fault that the wagon was there,' Louisa said quietly. What Venetia Ponsby-Smythe had done was unforgivable, twisting his memory and then piling the guilt on to ensure he would marry Clarissa.

'If I had been going slower, I would have had time. I was distracted…' He gave a bitter laugh. 'I wanted my life to start.'

'Simply because it happened then…' At his look, Louisa's voice trailed away.

'Are you always this arrogant? Do you know what the future holds, Louisa?'

'Not being wrapped in cotton wool for one thing.'

'It is for your own good. Think about how I would feel if anything happened to you as you waited here.'

It was unfair of her to protest; Louisa knew that, but he was being overly protective. Knowing about how that accident had happened, how could she be so cruel as to put him through the agony of what could happen? Louisa closed her eyes and concentrated. 'You worry far too much, Jonathon.'

'It won't take long,' the coachman called out. 'An hour, two at most. It is for the best, miss. You won't be out in this. And that there hut is right snug. There will be wood for a fire.'

Jonathon held out his hand and his expression had once again become smooth. The distress of earlier vanished as if it had never been. But Louisa knew somewhere deep inside him, Jonathon hurt. 'Be sensible, Louisa. Nobody planned on the carriage hitting the rut. Things like this just happen. Dexter knows the short cuts. He will be back before we know it.'

Sensible. She had spent the last four years being sensible. Sensible would be to walk over the fields and arrive back at Chesterholm full of self-righteousness and impeccable virtue. Sensible would be to spend as little time in Jonathon's company as possible.

Louisa knew she was not sensible. She did not want to think about what being alone in a hut with Jonathon would do to her already heightened senses. But there was merit in his suggestion—the hut was somewhere to wait. And she could resist her impulses. A supreme test of her resolve. It would demonstrate how much she had changed.

She reached out her hand and curled her fingers about his. 'I bow to your wisdom.'

The tension went out of his shoulders. 'Much safer, the hut is the most practical place under the circumstances.'

Louisa ignored the sudden trembling of her stomach. She was no longer a green girl who was head over heels in love. She knew the consequences. 'I would be a fool to ignore my security.'

He smiled a smile that sent pulses of warmth coursing straight down to the tips of her toes. As if he knew precisely what she was agreeing to and it entailed more than waiting patiently. 'I knew you would see sense.'

'Are you going with the coachman?' she asked, knowing her cheeks flamed. 'To get the carriage, I mean. There is no need for you to stay if you have something else to do.'

'Do you want me to?'

In the distance the clap of thunder sounded. Louisa stiffened. So much for a pleasant rain shower—this one threatened to be a violent storm, the sort she dreaded. She had never liked thunder and lightning, not since her parents' deaths.

Miss Mattie had used to throw the shutters open and watch the lightning forking down over the Bay of Naples, but Louisa had always pretended a deep interest in her book when in reality her entire body had trembled with each thunderclap. The likelihood was that this storm would never get near them.

Louisa took a deep breath, preparing to send him away, but the rain pelted down a bit faster and he stood there, bare headed with his hair beginning to curl at the ends. A single raindrop travelled down his cheek, tempting her.

Where had being sensible ever got her? Had being sensible ever helped her weather the storms?

She tightened her grip on his hand.

'Stay. Stay with me.'

His eyes became deep pools of blue-green. 'Only if you are certain.'

Sometimes, life had to be more than it might have been.

'I know what I want, Jonathon, and I want you with me. I do not want to be alone in this storm.'

## Chapter Ten

The hard stinging drops of rain splattered Louisa's bonnet, with one landing on her nose as she walked purposefully up the muddy track towards the shepherding hut.

True to the coachman's word, the hut was a few hundred yards from the road. Its slate roof and stone walls seemed solid and long lasting. As much as she hated to admit it, Jonathon was right. It would be a far pleasanter place to wait out the storm than in that little carriage.

As she reached the wooden door the thunder sounded again, closer this time. She flung the door open and launched herself inside. Her heart pounded in her ears. She was on her own in a thunderstorm. Jonathon had stayed behind for a few minutes to help move the carriage and she had to think that he would be fine. He would come to the hut when he was done. She would not be alone for ever.

When he arrived, what next? Louisa pressed her hands against her skirt.

Wait out the storm together. Alone. Without another soul to comment or remark.

Louisa licked her parched lips. Surely the coachman would be with him. The storm was far too fierce for him to go out in. With the coachman standing guard, the temptation to be with Jonathon would vanish.

It would solve the problem…for a little while. And after the storm, there would be no reason for her to stay in the hut. They could all walk together to Chesterholm when all around her the world would glisten and sparkle as the rain would wash everything clean.

Her breathing eased. If she thought clearly, there was always a solution. She simply worried far too much, saw too many possibilities.

The hut was small and barren. A straw bed lay in one corner and there was the bare minimum of supplies: a rough table, a chair and the remains of half a candle. The barest hint of daylight trickled through a badly fitted shutter. She took off her bonnet and gloves, placing them on the rough-hewn table next to her reticule. The simple act went some way towards restoring her sense of well being.

Logically, nothing could harm her here.

She was safe within these four walls. She had been wrong to panic earlier. Her rules had kept her safe this far and Jonathon was a known quantity, even if the coachman stayed with the horses. Nothing would happen to her that she did not desire. Desire. Her pulse raced faster and her breasts grew heavy as she remembered that once Jonathon had fuelled another sort of desire.

The rain pelted down against the shutter and the

distant rumble of thunder sounded again. The hut might be safe but she worried about Jonathon being caught out in the storm. Her mind kept inventing reasons why he was delayed. She watched the door as one of Jonathon's sheep dogs might watch a stick, waiting for the movement, the signal that she was far from being alone.

'I see you found it easily enough,' Jonathon's voice called out. 'Snug and dry as I promised.'

'I have a good sense of direction, particularly when following a straight road,' Louisa called back, the tension rolling off her back. Straight and narrow—she had followed that road metaphorically for a long time now. It had kept her safe. She was familiar with its landmarks and signposts, but hearing Jonathon's voice, she knew she had reached a crossroads.

'We use it in lambing season,' Jonathon said, ducking his head as he entered, at once filling the room.

He had removed his coat, stock and hat to help move the carriage. The rain had turned his hair dark and his shirt translucent. It clung to his body, revealing the sculptured definition of his muscles, firm and hard, the muscles of an active man, not one who spent days lifting cards in club rooms. Louisa sucked in her breath as the memory of how his skin had felt under her fingertips flooded through her.

He lit the candle using a lucifer match. The yellow light made strange shadows on the roughly plastered walls and turned his rain-soaked skin to a gleaming golden. A single drop gathered in the hollow of his throat, begging to be tasted. Louisa pressed her fingertips together and concentrated on the flickering light. The memories of how she had taken off his shirt once and revealed his smooth chest came flooding back. His skin then had been golden and warm beneath her fingers. Unable to resist the temptation, she had tasted, savouring the heady taste of sunlight and pure masculinity. She forced her shoulders to relax and her mind to focus on the single flickering candle.

'It is good that the coachman remembered it was here.' Her voice was far too high and stilted. She swallowed and tried again, being careful not to watch the shirt as it clung and then slid across his chest. 'You were right. I would not like to be out in the storm.'

'Its four walls and roof will keep the rain off you until the chaise can come.' His hand ran through his hair, sending droplets spraying out in the room. A single drop touched her cheek, just before another fell on her breast causing a damp patch, cooling her fevered skin, but igniting the blaze inside her. 'You were lucky. You made it to shelter before the rain really started hammering down.'

'My bonnet will never be the same again.' Louisa gave a rueful look at the sodden bit of straw, pleased to concentrate on something other than him and the growing ache inside her. 'Not even the new trimming will mend it.'

'Perhaps I can help. After all, you came on this journey to help me.'

'It is not necessary.' Louisa started to rearrange the objects on the table, moving her bonnet to the right and her reticule to the left. 'Has the carriage been moved?'

'The carriage slipped and slid in the rain and its wheel is truly ruined.' A satisfied smile crossed his lips. 'However, in the end, I got what I wanted.'

Louisa carefully moved her bonnet closer to her reticule. *What he wanted*—that was the problem and the temptation.

'Do you generally get what you want?'

'In most cases, it is part of the privilege of being a baron.' His eyes became deep pools of blue-green that enticed her to drown in their depths. 'The carriage is not a danger to anyone now.'

'And the storm?' Louisa swallowed hard, hating the tremor in her voice. The carriage might not be a danger, but he was certainly dangerous. And like a moth to a flame, she was attracted to the danger. It made her feel alive in a way she hadn't been for years. Not since the last time she'd been with him, since the last time they'd made love. 'How long will the storm last? Maybe after it has blown out, we could walk along with the coachman.'

The excuse sounded feeble to her ears. Her gaze locked with his and she hoped he understood what she was saying. Not only understood, but acted in a way to keep them both safe. Why she needed to get away from this cottage before it overwhelmed her good intentions.

'There is no need when shelter is here.' He wrung the bottom of his shirt out, sending a fresh shower of droplets scattering on the floor. 'We are in for an incredible storm. Sometimes, the thunder rumbles for hours as the storm circles the valley. But this hut has been around for years. It will shelter us from the storm. Nothing will harm us here.'

'Where's Dexter the coachman? I had expected him to wait.' Louisa began to pace the floor, but with each turn, the room seemed smaller and Jonathon's chest more inviting. 'Surely you have not sent him away in this.'

'Dexter has set off leading one of the horses. He will ride if the weather clears up a bit. He should make it back home without too much difficulty.'

'But the storm is dangerous.'

'He loves being out in storms. Something about seeing the sky light up. It makes him feel like he is alive, he says.' Jonathon smiled a heartbreaking smile. 'I could not have stopped him if I had wanted to. He knows the risks, Louisa. It was his choice.'

'He will be drenched to the skin and will catch lung fever.' She caught her bottom lip between her teeth. She knew the risks as well. Suddenly that straight and narrow road was long and lonely. 'Like you. Perhaps...'

'You are showing a lot of concern for a man you barely know.' His eyes softened, beckoned to her. 'He wanted to go, Louisa. I did give him the option. There was no dissuading him.'

'You wanted him to go. You are his master. You could have commanded him to stay.'

'And what would that have achieved? A delay? We need another carriage to continue.' He smiled a half-smile and caught her hands between his warm ones. 'Stop worrying about Dexter. He is a sensible fellow.'

'You wanted to be alone with me.'

The pulse quickened in the hollow of his throat. 'Yes, I did.'

'And the horses? Are they safe?'

'The remaining horses are tethered behind the hut.'

Louisa rearranged her reticule and gloves on the

table, concentrating on the little details that showed she was respectable and that the girl who had blithely thumbed her nose at convention was no longer. The only trouble was that it appeared her former self had been resting rather than dead. And she wanted everything— respectability, safety and Jonathon. But experience dictated that it was impossible. 'Hopefully he won't take very long.'

'He will be back as soon as he can, but I would imagine that it will take a few hours. We are here for the duration.'

The duration. Just the two of them. Alone. With no chance of interruption. The knowledge made her quiver with anticipation. She could make a small detour on her straight road.

A rumble of thunder shook the hut, bringing back all of Louisa's fears about violent storms and their destructive power. Intellectually she knew that the lightning had little chance of striking the cottage, but it still made her knees weaken and her insides tremble. In her mind's eye, she saw the ruined burned-out carriage. Her father had taken the risk, her uncle had always said, and he should have stayed put. God's judgement.

How would God judge her?

She paused. Hadn't he already? He, along with the rest of society, had judged her unworthy. It was why she had lost the baby.

She had spent years trying to believe differently but for what? Simply to discover that she need not have struggled. She was back to where she had started, destined to repeat the same passion with the same man.

Except this time she no longer believed in for ever

or for always. And she asked for no more than a few hours. No words of love had passed between them and this was no prelude to marriage. It was about the here and now, because the future offered no guarantees.

'It is good of you to wait with me.' She gave a nervous smile as yet another clap of thunder bounced off the walls. Jonathon stood there unflinching, seemingly unmoved by the crashing sound. Louisa watched with envy. She wanted to curl up in a small ball. She had to keep talking or she'd beg him to put his arms about her and put an end to this terrible waiting for him to make the first move.

'It is my pleasure.' A faint smile touched his lips. 'Does the thunderstorm bother you that much?'

'I hate thunderstorms, always have. Ever since my parents died.' Louisa wet her lips. It was easy to admit that fear.

'You think I have forgotten everything about you, don't you?' He put out a hand and touched her cheek with a brush of his fingers, a featherlight touch, but one that made her blood fizz with anticipation. Despite the soaking he'd received, his fingers seared her skin. Her breasts strained against the confines of her stays.

'There was no reason why you should remember such a little thing.' Her voice held a husky note.

'You have no idea what I remember.' His words wrapped themselves around her insides, holding her in their warmth. 'Losing your parents was tragic.'

'I had assumed...' Louisa pressed her hands against her skirt and tried to regain some control over her body. 'I had assumed if you remembered anything, you remembered only the physical.'

'Your parents died in a thunderstorm after their carriage was struck by lightning. A judgement from God, according to your uncle, but then your uncle was always quick to invoke God when things did not go as he had planned.'

She gave the briefest of nods, not trusting her voice to speak. He had remembered everything, even the words her uncle had used to explain every misfortune. Her life after Jonathon had been built on the foundations of a belief that he would have forgotten. It made it much harder to stand there, pretending not to need him when he remembered how much she had needed him once before, how she had clung to him that summer's day in the gazebo, not caring who saw as the lightning sliced through the sky, hitting the great oak on the other side of the ha-ha.

'It was easier to think you had forgotten,' she whispered. 'I wanted you to forget.'

He took two steps towards her, so that their bodies barely touched. He made no attempt to take her in his arms, but simply stood, allowing her to make the choice. Their gazes locked and she found herself mesmerised by the shifting blue-greens in his eyes. Who would have thought so many colours could be contained in such a space?

'I wanted to, but I couldn't,' he said in a low voice. 'Louisa, did you forget me? Have you changed that much from the girl I once held?'

There was a catch in his voice that made him sound like a little boy begging for the moon. And she knew she owed him the truth. 'I remembered…everything. I tried to forget, but couldn't.'

She ignored the sudden fluttering in her belly. Right now all she desired was standing in front of her—Jonathon with gleaming golden skin, softly curling hair and shoulders wide enough to lean on. This man could protect her from the raging storm. He had protected her once before.

It did not matter what would happen two days from now, a month from now; all she knew was that she wanted to be kept safe from the coming storms—shelter from the storm outside, from the possible storm with society and to be able to face the passion raging inside them both without fear. She would think about her position in society and what the gossips might say after the storm had passed. Everything but the need to feel safe and secure faded into insignificance.

'Jonathon,' she breathed and held out her hand as she took several faltering steps towards him. He opened his arms and she tumbled into them. It felt like she was coming home.

He cupped her face with his warm hands and bent his head. His lips tasted of rain and summer sunshine, a promise of all good things. Then he lifted his head and his eyes became deep turquoise pools. 'Storms are helpful, Louisa. They are to be welcomed. They remake and reshape the world. We cannot stop them. We can only look forward to the world made new.'

'And will this storm remake the world?'

'It will change it in ways we can only imagine.' He pressed his lips to the nape of her neck. Warm tingles invaded her. 'But trust me to protect you from it. You do trust me, Louisa?'

Her hands touched his face, feeling the rough bristles

and then the softness of his lips under the pads of her fingers. She brought his head down next to hers, lifted her mouth. 'Yes, I trust you, Jonathon.'

She drank from his lips, opening her mouth under his gentle pressure and slaking her thirst. As their tongues touched, her fear about the storm faded, to be replaced by something far deeper and more primitive. Desire. For too long she had denied her need and now it raced through her blood, heating it and driving her onwards.

They stood there, lips entwined, tongues touching and the hunger grew within her. Her world had come down to no more than the four walls, and the man who held her against his strong body, protecting her from the sound of thunder. She didn't dare think beyond that. Later and a return to civilisation would happen whether she wanted it to or not. Neither Miss Daphne nor Lord Furniss would say anything, she was certain of that. The coachman, the broken carriage and the storm ensured that tongues would be silent. Now was about the storm they were creating inside.

He shifted his hold and pulled her tighter against his body, pressing up against her so she felt his arousal pressing against her stomach and knew that he wanted her as much as she wanted him. She moved against him, enjoying the feel of him. The small action sent a pulse of heat throughout her body, which coiled around itself to become a deep aching need.

A small moan came from the depths of her throat.

His hands tilted her head back, scattering hairpins, allowing her hair to tumble about her shoulders.

'Your hair—so many different shades of red,' he whispered at her temple.

'I have always hated the colour,' she said with a strangled laugh. 'I am afraid it will not make a cloak for us any longer.'

'But I like it this way as well.' He brought a strand of hair to his lips. 'There is more to you than your hair.'

Inside her, a rampant storm built and grew, urged on by the inexorable pressure of his mouth and the lap of his tongue against hers. Thunder sounded again, closer this time, shaking the door and rattling the single shutter as the rain pelted down on the roof.

A blinding light filled the darkened hut, illuminating Jonathon's intense features—his high cheekbones, the burning pools of blue-green reminding her of the Bay of Naples on a summer's day, the strong column of his throat. But somehow, with Jonathon holding her, she knew it would be fine. The storm would not destroy her; the storm would remake her. She gave in to her earlier temptation and tasted where the drop of water had gathered at the base of his throat. His skin tasted of warmth and something that was indefinably Jonathon. She suckled, feeling his pulse quicken under her tongue.

His lips nibbled down her neck to where her bodice started.

'Shall I stop?' he murmured, his breath teasing the sensitive part of her neck.

She stilled, amazed.

He was offering her an escape, but the way his hands moved on her back, kneading and stroking, escape was the last thing she desired. She wanted to be in his arms and experience passion once more. Some might say that she lacked will-power, but she knew the regret of what might have been was far worse than the worry about respectability.

She buried her hands in his hair, glorying in the crisp firmness. All around them, the thunder ebbed and surged, circling the valley, calling to her and telling her that life was short and fleeting. What was possible now would not be tomorrow. Tomorrow she would follow her respectable road again.

'Don't stop. Don't ever stop.'

He cupped her breasts with his hands, gently flicking the nipples over the cloth, rolling them between his fingers. The nipples instantly hardened into sharp points. A soft moan emerged from her throat as her breasts strained against the cloth and ached to be free. He seemed to understand her wordless plea.

Slowly he undid the tiny buttons and exposed her chemise and corset. With probing fingers, he slipped between the lace-edged material and her quivering flesh. Her nipples tightened still further and her back arched forwards, seeking his touch.

He bent his head, captured a nipple between his teeth and suckled, creating wet patches on the thin cotton chemise, making the areola appear dark rose under the now translucent material.

Louisa's knees weakened and she clung to him. He finished undoing the buttons of her dress and then with expert fingers untied her petticoats. They fell to the floor with a soft swoosh. And she stood in front of him, dressed only in a chemise and drawers, free from the confines of society's requirements. Here the world became two.

Gently he eased her down amongst the profusion of petticoats.

'I want you, Louisa. I want all of you,' he said, pressing kisses on her temples. 'Dear God, please do not tell me I am dreaming.'

'You are awake.'

Her hand grasped his neck and brought him down with her so that their bodies were nestled together. It all came back to her—the taste of his skin, the pressure of his legs intertwined with hers, and most of all the thrumming that echoed through her body. Her hands clawed at his shirt, pulling at the damp linen. With an understanding smile he quickly divested the garments and stood before her—naked, his skin gleaming golden in the soft candlelight, better than her memory.

Slowly he moved his lips down her neck and returned once more to suckle her breasts. This time he moved the material aside and feasted, tugging and swirling the nipple in his mouth. And with each tug, the rising ache between her legs grew.

Her hand stroked his hair, holding him against her body. His hard planes hit her soft curves and it was somehow far more wonderful than she remembered. Every single part of her was alive.

His hand ran along her drawers until his questing fingers found the opening. Her body arched upwards, allowing his fingers to slip inside and play. His fingers followed her unspoken command—gliding along her inner surfaces with a lazy grace, tantalising her senses. The great aching want grew within with each movement of his finger against the slick surface. Her hips lifted off the bed of petticoats, seeking the release that she knew only he could give her.

He slipped one finger, then two inside and instantly she clenched against the fingers as they slid in and out of her.

She grasped his face with her hands and a moan came from her throat as her body arched towards his questing fingers, desiring the ultimate release.

'Jonathon.'

'Soon,' he rasped in her ear as his fingers continued their play, sliding and stroking her, making the want within her grow until she thought she must break into two from the need to join with him.

'Now.'

Her hands tugged at his back and urged him forward, urged him to fill her with more than his fingers. She wanted him inside and his body covering her.

He wedged her thighs wider and positioned himself between them.

As a crack of lightning lit the room with its white-hot heat, he thrust forwards and her body opened to meet him, enveloping him as he filled her. This time, unlike four years ago, her body stretched and welcomed the full length of him. She gave a soft cry and clutched at his back as he drove forwards. He collapsed on her, and lay there unmoving.

She looked up at him, her hand touching his eyebrows, and cheeks, memorising his features.

He rained kisses on her face before raising himself up on his elbows. She lifted her hips, wordlessly urging him to stay with her.

'At your pace,' he rasped in her ear as he rested deep within her. 'You know what you want.'

What she wanted. What she had to have. And it was the same as him. They were joined.

She began to move her body, giving in to her instinct. Faster and faster until they were both spent and with a cry, she reached the edge and plunged over as all around her the thunder sounded, no longer frightening, but somehow echoing and rejoicing in their cries of pleasure.

Jonathon twisted the red-gold hair about his fingers, revelling in its silky texture and flower-scented smell. Her hair had darkened and changed over the past four years. He had not realised that so many shades, from dark auburn to burnt copper, could be contained on one head—a colour to suit any mood. Every time he looked, he found something new to admire.

Joining with Louisa had surpassed his memory of the last time.

He had never lost control in that way with any other woman. And he knew he had lied to himself—once would not be nearly enough. He did not want it to be a short affair where two bodies collided. He wanted to wake up with her by his side. He wanted her to be in his life, rather than simply being a memory.

He had not planned to make love to her in this spartan hut. Today was supposed to be one more baby step in the seduction. But the storm had intervened and the desire to comfort her had overwhelmed him. She had turned to him because of her fear. The next time, he wanted her to turn to him because of her desire for him.

He pressed his lips against her auburn hair. Her eyes were sated and wide. He started to speak, but she laid two fingers across his lips. 'Hush, after what we shared, neither of us should keep secrets from each other.'

Jonathon ignored the slight twinge of guilt. Louisa would learn of Venetia's arrival soon enough. He gave her an indulgent smile. 'What dark secret have you been keeping from me?'

'I was pregnant with your child when I went to Italy.'

Jonathon stared at her in astonishment. He had expected something little, not this. 'You were pregnant with my child? And you left?'

'It seemed the best option. I was not going to give the child up, Jonathon. You were getting married.' Her lips trembled. 'I was certain that your stepmother was right.'

'It was a lie.'

She laid her head against his chest. 'I know that now.'

He put a hand on her shoulder and held her away from him. His insides churned. Louisa had had their child. 'Where is the child now? Sorrento?'

'I lost our baby, Jonathon. Me! Not anyone else.' She gave a shuddering gulp. 'I...I caught a fever on the boat and the baby was born too soon. My body could not hold her.'

*Born too soon*. The words echoed about his brain. He put his arms about her and held her as great shuddering sobs racked her body. Anger, regret and remorse surged through him. He wanted to take the hurt away from her, but there was nothing he could do except hold her. 'I want to know everything.'

'They said I was lucky to be alive. I wanted to die.' She stared at him with tear-stained eyes. 'That Louisa, the girl you loved, I thought she was gone, but now I am not sure.'

'Hush, it is all right.' He kissed her temple and willed her to believe. 'You are safe in my arms. Nothing bad will hurt you again.'

'You broke my heart twice that year, Jonathon,' she said, breaking free. Her face was pinched, white and vulnerable, but there was dignity about her. 'Once when I did not hear from you and the second time when your baby, our baby, left me. The little girl never breathed. Not one breath. She was beautiful, though.'

'Did you give her a name?'

'Elizabeth Claire after our mothers.'

'I would have chosen the same name.' He drew her firmly into his arms and held her, longed to do more. 'I am glad you gave her a name.'

She squeezed his hand and then moved away from him. 'Thank you. I am fine now. The storm has passed. I need to dress.'

Silently Jonathon handed Louisa her chemise, allowing her time to recover. His entire being ached. Louisa had gone to Italy because she was pregnant. Because she thought… His mind reeled and bile rose in his throat. He could not change the past as much as he might want to. 'No one told me. I would never have abandoned you and the baby. Ever.'

'I know that now.' A final tear ran down Louisa's cheek. She wiped it away with impatient fingers. 'You would think, after all the years, the hurt would have stopped.'

'You have someone to share it with now.' Jonathon forced his shoulders to relax. One more thing to confront his stepmother with. One more thing she would have to atone for.

'I thought I would die when it happened. I wanted to, but stupidly I lived. Then one warm spring morning, I laid a flower on her grave and I found I wanted to go on living.' She lifted her chin and met his gaze full on. 'I put my past behind me. I changed and became the person I am now.'

Jonathon started to pull her back into his arms, but she moved away. 'Louisa, I am sorry. The words are inadequate, I know. If anything happens this time, I am here. We face the future together.'

'It won't.' She looped her hair behind her ear. Her voice became dull and without emotion. 'The doctor said I would never have children again. Or at least that's what I understood. My Italian was not so good in those days.'

Jonathon closed his eyes. It explained why Louisa had been reluctant to play with his son. The Louisa of his memory had loved children and had wanted a large family. His careless driving had destroyed her life even though she had not been in his carriage. That she was willing to forgive him was a miracle. 'Louisa...'

'I must dress, Jonathon. The storm is over. All my tears are shed.'

'Dress?' He stared at her in disbelief. There were things they had to discuss. 'Listen to me, Louisa.'

'Unless you want everyone to know what we have

been doing, we will have to dress.' She pointed towards the window. 'The sun is shining and the sky is blue. The storm has cleared the air. Even now, the chaise will be making its way towards us.' She scrambled to her feet. Her cheeks flamed. Red. It pleased him that she still knew how to blush. 'No one must know. Tell no one how we sheltered from the storm.'

Jonathon narrowed his gaze. It would be very easy to force her to make the right decision, but that would not win her. Jonathon knew he wanted all of her, not just her body and not just because they happened to be discovered together. 'Are you going to deny that you were an equal partner in what just happened? You were the one who asked me to stay with you.'

'It was an aberration and best forgotten.' Her hands worked feverishly, collecting the various garments. 'The storm has passed. I am no longer in need of comfort. I have the rest of my life to live. I cannot go on wishing for what might have been. This was goodbye.'

Was that all he was—a temporary shelter from the storm? Jonathon's mouth tasted bitter. What happened here was supposed to be a beginning, not an ending.

'I want to be with you again, Louisa. In a bed, properly, and with time to enjoy all the sensual delights.' He half-closed his eyes, picturing the large four-poster bed in his room, the firelight, and Louisa naked, spread out for his delectation, her auburn hair contrasting with the cream of the sheets. But he wanted more than that. He wanted her in his life. But right now, he had to settle for what she was prepared to give. 'Do you think our passion would be satisfied with just this once?'

Louisa's hands tried to shove the final button of

her gown through its buttonhole. It broke off and went bouncing on the floor. He wanted to be with her, even after she had told him about their baby. He had not recoiled in horror. And she knew if she had stayed in his arms then, her heart would have been lost for ever. She was not prepared to take the risk. 'What you want is not going to happen.'

'Why not? We are adults.'

'I will be beholden to no man.' She reached down and picked up her dress. 'Jonathon, I have a life in Italy. There is a little cottage with grapes and lemons growing in the garden, and if I crane my neck just right, I have a view of the Bay of Naples and Mount Vesuvius beyond. I am going to return there. You might not consider it much of a life, but it is safe and respectable. And, most importantly, it belongs to me. I created the garden. It is my true refuge from life's storms.'

Pain flickered across his face, but she also spied more than a hint of relief. Her stomach tightened as the bitter knowledge flooded through her. He was not offering to become a permanent fixture in her life.

'We will have to make the most of our remaining time together.' He put his arms about her and drew her back against his body. Her curves melted into him, making her want to give into him.

'I knew your intentions are far from honourable. You are seeking to cause a scandal.' She kept her head still. The need for him was welling up again, so fiercely that it scared her. Jonathon needed to marry a woman who could give him everything and she was barren. All he offered was an affair—that was his unspoken message.

His hands loosened, allowing her to stumble away from him. His face became cold and remote.

'Shall we forget about intentions and concentrate on being?' His eyes glittered with dangerous fires. 'You were the one who seduced me. You were the one who wanted me. You used me when it suited.'

Her fingers quickly twisted her hair into a semblance of a knot. She spied several hair pins, pounced on them and jabbed them into her head. Then, feeling more in control of her emotions, she put on her bonnet and turned back to him.

'There is no future, Jonathon, for us. I have my future mapped out.' She gave a little smile, but inwardly she died a little.

'There does not have to be a plan or rules. We can simply be together. We are adults, Louisa.' He held out his hands and a slow sensuous smile that promised hot nights amongst tangled sheets caressed her.

'And no one will know,' she said, reaching for her bonnet and gloves. 'I have heard those words before, Jonathan. I learnt the lesson. Someone always knows.'

His lips twitched upwards as he acknowledged her statement. '*I* am not planning on telling anyone.'

'Good,' she lied and then stilled, listening as she heard the distant rattle of a carriage wheel. Relief flooded through her. She was not going to have to pretend an indifference any longer. She held up her hand, silencing him. 'I cannot deny what happened this afternoon. But here it stays. You and I must go on as if this never happened.'

'But it did happen,' Jonathon said.

'Then forget.' Louisa gave an imperious nod. Her

insides ached with knot upon knot. If Jonathon whispered one word of love or caring about her, she would go to him, and that would be wrong. She stopped believing in dreams four years ago. 'It is the only solution, Jonathon. Maybe it is time you learnt that you cannot have everything you desire.'

'I learnt that lesson years ago, Louisa.' Jonathon turned his back on her, hiding his face. 'But we will play it your way…for now.'

Louisa bowed her head and the brim of her bonnet hid her face. 'Thank you for respecting my decision, Jonathon.'

'I was always a gentleman, Louisa.' He caught her arm and turned her so that her heart-shaped face faced him. He wanted to shake her and get her to listen to what he was saying, but he also knew she was right. He would not stoop to causing a scandal. 'I will give you the privilege of changing your mind.'

'That won't happen.' Her voice shook with the faintest of tremors. 'I can assure you.'

He straightened her bonnet with a twitch of his fingers, allowing a single strand of hair to wrap itself around his thumb in the process. He resisted the temptation to bring it to his mouth. 'I wonder what excuse you will use the next time.'

'There will be no next time.'

'You were never good at wagering, Louisa, so do not even start.' Jonathon gave her a bow. 'You will be the one who begs for my mouth. We are meant to be together.'

## Chapter Eleven

$\text{B}$eg. She would never beg for his touch. Louisa gritted her teeth and concentrated on the dining-room chandelier's flickering light. Jonathon's arrogant prediction as the replacement coach had arrived continued to echo in her brain several hours later. No flimsy excuse would cross her lips but she might find a reason to surrender.

Louisa released a breath the moment she reached the corridor, expanding her lungs until her breasts were tight against the *décolleté* green evening dress. She had made it through supper. It had been sheer torture to sit at the table with Jonathon presiding at the other end.

She had tried very hard to pay attention to the dinner-table conversation, but her mind had kept drifting back to the afternoon.

Forgetting about him was proving harder than she had thought possible, little short of torture. With each turn of his head at supper, every time his fingers had curled around the wine or water glass, a warm heat had infused her body, curling around her insides.

What was worse was that several times their gazes had met and he appeared to know precisely what she was thinking. Having an affair was tempting. It would be a way to banish him from her system.

'Miss Sibson, that shade of green suits you. You must tell me how you do it,' Miss Blandish said, taking Louisa's arm as she entered the drawing room and leading her away from the chair she had occupied the previous evening and towards the centre of the room.

'I like the colour and the colour likes me.' Louisa dipped her head. What was Miss Blandish playing at now? The woman had scarcely spoken more than a few words to her and suddenly she was behaving as if they were bosom friends.

Miss Blandish gave a little trilling laugh. 'The country air must be good for you. It has certainly put the roses in your cheeks over the last few days. When we were in Newcastle, I thought you were pale and insignificant, but now I can see I was utterly wrong. You appear as if you were lit by a thousand candles.'

Louisa stopped and stared at Miss Blandish. A compliment—a back-handed compliment, to be sure, but a compliment all the same. She swallowed hard. Hopefully what had happened this afternoon did not show on her face! Even the maid had said something about her heightened colour and how much better her complexion was for spending a few days in the country.

Her breathing eased. The notion that Miss Blandish had guessed was misplaced guilt.

Despite Miss Daphne's eyes twinkling, she had not asked about the details of Louisa's misadventure when she'd gone to see her and explain about the unexpected delay. Thankfully, Dexter the coachman had given a very graphic account of the accident, playing up his part. And Miss Daphne knew how much Louisa hated thunderstorms.

She inclined her head and accepted Miss Blandish's compliment as an overture of friendship. 'The right shade can do wonders for one's complexion.'

'You are lucky to be able to wear green.' The blonde woman linked her arm with Louisa's. 'I have always wanted to wear green but my dear mama keeps me in pink. She says that green makes me look bilious. What is worse is that Prunella agrees. This afternoon while it was raining she said so very loudly. And Lord Furniss overheard, I'm sure of it. He was reading in the library.'

'You are imagining things.' Louisa leant forwards and dropped her voice. Now was the perfect time to matchmake. 'Lord Furniss tends to concentrate quite hard when he is reading. He will not have heard.'

'You are sweet. You have no idea what a trial Nella has been and how it has preyed on my mind. I would hate for Lord Furniss to think me bilious in anything.'

'It is one of the good parts about having no siblings,' Louisa said with the slightest catch in her throat. 'Not having to worry about one's younger sister.'

'Yes, I have never thought of it in that light. No one to tell you what to do or wear. Now that has a certain appeal.' Miss Blandish giggled like a young girl. 'When I get married, I am planning to wear green simply to spite my mother.'

'Lord Furniss appears to like you in pink.'

Miss Blandish's cheeks coloured slightly and she

lowered her voice. 'Do you think so? Lord Furniss is, well…very pleasant and amenable. I know Mama would prefer Lord Chesterholm for me, but there is just a certain something about Lord Furniss. I think it is his hands with their clean nails and tapering fingers. I noticed them when he was teaching me the proper way to bowl.'

'It sometimes happens that way.' Louisa glanced over her shoulder towards where Miss Daphne sat seemingly engrossed in an animated conversation with Nella. Her matchmaking scheme was progressing far better than she had dreamt possible.

'Shall we take a turn about the drawing room?' Miss Blandish said, lowering her voice and gripping Louisa's arm tighter. 'I simply cannot face another moment at the spinet. Miss Daphne kept me at my scales for hours and hours until my voice was beyond hoarse. Dear Mama has had me take some of her tonic in preparation, but I cannot face another warble. I can't remember ever practising that much.'

'Just think about Lord Furniss and the pleasure he took in your voice.'

Miss Blandish brightened and then a frown marred her features. 'Of course, it might all change when Margaret Ponsby-Smythe arrives tomorrow.'

Louisa froze. The room swayed slightly and then righted. She swallowed hard and tried to keep from being ill as a sense of supreme betrayal coursed through her. Margaret was expected tomorrow. And that would mean Mrs Ponsby-Smythe arriving as well. She could not see Margaret being allowed to travel on her own. Jonathon had kept that intelligence from her. Despite everything they had shared, despite her sharing her secret, he was still playing games.

He had been the one to send the driver away. He'd known where the hut was. Louisa pinched her brow. He could not have predicted the broken carriage wheel or the storm, but he had taken advantage of her. He had sought to bind her to him before she had a chance to confront Venetia. He had kept it from her.

'Miss Sibson? You have gone pale.'

'I wasn't aware that Margaret was arriving so soon.' *Or at all.* All her excitement tasted like ash in her mouth. She remained a naïve fool. Louisa stiffened her shoulders. No, that was wrong. She had been deceived.

'Apparently Lord Chesterholm has been put out at her taking so long. He anticipated her and Mrs Ponsby-Smythe this afternoon. You must sit down, Miss Sibson, before you fall down.' Miss Blandish put a hand under Louisa's elbow and led her to the sofa.

Louisa gulped in air. 'How did you learn this intelligence?'

'My sister overheard Lord Chesterholm when he returned from your journey. She listens at doors. Apparently he let out a roar that could be heard two counties away.'

Ice-cold shock coursed through Louisa, closely followed by white-hot anger. Why had she learnt nothing? Once again she had been living in some fantasy world of her own making. She had even considered his disreputable offer.

'It is a terrible habit to listen at doors,' Louisa said, concentrating on the candles above the mantelpiece and how they glowed and tried to remember Miss Mattie's mantra: calm, cool, reasonable. Jonathon could only hurt her if she gave him the power to do so and she refused to allow her heart to be broken a third time. She should have remembered that storms always pass.

'But a useful habit.' Miss Blandish tapped her mouth with her fan. 'Lately Nella has proved invaluable with certain information. I wish she would learn to hold her tongue on other matters, though.'

Louisa allowed Miss Blandish's words to flow over her as she concentrated on a single candle flame. The knowledge of Jonathon's betrayal kept circling through her brain. He was seeking to use her. She had been wrong to think that there was anything real or lasting between them. He wanted all her secrets, but was not even prepared to tell her that his stepmother was expected.

'Miss Sibson, are you sure you are quite the thing? Your cheek grows paler and paler.' Miss Blandish waved her fan in front of Louisa's face.

'I never faint.' Louisa pushed the fan away. 'We were speaking of Lord Furniss. I'm sure he will prove a faithful squire to you.'

'You are good to say that, but until he actually makes an offer, I cannot count on the faithfulness of his heart. There have been many a slip between cup and lip.' Miss Blandish gave a little high-pitched laugh, but Louisa could see the fear in the young woman's eyes. 'I have no idea what Miss Ponsby-Smythe is like and I would hate to give my heart only to have it broken.'

'If you never give your heart, how can you expect him to give his?' Louisa kept her voice light. Miss Blandish would make a good match with Lord Furniss. At least some happiness could come from this house party.

'But is she pretty?'

Louisa closed her eyes, remembering Margaret's somewhat mismatched features. Clarissa had been cruel, and often pointed out what a graceless elephant Margaret was and how her nose was far too large for her face.

'Not conventionally so, but she had a certain liveliness to her conversation.' Louisa tapped her fan against her teeth. 'But knowing both of them, I would be surprised if Lord Furniss would find Margaret a compatible companion in life.'

Miss Blandish pressed Louisa's hand. 'You do not know how it does my heart good to hear this. I have no wish for Lord Furniss to become distracted. A man with a title is sought after and he does have the dearest smile. When he smiles, my entire being lights up.'

'It all depends on the woman.' Louisa squeezed Miss Blandish's hand. 'Some women have lots of proposals and others need only one. But I am sure the right man is out there.'

Miss Blandish's colour rose and she pressed Louisa's hand tighter. 'But I do think he could be the one. He has even praised my singing. I mean, it is as if he looks at me and sees *me,* rather than my dowry. It is amazing how many men simply see my father's mills and factories. I want to be loved for me. Is that too much to ask?'

'I am sure the right man will find you,' Louisa said quietly as she disentangled her hand. To be loved and cherished for oneself—wasn't that what everyone hoped for? It was that sometimes what one wanted, one could not have.

She had misjudged Miss Blandish. Miss Blandish was more than a feather-brained débutante. She was a woman who wanted love. Louisa was as guilty as those who looked at her and saw a former governess. It was the person who mattered and not the label. 'You are quite beautiful, Miss Blandish. When I was younger I yearned to have your sort of complexion—all roses and cream, the sort that suits ball gowns.'

'I can't afford another scandal. Not one little hint. I have to be so very careful.' Miss Blandish gave a soft sigh and raised her handkerchief to her eye. 'If that happens I might as well give up and go to the Continent. Lord Edward—'

'The man who died earlier this summer. You must be upset about that. Did you love him very much?'

Miss Blandish blinked at her, shocked. 'I never loved Edward Heritage. I would have like the title, but as a man, no, not in the same way I feel about Lord Furniss, you see. There is just a connection between us. I find it impossible to explain. Have you ever loved someone, Miss Sibson?'

'I thought I did,' Louisa said without thinking. 'Then I was sure I didn't.'

'And now?'

'Now everything is muddled,' Louisa admitted. 'And you?'

'I was sorry, of course. The aftermath was dreadful. No one seeks another's death, even if it was heroic.' Miss Blandish's eyes widened. 'Mama encouraged me to be

far too free with him. It could have been much worse.
We were never caught together.'

Louisa pasted a smile on her face and tried to ignore
the butterflies in her stomach. Much worse. She knew
all about much worse.

She had stumbled blindly into a trap of Jonathon's
making again, and she knew that it would be impossible
to blame anyone but herself.

'It is why I have to avoid darkened garden paths and
moonlit walks. Lord Ravensworth gave me the advice
before he left, and I suppose he should know. Nella said
that his list of conquests was legendary.'

'But he has settled with Daisy.'

Miss Blandish's brow furled. 'I do not believe she
ever walked down a garden path with him. Miss Milton
was quite the stickler for convention. Her curtsies were
always the correct height for the occasion. I always
admired her for it.'

*Darkened paths. And cottages in a rainstorm.* She
should have insisted on walking with the coachman,
anything but staying with Jonathon. And yet an insistent
voice in the back of her mind whispered that given the
chance she would do it again. Every part of her hummed
with vitality. Before now she had existed, but suddenly
the impossible seemed possible.

'They are coming into the room.' Miss Blandish's
whisper held a note of excitement. 'They did not linger
over the port tonight.'

'We are agreed. We will not give into the temptation
of a stroll in the garden,' Louisa whispered back.

'Thank you, Miss Sibson.' Miss Blandish squeezed
Louisa's hand. 'I felt you had a kind and understanding

face. I have no wish to spoil my London Season unnecessarily. A good marriage means a lot to Mama and Papa. Lord Furniss has not declared his intention and I understand his mother is a great friend of two of the Lady Patronesses of Almack's.'

'Where I can help, I will.' Louisa unfurled her fan and hoped the gesture would make the gentlemen think her heightened colour was due to the temperature in the room rather than the heat from Jonathon's glance. Seeing how Miss Blandish's eyes sparkled, Louisa knew she had been right in refusing to allow Lord Furniss to speak the other night.

'Susan!' Mrs Blandish called out from where she sat. 'I believe you were going to sing an air for Lord Furniss. The one we practised this morning. Now there's my girl. A simple country tune.'

Louisa's gaze tumbled into Jonathon's amused one as he and Furniss stood framed in the doorway. The conversation about the singing seemed such a long time ago.

Louisa rapidly sat down and concentrated on breathing steadily. It was hard not to remember the way Jonathon's skin had felt under her palms. Or how his mouth had absorbed her cries earlier. But it was under false colours. He had planned on springing Venetia Ponsby-Smythe on her without warning or consideration.

'It appears rather warm in here, Miss Sibson,' Jonathon said, coming up to her. 'Furniss, do you not think it is warm in here?'

'Stifling.' Furniss ran a finger around the edge of his stock. But Louisa did not miss the significant glance between Jonathon and Furniss. It was all too easy to guess what the topic of conversation over port had been. And she could easily imagine what would happen. They would start off as a foursome, but one or the other of them would find cause to linger and become lost.

'I thought it rather chilly,' Louisa said, looking hard at Miss Blandish. 'And it rained earlier. The pathways are bound to be muddy.'

'There might be another storm,' Miss Blandish agreed. 'Rain is in the air and I would hate to think of my hairstyle being spoilt. Or my dress being ruined.'

'Aunt Daphne, do *you* think a turn about the garden might be in order?' Lord Furniss made a bow. 'As the younger ladies appear to be melting in front of a rainstorm.'

'My bones are old, Nephew.' Miss Daphne pulled her shawl tighter around her and stayed seated. 'English summers are far colder than Italian ones. I long for indoor entertainment.'

'It is settled, then,' Louisa said, giving Miss Blandish a significant look. Miss Blandish gave a wide smile back. 'We should open the French windows if the gentlemen feel rather close. And perhaps a game of cards would be in order. Miss Daphne, shall we have a game of whist?'

'What a clever idea, Miss Sibson—whist,' Mrs Blandish said with a smile. 'It is the perfect thing to pass the time. Perhaps Lord Chesterholm will be so good as to partner me in this endeavour.'

Jonathon lifted a brow and mouthed *coward* at her. Louisa smiled her brightest smile back at him. Round one to her.

'A game of cards would be an admirable suggestion.'

'Is it true, Lord Chesterholm, that your stepmother and sister are expected tomorrow?' Mrs Blandish asked, shuffling a pack of cards with expert hands. 'Mrs Pons-by-Smythe is reckoned to be an expert card player.'

'Your intelligence is admirable, Mrs Blandish. I was unaware my stepmother's proposed arrival was common knowledge.' Jonathon's eyes became cold and Louisa knew that he had not intended for the news to get around.

'But will she arrive tomorrow? I believe your half-sister and my Susan are about the same age. They might be companions during the Season,' Mrs Blandish persisted.

'My stepmother arranges her schedule as she sees fit and travelling tires her. I have learnt through experience only to look for her after she arrives,' he said, making a low bow.

'It is impossible to keep a secret in a house this size. The very walls hum with anticipation of such momentous events,' Miss Daphne called out from where she sat next to Nella Blandish. 'It always amazes me when people forget that their voices carry or that servants will talk, even in the best-regulated households.'

'I will try to remember that for the future.' Jonathon lowered his brows and glowered at Louisa. 'Listening to gossip without seeking clarification can lead to grave misunderstandings.'

'Or enlightenment, when someone persists in keeping secrets,' Louisa replied, lifting her chin.

'Sometimes, things are withheld to protect others.'

'I believe there was a game of whist in the offing,' Louisa said smoothly. She intended to behave as if Mrs

Ponsby-Smythe's arrival meant nothing to her. Calm and dignified.

'A game of cards is the proper way to pass an evening,' Mrs Blandish commented.

Louisa tilted her head to one side. 'Respectability is everything, particularly when there is gossip in the air.'

'Except during thunderstorms,' he said in a low murmur as he pulled out her chair for her.

'That was unworthy, Jonathon.' Louisa glanced back at him.

'But the truth, Louisa. Why are you so afraid of the truth?' he murmured in her ear. 'Try trusting me for once. We are friends. My intentions are good.'

His fingers traced a line down her back. Louisa forced her body to stay still and her lips to smile sweetly at Mrs Blandish.

'I have no need of that sort of protection.'

'I will keep it under consideration.'

The ominous roll of thunder woke Louisa from a sound sleep. In the end, the game of whist had been unsatisfactory, particularly as Jonathon had readily agreed to it and seemed to relish in each hand that he and Mrs Blandish had won.

At Miss Daphne's suggestion, Lord Furniss and Miss Blandish had spent most of the evening going over possible songs for a recital later in the week.

Every time Louisa had glanced over, Lord Furniss had inched closer to Miss Blandish; then, when he considered Mrs Blandish's attention engaged elsewhere, he had attempted to put his arm about her under the pretext of turning pages.

Louisa hugged her knees. It was good to see an attraction blossoming and to know that she had had a small hand in it.

Worse was the knowledge that Jonathon had intended keeping Mrs Ponsby-Smythe's arrival a secret until the last possible moment. They might have been intimate that afternoon, but he had still kept secrets from her, even after she had shared hers. There was no need for explanations. This was no simple misunderstanding of intentions.

With another roll of thunder, Louisa knew staying in her bedroom with the blue flashes lighting up the walls was impossible. She grabbed a wrap and lit her candle, heading for the library. Sometimes, the only thing to do was to read and hope the storm blew itself out.

As she walked through the halls, her bare feet sinking into the thick carpet, she was surprised at how quickly the house had become familiar. She could never make the mistake of going to Arthur's nursery now. The outside of the house might be austere, and overly formal, but there was respect and security in these walls as well. It had a way of winding itself around her heart.

When she got to the library door, she saw a sliver of gold light coming from Jonathon's study.

She struggled to breathe. He was in there. Awake.

Three times she tried to walk past, but each time her feet stopped. She closed her eyes. There was a thunderstorm outside and the only thing that had made her feel truly safe was Jonathon.

Golden gaslight lit the room, through long shadows.

A full decanter of port and an empty glass stood beside a winged chair. Soft breathing emanated from the chair and the tips of Jonathon's boots were just visible. He was asleep.

Louisa started to back out quietly.

'Stay, Louisa.'

Louisa gripped the shawl tighter about her shoulders. She wished now that she had stayed up in bed. She certainly should never have given in to the temptation to enter his study. 'How did you know it was me?'

'Recognised your footsteps. At first I thought you might be a ghost that I had conjured up, but then I knew you had to be real.' His hand lifted the decanter and poured two glasses of port. 'Come, join me. Pass some time with me.'

'Were you waiting for me?' Louisa ignored the ruby-red liquid. Her blood was fizzing enough without adding alcohol to the mix.

'Should I have been?' He shook his head. 'I am not clairvoyant. You made your intentions clear this evening.'

'I changed my mind.' Louisa shifted on the balls of her feet. He had been waiting for someone, not her. Venetia? Had he thought that she would arrive tonight? 'Another storm has got up…and I went…'

'In search of comfort and security.'

'In search of a good book. Is there anything wrong with that? I like having security.'

'If you had truly wanted security, you would have accepted Sir Francis's marriage proposal rather than coming to England with Miss Elliot.' He tilted his head.

'You want something else, Louisa, and you are too much of a coward to admit it.'

'A coward? Me?' Louisa balled her fist. 'I have weathered thunderstorms on my own. I buried our child on my own.'

'It is not a case of any pair of strong arms will do?'

Mutely Louisa shook her head.

Jonathon stood up. His shirt was slightly undone and there was a distinct gleam in his eyes. 'I am very pleased you came down, though.'

Louisa gave a little shrug. 'The thunder made me restless. Reading helps take my mind off the noise.'

'There are other ways.' His lidded eyes became beckoning pools of sea green blue. He took a step closer. In spite of all her vows, Louisa's insides turned to molten heat. She wanted his skin against hers again. 'Allow me to keep you safe from the storm, Louisa. Allow me to keep you safe for always.'

Louisa backed up, holding the candle in front of her as a sort of shield. Desire was not the same as doing. She could resist the temptation. It was a test. He did not want to keep her safe. He wanted to bend her will to his. But now she knew that he did not intend to share his life with her. 'The very walls will scream the news, isn't that what Miss Daphne said? We must be careful, Jonathon. No scandal.'

'The news carrier has gone to bed.'

'Meaning?' She tilted her head and put her candle down on the table.

His smile widened. 'Nella Blandish. I saw her standing in the hall when Roberts gave me the news about my stepmother.'

'You kept me in ignorance.'

He stilled and his face became a mask. 'It was none of your business. My stepmother's impending arrival has nothing to do with you.'

'That was wicked of you, Jonathon.'

'Selfish, maybe, but listen to my side of the story before you judge.' He came forwards and put his hands on her shoulders. 'Venetia has Margaret with her. I want Margaret under my roof where I can keep an eye on her. Knowing what Venetia did to me, to us, I am determined to let Margaret make her own choices in life.'

Louisa examined the carpet, rather than looking into his eyes. 'You should have told me that she was expected today.'

'What would you have done? Packed your cases? Left without warning?' He reached out, his fingers closing about her elbow, and pulled her against the hard planes of his body. He rested his chin on the top of her head. 'I refused to take that risk. I refuse to lose you, Louisa. Again.'

'You are impossible.' Louisa pulled herself out of the embrace. She gathered up the candle and held it with a trembling hand, intending to sweep out of the room. 'You have treated me in the most high-handed fashion. You simply assumed that I would fall in with your wishes without a "by your leave". You should have warned me, Jonathon, and that's all there is to it.'

He gave a tiny smile. 'You are getting cross over nothing.'

'Nothing?' Louisa waved her hand. Hot candle wax fell on to her wrist. A small cry came from her throat. She would now have a scar to remember her folly with.

'Let me see that.'

'It is a burn. It happens all the time. I was careless.'

'You are annoyed with me and weren't thinking.'

His fingers reached and held her wrist for a moment before bringing it to his mouth. His cool breath soothed the hurt. The pain receded, replaced by a growing, insistent warmth. Louisa was aware that her hair was loose beneath her nightcap, her feet bare and she wore a linen shift covered by a shawl.

'I don't think this was my best idea,' she whispered, trying to ignore the warm sensation that raced from his touch to the furthest tips of her body, lighting every particle of her along the way.

'Idea? What is your best idea?' His grip changed and became more seductive as his fingers moved slowly over her skin, travelling up her nightdress to her shoulder.

'Me being here. With you. Alone.'

'I think it is an excellent idea.' He tilted her chin so she was forced to look into his eyes. 'Lean on me, Louisa.'

'I learnt not to make that mistake.'

His hand undid her nightcap, pushed it until it fell off and brushed her hair. 'What is wrong with seeking another's help, Louisa? Help makes you stronger.'

Louisa found it impossible to move away from his hand. 'Everything.'

He tangled his hands in her hair, loosening it from its plait. 'You are a woman. You know how this particular game is played. Why did you come into my study?'

'Because…' Louisa groped for the right words. How

could she explain that she wanted his company? She wanted to feel the strength in his arms again. When his arms were about her, she felt as if nothing bad could happen in the world. Her heart skipped a beat and she knew she had fallen in love with him. Not the Jonathon she had once known, but the man standing in front of her. And she wanted to be loved by this man. The knowledge was enough to bring her to her knees.

Silently she cursed.

Why was it that the one man in the world who she loved was also the one man who was most likely to betray her dreams and shackle her independence? Her dreams were no longer grandiose ones of marriage to a peer, but simple ones about a home and respectability. His plans for her seemed to be very different and she did not dare ask.

'Because you were seeking shelter and needed me, despite your earlier words. There is a connection between us, Louisa.' He traced a line around her lips. 'You are very good at mouthing words, Louisa, but when are you going to admit the truth? When are you going to grow up? When are you going to approach me with a woman's heart and mind?'

'I am well grown, thank you.' She moved her face from his questing fingers. But they simply went instead to her shawl and loosened it. It made a soft swoosh as it fell to the ground. Louisa stood there, clad in her nightdress, aware that her breasts were clearly visible through the thin lawn material, thrusting upwards with hardened points.

'Then when are you going to stop finding excuses for your behaviour?' He ran a seductive hand down her arms. 'Do you always have to find a reason to come to me? Why not admit the truth?'

Louisa stared at him as warm tingles pulsated through her. Surely he should be kissing her and preventing her from thinking about her rules. 'What truth is that, Jonathon?'

'I have no wish to be your port in the storm, Louisa, not without you giving something in return.' He dropped his hands to his side and stepped back. 'Go back to your bed before we both do something we regret.'

A shiver went through Louisa. The air about her was suddenly ice cold. He was sending her away, back to her room with the booming thunder.

Back to her bed where she'd suffer. Where she'd be forced to re-examine her dreams and see if they were in fact empty and devoid of love.

'Jonathon, don't…don't make me leave. I am frightened…of the storm.'

'I want you, Louisa, but I want you to want me for myself, not simply because you are frightened of thunder.' He stood there, looking at her; his brown hair fell over his forehead and his hands were at his sides.

'You want me to leave,' she said slowly, trying to understand. She held out her hands. 'But I thought…'

A groan came from his throat. 'When we make love again, it will be because you desire me, rather than because you are running from your fears. When we make love, I do not want accusations of seduction or protestations that it happened this once and never again because you need to be free.'

He had not uttered one word of love or tenderness. It was worse than four years ago; then she had had the promise of marriage. Four years! She did not doubt that she'd have run to his arms, but now her feet refused to move. For some reason she had been offered a choice and she knew she was not ready to make it. Go to him now and she'd lose any chance of independence. 'I want more than an affair.'

'You have no idea what you want and until you do, what is between us is impossible.'

She stooped to pick up her shawl, but he was there before her, taking the shawl and placing it tightly over her shoulders. Her stomach plummeted. He meant it. He was sending her away. He was not going to seduce her into staying. If she wanted to stay, she would have to seduce him. She would have to admit that she was an equal partner.

Her hands curled about her shawl.

The temptation was there, but it would mean she had become the person she had always feared being—a wanton without thought of propriety or gentility. And yet her heart whispered that she should take the chance.

Her eyes filled with tears of frustration. 'Jonathon.'

His mouth twisted and he gave her a hooded look. 'Run back to your room. Before you do something we both regret.'

# Chapter Twelve

Jonathon sat in the breakfast room, staring at the remains of his breakfast. According to Roberts, Louisa had breakfasted early and set off on an expedition with Miss Elliot and the Blandishes to visit a few of the Roman remains. She had neglected to consult him. Her answer to last night was clear and unambiguous.

Right now, as much as he wanted to go after her, he had other duties. Surely today Venetia would arrive and he would be able to ensure Margaret was protected.

The problem haunted Jonathon, driving the sleep from his brain. Margaret deserved a bright future, not being tied to some man simply because Venetia deemed it correct. He knew now the depths Venetia would sink to. And he had been right to keep it from Louisa. The fight was between him and his stepmother. Louisa had no part in it.

His stepmother's strident tones berating Roberts resounded from the hallway. She had arrived. Jonathon's shoulders eased. The final battle had begun. He said a silent prayer, thanking God that Venetia always found fault with whichever servant crossed her path when she first arrived. He made a mental note to increase Roberts's salary.

'What are you doing, Jonny, giving a house party without informing me?' His stepmother bustled into the study, her starched petticoats crinkling with every step she took. His stepmother was the only person on the face of the planet to call him Jonny, as if he remained in short trousers. He could remember the first time they had met. He had been absolutely terrified, but she had taken his hand and pledged to his father that she would be the right sort of mother for him, one who would look after him and keep him on the proper paths. 'It is really too bad of you!'

'It is my house,' Jonathon commented and forced his voice to be even, though anger surged through him. Venetia presumed much.

'It is really too bad of you not to consult me. The servants are all in a twitter.'

'Is Margaret with you? Or did you travel on your own?'

Venetia's gaze narrowed to glacial blue slits. 'Does it matter to you?'

'I requested that you bring Margaret.'

His stepmother trailed a finger down the table, inspecting it for dust. She frowned as her finger came away. 'I have no idea why you keep Roberts on. He was most insolent about who was here. As the hostess, I need to know. You will probably have muddled all the room arrangements. It is not simply a matter of people arriving, but where they are staying and being careful not to have certain people get ideas above their station.'

'Are you the hostess?'

'I am your nearest living female relative. Who else would be? Poor dear Clarissa…she must be turning in her grave. She was so proud of the house and its reputation for hospitality. Are your guests fit for Margaret's company? She is a gently reared child and has expectations.' Venetia gave a superior smile.

'I have managed to cope in your absence, Venetia. Chesterholm is *my* house. The servants keep the house to my requirements.'

Her shoulders sagged and she reached into her reticule for smelling salts. 'But to have a respectable party without a hostess is unconscionable.'

'Where is Margaret? In the carriage?'

'The hoyden ran out of the carriage and down to the garden before I even managed to speak to Roberts.' Venetia clicked her tongue. 'Margaret's manners are sorely wanting. She must be brought up short if we are to catch her a duke.'

'Margaret will marry whom Margaret wishes.'

'No, no, the choice of a husband is far too important to be left to her. What if she meets and marries an unsuitable person!' His stepmother's lashes fluttered. 'How would you feel then? Your little experiment in allowing youthful folly will have ruined your sister's prospects and her life and very probably her children's.'

Jonathon's neck muscles ached as he struggled to keep control of his temper. 'The only person who has mentioned ruin is you.'

'You were always unfeeling.' His stepmother sniffed. 'Roberts—'

'I will not hear another word against Roberts. He

served under my great-uncle for years. Simply because he is not your creature, Venetia, does not make him insolent or a failure. Kindly refrain from addressing my servants in such a manner.' He gave her a stern look and Venetia had the grace to bow her head in submission.

'You are becoming more like your great-uncle every day.' Her mouth pursed like she had swallowed a sour plum. 'And I do not mean that in a good way, Jonathon.'

'I will take it as a compliment. I have the utmost respect for Uncle Arthur and his integrity.'

'You have invited the oddest assortment of people. Miss Elliot of all people! She must be nearing her dotage.' His stepmother began to lift the lids on various dishes, poking at them, rather than meeting his eye. 'I don't mind Rupert Furniss, but the Blandishes... They are people on the make. You must have seen the mother...' She shook her head. 'What Honoria Furniss will say about her son making sheep's eyes at Miss Blandish, I have no idea. He might do for Margaret if no one else comes up to snuff.'

'I enjoy the Blandishes.' Jonathon waved his hand, cutting her complaints short. His stepmother liked to forget her own background was not quite top drawer. She preferred to concentrate on his father's and late mother's connections rather than the fact that Venetia herself was the daughter of an impoverished third son of a minor baronet. 'Margaret will marry whom she chooses.'

His stepmother's cheeks coloured slightly. 'Margaret deserves the best and in order to get the best, she must be able to take full advantage of the Season next year.

With a young and vibrant queen on the throne, the balls are certain to be without parallel. She must have the correct counsel.'

Jonathon schooled his features. He had waited long enough. It was time.

'I met an old friend recently,' he said evenly, watching Venetia's face for any sign. 'I had been under the impression that this person was dead. You can imagine my shock.'

His stepmother's reticule tumbled from her hand, falling to the floor with a thump. 'Who is that? Do I know this man?'

'Not a man, a woman. Louisa Sibson. It was most peculiar as I am positive you told me she had died. That her death was connected to my accident.'

His stepmother sank down gracefully into a winged chair. Her shoulders shook slightly as she went to retrieve a handkerchief from her reticule and discovered that it was on the ground and she had to reach for it with her foot. She made a practised flourish with her hand and withdrew the handkerchief to furiously dab at her eyes. 'You might have warned me, Jonny, before I set out.'

'Warned you about what?'

'Your discovery… I cannot stay in the same house as that woman. She is a dreadful parvenu. She has ideas above her station.'

'Why did you tell me that she died?'

His stepmother got up and went over to the morning-room window. She stood there looking out for a moment.

'Why, Venetia? Surely you remember.'

'I can't rightly recall. What was I supposed to tell

you? She left our house, disappeared.' Venetia spun round and said in a furious undertone, 'The woman had loose morals, Jonny. She was a jumped-up nobody who was out to trap you. You just needed a push to fall for the right woman, one who was worthy of you and this house.'

'You told me she had died in the accident, the accident I caused. You said that you had wept at Louisa's memorial service. You put a gravestone up,' Jonathon continued remorselessly onwards. 'Why did you do that if she was a jumped-up nobody?'

'Maybe you simply assumed it. This was years ago. You were struggling for life.' She paused, hiding her face behind her handkerchief before peeping out. 'Did she say where she had been?'

'Italy. You gave her money for her passage. Why?'

'Why did she return?'

'Is that any concern of yours?'

'I think it is, Jonny.' His stepmother stepped forwards, her face eager like a vulture seeking to scavenge. 'A number of items disappeared when she left. I have never—' Venetia pressed the handkerchief to her face again. 'I know you always felt Lily, my old maid, took them, but I was always convinced it was Louisa.'

'Louisa. Carried. My. Child.' Jonathon bit out each word. 'Louisa never stole anything. Stop your self-serving lies, Venetia.'

'She carried *a* child.'

'It was mine. Mine!'

'Was?' The corner of Venetia's mouth twitched.

'The child is dead. Born too soon, she never even breathed.'

'Surely you cannot have feeling for something that never lived, that you never knew.' She put her hand to her throat.

'You knew Louisa was expecting and you never even bothered to discover what happened.'

'You must believe me, Jonny, I acted for the best. It was better for everyone that you thought her dead. And the child's death was providence, a punishment for the mother's sin if you like.'

Jonathon stared at his stepmother in astonishment mingled with disgust. 'What sort of creature are you?'

'What was she to you until you knew of her death?' His stepmother snapped her fingers. 'A misalliance that you would grow out of, that you were tiring of. That one little lie turned you from being a rather dissolute young man to a model gentleman. This estate has gone from strength to strength. You had the perfect hostess in Clarissa, a woman who was born to the role.'

Jonathon flexed his fingers, itching to shake her, but he had never laid a hand on a woman in anger. Never would. With effort he regained control of his temper. 'Did you ever regret what you did to Louisa?'

His stepmother's ear bobs swayed slightly as she caught Jonathon's hands between her ice-cold fingers.

'I have never lost a moment's sleep. I saw you lying there, all distressed, calling for a woman who would never come, when a good…no…an excellent woman stood by your bedside, waiting with bated breath for you to live. Clarissa possessed every attribute you needed, if only you could be made to forget flame-coloured hair and an ingratiating manner.' She lifted her chin and her eyes glittered like a snake's. 'I would do it again in an instant. You should be thanking me for releasing you from purgatory.'

Jonathon pulled his hands from her grasp. Cold fury swept through him. This woman had abused his trust in the worst possible way. She had harmed Louisa, had indirectly caused the death of his baby and she had no remorse. Even now, she was attempting to justify it. 'You are insane.'

'You can believe what you like, but my conscience is clear.' His stepmother met his gaze with a proud tilt to her chin, but there was something about the way that the corner of her mouth twitched.

'Get out! Go before I do something we both regret, but you richly deserve!'

'If I go, you will never see Margaret again. And I will marry her to whomever I see fit.'

'I think not. Margaret stays with me.' A white-hot rage filled Jonathon, but he damped it down. His revenge would be served ice cold. 'I am her guardian. Margaret is the only reason I allowed you and your stinking lies in this house.'

'You tricked me! I would have never come here!' His stepmother's face crumpled and she fumbled for a handkerchief. 'I love my daughter. I want to see her.'

'That is your problem.' Jonathon regarded her and forced all pity from his heart. Waited.

Venetia replaced the handkerchief in her reticule, went over to the door and closed it with a click.

'Is she here? Is that witch here in this house, listening to every word? Did she seduce you?' She paused and looked him up and down. 'Not yet, I think. Men are such fools when they think with their nether regions. One can make them do anything.'

'Is that what you did, Venetia?' Jonathon enquired, fixing her with his eyes. All these years and he had never guessed what a twisted person this woman was.

'What has that woman been saying?' His stepmother stopped in the centre of the room and held out her hands. 'Do you not think, Jonathon, that if I had felt there was a spark of honest and genuine feeling in that chit that I would have moved heaven and earth to bring her to you?'

Jonathon's stomach revolted at his stepmother's self-serving words. 'Stop lying.'

His stepmother's eyes widened. 'I saved you the trouble of ending the affair. You should be grateful. In the end, you had the perfect wife, a woman far more suited to withstand the rigours of being a baroness. You were happy with Clarissa and now you have a wonderful little boy. You should have left Louisa in the past where she belongs.'

'Whose idea was it? Yours? Clarissa's? Her mother's?'

'I have no regrets, Jonny. The idea was mine and, what is more, I'd do it again in an instant.'

Jonathon flexed his hands, longing to throttle the woman. She knew nothing of his hopes and dreams. He had thought her wonderful once, but now he could see that she only ever thought of herself. The only thing he had to be thankful for was that Louisa would never have to confront this woman. Louisa would not have to hear self-serving filth. 'This interview is over. We have nothing more to say to each other. Ever.'

'Jonathon!' His stepmother lifted her hands in supplication. 'I have only ever had your best interests at heart. You have no idea of the sacrifices I have made on your behalf.'

'I believe I understand well enough, madam.'

'You understand what?'

'Your self-serving lies. It was none of your business whom I married or how I lived my life.'

'I have no regrets.' Venetia gave a half-smile. 'Louisa's death was the making of you, Jonathon. Think about that.'

'No, her life is.'

Louisa trudged along the path towards the ruined Roman bath. The entire world sparkled with the remaining raindrops reflecting the sun. Jonathon had shown common sense and restraint last night. The last thing her heart needed was a dead-end affair with Jonathon. And he had never pretended that he wanted anything more.

The opportunity of accompanying the Blandishes and Lord Furniss on the proposed expedition to the Roman ruins was the perfect chance to clear her brain.

'Miss Sibson, we must speak,' Lord Furniss said, taking her arm as they went around the ruins. 'I have a confession to make.'

'Do you?' Louisa kept her voice light, but her stomach churned.

'The other evening you prevented me from speaking...'

'I had no wish to fall out of civility with you.' Louisa regarded where Miss Blandish was laughing with her sister as they clambered over rocks. 'I value your friendship too highly.'

'You are truly a pearl amongst women, Miss Sibson, and perceptive beyond measure.' He gave a short laugh as his countenance flushed bright pink. 'I shall be on my knees—'

'Lord Furniss, please do not.' Louisa withdrew her arm from his grip and examined the stone from a disused altar. She forced her breathing to be steady. 'Why are you doing this, Lord Furniss?'

'Because this is the first time we have had an opportunity to speak privately.' He gave an overly pleased smile. 'Thanks to you, my heart has found its true life-mate, whatever my mother may think about Miss Blandish.'

'Your mother knows about Miss Blandish?' Louisa said, as relief ran through her. He was enamoured of Miss Blandish.

'Before I left Newcastle, I penned a quick note about the house party. I had her response this morning. She casts aspersions on that innocent's character!' Lord Furniss tucked his chin into his neck. 'To my certain knowledge, my mother has never encountered Miss Blandish. And thanks to your perception, I remain a free man to pursue her.'

Louisa placed her hand on his arm. 'I appreciate your understanding but I have done nothing.'

'Miss Blandish confided that you put forward my suit last night. I could not have hoped for a better friend. She is an angel. I know she wants a Season but I intend to be her faithful squire.'

At his eager face, Louisa's heart squeezed. Lord

Furniss deserved some measure of happiness. Perhaps she had misjudged Miss Daphne and her matchmaking tendencies. But simply because she'd had a success with Miss Blandish and Lord Furniss, it did not mean there was to be a match between her and Jonathon. The past stood firmly in their way.

'Miss Sibson! Oh, Miss Sibson!' Annie Sims hurried towards the group. 'Please wait!'

'Is there a problem?' Louisa motioned for the group to continue on. Miss Elliot appeared to understand and began to talk very loudly to Nella Blandish about the Romans, speculating why they might have built a wall in Northumberland and when.

'I need your help with a problem.' Annie drew a piece of paper from her pocket. 'I have heard from Trevor.'

Louisa stared at her in astonishment. 'You have heard from him.'

The woman dropped a quick curtsy. 'I left him a note, you see. I could not leave without saying anything. And he guessed that I might return to me family. He wants me back. I jumped to the wrong conclusion. He wants a chance to explain. Is that too much to ask? But I don't see I could have made a mistake, like.'

Louisa closed her eyes. That man had written to Annie. He must have worked out that Annie had taken the snuffbox. 'Do your parents know?'

'How could I tell them? They hate him! They'd only turn me against him. And what if I did make a mistake? What if I turned my back on love?'

'You brought the snuffbox back. He might consider it his property. That could be the reason he contacted you,' Louisa said calmly. 'He lied to you before.'

The woman's eyes widened. 'I hadn't thought about that. He did not even mention the snuffbox, you know. Maybe he doesn't know that I took it.'

Louisa concentrated on the tree behind Annie. Surely the woman was not that naïve. Of course this man knew. 'Does he say where he is?'

'He writes that everything is not as it seemed and… wants to come. My ma and da will skin me alive if he does. Promise me you won't say nothing to Lord Chesterholm. He was good about the reward. But…Trevor might not know who the snuffbox belonged to. He might have bought it off a man at the post inn. I did not give him a chance to explain. That was wrong of me.' Annie gave a heartfelt sigh. 'He promised me so many things and, oh, the way he made me feel. I have to give him a chance, don't I, miss?'

Louisa put her hand on Annie's shoulder. 'He is a married man with children. He abandoned you in a flea-infested boarding-house. The man used you and abused your trust.'

'He misses me.' Annie gave a half-shrug. 'But I knows what you mean about his wife and children. He don't have time for them. He loves only me. Me! And he wants me back.'

'You need to think very carefully, Annie. Lord Chesterholm…'

'You have a kind face, miss.' The woman gave another small curtsy. 'But you don't understand. My man loves me.'

'Annie, tell your parents. They do love you.'

The woman sucked in her breath. 'I will think about it, like, miss. But me da is up Wark way, seeing about

some horses for Lord Thorngrafton. Now that there was
a right scandal. The nephew ran off with his lordship's
young wife.'

'Annie, will you let me know if your Trevor shows?
Before you do anything?' Louisa asked.

'I'll think on it, miss.'

It was not until Annie hurried away that Louisa
realised that she had never actually seen the letter.
Whatever happened when she returned to Chesterholm,
Louisa resolved, she would explain to Jonathon about
the encounter and her unease.

Louisa concentrated on the Roman ruins. From the
log book and the ropes on the ground, it was clear that
Jonathon was taking the time and trouble to excavate
properly, rather than behaving like many amateurs who
went out for an afternoon's digging with a spade. Miss
Mattie would have approved.


On the way back from the diggings, Louisa spied a
young woman running towards them. Her bonnet was
askew and she had picked up her skirts to run. Jonathon's
dogs ran behind her, barking. Louisa bit her knuckle,
torn between the panic that Margaret's arrival meant
meeting Venetia Ponsby-Smythe again and the sheer
pleasure of seeing her former charge again.

'Margaret. You have arrived.' Louisa caught Margaret's hands. The young woman spun round and round,
making Louisa quite dizzy as the two dogs lay down
panting at her feet.

Louisa rapidly made the introductions to the others in
the party. Miss Blandish and Margaret eyed each other,
but then Nella made one of her more outrageous remarks

and both women laughed. With that brief gesture, Louisa knew it was only a matter of time before the trio became friends.

'How did you know where to find me? Or indeed that I was here?' Louisa asked, as the group began strolling back towards the house.

'I asked Roberts who was here and he gave me your name. Then I had to run and run and see if it was indeed true. Mama was not even out of the carriage and I was gone before she could say anything.' The young woman clasped her hands under her chin. Her grey eyes shone. While she would never be an English rose, Margaret Ponsby-Smythe possessed a certain liveliness and vitality. 'Oh, I always knew you weren't dead, despite what Mama and Clarissa said. Jonathon simply would not listen. I was cross with him for ages and ages. I told him that you left after he did, that Mama had seen you and I watched on the stairs. But by then…well, Clarissa had her claws in and I'm sure you know the rest.'

Louisa kept her face bland, but her insides churned. She had thought it was going to be straightforward, but all the feelings from four years ago were there, as well as the knowledge that, had she been more forceful, the whole mess need not have happened.

'I am pleased to see you as well, Margaret. It has been a long time.'

Margaret linked her arm with Louisa's. 'Was my brother surprised? I would give anything to have seen his face. He must have thought you were a ghost.'

'Astonished.' Louisa gave a brief and edited version of the concert. She regarded the group, who were busy looking at the remains. 'And your mother, is she with your brother?'

Margaret scraped her toe along the dirt. 'I suppose so. Mama gets worse and worse. Nothing ever pleases her.'

Louisa dropped Margaret's arm. She had to go and confront Venetia Ponsby-Smythe. And she had to do it now, before anyone else was around. It was her problem to solve, not anyone else's and certainly not Jonathon's.

'Where are you going?' the young woman called after her. 'You have gone as white as a ghost.'

'There is something I forgot. Miss Blandish will entertain you.' Louisa picked up her skirts and ran. This time, she would prove that she could weather any storm and demonstrate that she had not only survived, but thrived. This time, she would finally be rid of the past and turn her face towards the future.

## Chapter Thirteen

Louisa marched towards the main house, her fury at Jonathon's high-handed behaviour growing with each step. In many ways, she had behaved like poor deluded Annie. She had even begun to believe that she could return to that innocent girl she had been all those years ago.

Already it seemed like the battlements were frowning at her, telling her that she had no place at Chesterholm. Louisa angrily shook her head. Today was her chance to finally slay demons and to demonstrate how far she had come.

She started towards the terrace doors, but Jonathon appeared in the centre of them. His face was drawn, but fire flared in his eyes when he spied her.

'You have returned far sooner than I thought you would,' he said, coming forwards and taking her arm, leading her towards the little summer house at the end of the terrace.

'Is that a problem?'

'You are never where I want you to be. You left this morning before I had a chance to learn your plans.'

'Roberts knew,' Louisa replied evenly.

'It was supposed to be all day. Roberts informed me that you were picnicking at the ruins. I had hoped to join you. Why did you return?'

'I had to.' Louisa regarded the flagstones. The speech she had carefully composed in her head only a few moments before had disappeared utterly from her brain. The only thing she could think of was Jonathon standing next to her, looking at her with concern in his face. 'I met Margaret.'

'My sister has not yet done me the pleasure of greeting me.' His eyebrows knitted. 'She chose you instead.'

'She will greet you, but she is busy forming an alliance with Miss Blandish.' Louisa tilted her head. Her stomach ached from its knots. He had to know why she had come back. He had to tell her where to find Venetia. 'But will your stepmother approve of Miss Blandish? Her antecedents are hardly top drawer.'

'Margaret is my concern, not my stepmother's,' Jonathon said in a low furious voice.

'Your concern?'

'Margaret is my ward.'

'Where is your stepmother?' Louisa said, unable to bear it any longer as the pain in her stomach became unbearable.

'She is in the house.'

He moved swiftly, coming over to her. His hands lightly skimmed her shoulders. 'For the moment. She will be leaving shortly. I have permitted her time to say goodbye to Margaret. I am not vindictive. I only seek to protect those I care about.'

*Protect those I care about.* She crossed her arms and took a step back despite the overwhelming urge to rest her head against his chest. He was right last night when he accused her of using him as a shield. She did not want that. She had never asked him to fight her battles. Her entire life was based on her standing on her own feet. His arms fell to his sides.

'Do you mean me?' she whispered.

'Yes, I promised to protect you. There is no need for you to confront her. You have suffered enough.'

Louisa clenched her fists as a fierce anger swept through her. He sought to protect her by keeping her in ignorance! Was she so pathetic in his eyes that she could not even face speaking to the woman? How dare he! She slowly counted to ten and regained control.

'Did I ask you to confront Venetia for me?' she asked between gritted teeth.

'It had to be done, Louisa, and done quickly. Venetia will no longer trouble us.'

Louisa stared at Jonathon in astonishment. He was serious. He thought she'd be pleased with what he had done. 'You explained the situation to Venetia,' she said slowly. 'For my sake? Or for yours?'

'You continue to underestimate me, Louisa.' His voice turned cold. 'I refused to have my sister Margaret used as a pawn in a game between my stepmother and me. The confrontation had to be done before Venetia could suspect a thing.'

'Where is your stepmother?'

'She has gone to wait for her daughter to say goodbye.'

He paused. 'Travelling does not agree with Margaret, and Venetia shall be departing soon…for an extended journey to France and then to Switzerland. Arrangements are in hand.'

'Truly?' Louisa found it difficult to breathe. Mrs Ponsby-Smythe was leaving. There were a thousand questions she wanted to ask. And a stab of regret ran through her. Jonathon was not telling her what they had discussed. He was simply informing her that his step-mother had lied.

'We agreed to differ. Margaret is to stay here with me. I am her legal guardian. My stepmother understands the law.'

'Did you speak to her about me?'

He raised a brow. 'It was unavoidable.'

'I wish you would have waited. I wanted to be there. I wanted to speak to her, Jonathon. I surely have earned that right.'

'You are determined to have your pound of flesh.' He ran his fingers through his hair. 'I cannot undo the past as much as I would like to.'

What exactly was he saying? That she was free to go? She hated the way her heart panged. 'I live in the present, Jonathon. The past is something that happened.'

'Ah, yes, the future. I presume you are running towards it with arms wide open.'

'It is my future, Jonathon.' Louisa wished he would take her in his arms and whisper words of love. He failed to understand that allowing him to fight her battles just made her dependent. 'Is that all you wanted to say?'

'Arthur needs a mother.'

'No. I have no plans to marry you or anyone else.'

She hated the way her heart screamed, but she could not do that. She refused to be tied to a man who kept her in ignorance, who decided what was best for her. She wanted to be an equal, not a doll.

'I was wrong to make you come here.' He pressed his fingers against the table.

Louisa concentrated on keeping upright. When she got to her room, she'd weep. Her future would become as she had planned—no marriage, no large house, simply a cottage in Sorrento and the people she knew there. She knew she should be happy, but it felt as if all the light and bubbles had gone from the world. 'I am pleased you have seen sense.'

'I only wanted to do what was right, Louisa.' He inclined his head. 'I would have protected you if you had let me.'

'By keeping me in ignorance! No, you wanted to protect the girl you thought I was. This type of protection would have destroyed me.' She gave her head a small shake. 'You know little about me and my life now. What I truly desire.'

'If that is what you want to believe.' He stood with the cool shadows of the summer house obscuring his features. Louisa longed to lay her head against his chest and say that she wanted him in her life, but she did not dare, not when he was in this mood.

'And how much do you know of me? The man I am now? Or do you still mourn your long-ago lover?' A faint smile touched his lips. 'Give me a chance to prove that I do know this new you. Let us face the future together.'

'I gave Miss Daphne my word. I will stay as long as

she stays.' Louisa gathered what dignity she had left. She had to go from the summer house, or she'd be in his arms. 'I expect to speak with your stepmother before she leaves. Please arrange it for me. You owe me this, Jonathon. I deserve the chance to face her.'

'It will be arranged.' He made a perfect bow. 'Is it ever lonely standing on your pedestal, Louisa?'

Louisa used the strength remaining in her legs to carry her away from the summer house and into the hallway. She laid her cheek against the smooth wooden panelling. Half of her hoped he would come after her and the other half was delighted when he didn't.

'You are being awfully quiet,' Miss Daphne said, reaching for her cameo brooch. 'You have scarcely said a word since I returned from the Roman remains. I thought you would be bubbling over with news. You were wrong to worry about that long-ago mishap. Margaret Ponsby-Smythe was overjoyed to see you. It is a pity her mother is ill, but then Venetia Ponsby-Smythe always hated travelling.'

'I understand Mrs Ponsby-Smythe is leaving for France.'

'Curious, that.' Miss Daphne tapped a finger against her mouth. 'I wonder if Nella knows the reason.'

'I doubt it.'

Louisa thought about the packed valise in her room.

'Would you mind very much if we returned to Italy soon?'

'Does it have to do Mrs Ponsby-Smythe's arrival?'

'There are other considerations.'

Miss Daphne's gaze sharpened. 'If you blame my

nephew's infatuation with Miss Blandish, I shall not believe you, Louisa. You encouraged it. You only have yourself to blame.'

'It has to do with keeping my heart guarded as Miss Mattie admonished on her deathbed.' Louisa regarded her hands. It was impossible to explain about her earlier fight with Jonathon and how he'd accused her of using him as a shield against her problems rather than really seeing him.

'My sister had no idea what she was asking. Never risking your heart makes for an unhappy, unfulfilled life. If you need proof of that, look at Mattie's life.'

'She was well respected. Content.'

Miss Daphne waved an impatient hand. 'You are attempting to distract me, Louisa.'

'I am seeking to reassure you.' Louisa rearranged the items on the dressing table, making sure the bottles of scent and the hairbrush were precisely placed.

'And what if someone needs you here?'

'Who?'

'I need you here, Louisa. It is vital. You must remain with me at Chesterholm. You promised.' Miss Daphne's bottom lip trembled and she looked little older than Nella Blandish. 'There are still things I need to do, things Mattie would have approved of.'

'But the plan has nothing to do with me.'

'Are you frightened by that awful Ponsby-Smythe woman?'

'How do you know Mrs Ponsby-Smythe is awful? Many in the *ton* fawn on her. She always has vouchers to Almack's. She is a friend of the Duchess of Kent, the new queen's mother. Or at least it is what I always understood.' Louisa's voice trailed off at Miss Daphne's amused expression.

'Venetia Ponsby-Smythe is considered to be a social climber *par excellence*. I remember when she made her début.'

'But…'

'If you listen to the servants, you can find out things. Half of the servants are already up in arms. Her imminent departure is being greeted as a miracle and a salvation. It is rumoured that she is going to a private clinic in Switzerland for her nerves.'

'You listen to servants' gossip?' Louisa stared at Miss Daphne.

Miss Daphne laughed. 'I listen to Nella. She listens. It is a terribly useful arrangement.'

'It makes no difference to me.' A steady ache grew behind Louisa's eyes. Before, when she'd been with Jonathon, she'd wanted nothing more than to see Venetia, but now she was not sure. She had lost so much the last time she encountered Venetia. And she knew how much she stood to lose this time. 'I have been too long from Sorrento. It is time for me to return. We should depart sooner rather than later.'

'You are running away, Louisa. You proclaim your independence, but you wear shackles. You are just like Mattie.' Miss Daphne shook her head. 'I wonder that I failed to see it before.'

'I am not running.'

'Then fight your demons and win. Why are you giving her the satisfaction of departing from the field before the fight begins?'

'It is my life to live how I please.'

Louisa put her hand to her throat. Miss Daphne knew that she cared. Did Jonathon? She hoped he had not guessed. But Miss Daphne was right. She needed to stand and fight. After all these years, it was her life to do with as she pleased. Mrs Ponsby-Smythe could not harm her without harming Jonathon or Arthur, or indeed Margaret's prospects.

'You want to take the coward's way out. Just as Mattie took the coward's way out all those years ago with Arthur Fanshaw. You are in love with Lord Chesterholm. Anyone who is not blind in both eyes can see that. And love frightens you.'

'You are being foolishly sentimental.' Louisa balanced the tincture bottle in her hand. 'I suspect you have been taking a sip or two of this. It does you no good.'

'And now you are going to try to start a fight by calling me an old fool or worse? Have you been fighting so long, Louisa, that you have forgotten who is on your side? I am. Always.' She reached out her gnarled hand. 'Always.'

Louisa tucked the white lace shawl more firmly about Miss Daphne's shoulders. 'I would never dream of fighting with you. I respect you too much. But England holds nothing for me.'

'By the time you reach my age, Louisa, you cease being amazed at people. I can see it in your eyes. Something happened between you and Lord Chesterholm when you were stuck in the storm.' Miss Daphne held up her hand, stopping Louisa's words. 'I have no wish to hear what it was, but it has unsettled you. You will not be able to truly put your past behind until you solve your differences with Lord Chesterholm. You are in danger of becoming exactly like Mattie. So afraid of being hurt that you are frightened to live.'

'Miss Mattie was the most alive person I knew.' Louisa gazed at the mirror. 'She took delight in telling the world around her. She was interested in so many things—cameos and Roman pottery. She carried on a vast correspondence.'

'Mattie was a disappointed old woman who let her pride stand in the way of her happiness.' Miss Daphne picked up one of the cameos.

'You are wrong about Miss Mattie and wrong about me.' Louisa crossed her arms.

'You have no idea what she threw away.' Miss Daphne gave a heart-wrenching sigh. 'Do not let history repeat itself, Louisa. One is seldom offered a second chance, but you have been. Take it and embrace it.'

Louisa started to explain that this was different, but at Miss Daphne's intent look she closed her mouth. 'I will consider your advice, Miss Daphne.'

'It is all I ask.' Miss Daphne extended her hand. 'Shall we go down to dinner? I declare listening to Nella Blandish and her stories makes me hungry. Oh, to be that young again and have my whole life in front of me.'

'Mrs Ponsby-Smythe. We meet again.' Louisa said, releasing her hold on Miss Daphne's arm as Mrs Ponsby-Smythe stood in front of them, blocking their progress. It was almost as if the woman had been waiting for her.

For years Venetia Ponsby-Smythe had haunted her dreams, but she was much smaller than Louisa had remembered. In person, she was less fearsome—her hair was askew and her breath smelt like alcohol smothered in peppermints. Louisa concentrated on the carpet pattern. This woman no longer had any power over her. She was a woman of substance, but there was also a very small part of her who remained the naïve governess.

'I expect you are feeling proud.' Mrs Ponsby-Smythe's lip curled. 'The cast-off disgrace has returned in triumph. Are you going to gloat?'

'Everyone will be gathering for dinner.' Louisa kept her voice steady. Surely Venetia Ponsby-Smythe did not want a public scene. Louisa would not shrink from one, but this was far from the place.

'Mrs Ponsby-Smythe. How delightful to see you again,' Miss Daphne said, coming to stand beside Louisa. 'I believe we last met at Eton—'

'You broke your promise to me. Your solemn oath.' Mrs Ponsby-Smythe jabbed her finger at Louisa, interrupting Miss Daphne. 'Explain yourself, Louisa Sibson. You were never to return to England, never to have anything to do with my family. I have sweated blood for you.'

The woman was clearly unhinged, obsessed. Louisa briefly wondered if she had always been that way.

'Do you wish to have a public confrontation, Mrs Ponsby-Smythe? This time there are witnesses.' Louisa was surprised at how calm and collected her voice sounded. 'I would think washing your laundry for all to see is something you would be advised to avoid if you wish to keep your reputation.'

'Are you threatening me?' Mrs Ponsby-Smythe drew back in amazement. 'Who are you to threaten me? Nobody will believe you. All you are is soiled Haymarketware.'

Louisa briefly glanced at Miss Daphne, who nodded back.

'No, I am stating the truth. I welcome the chance to speak with you. I have nothing to fear from the truth. Can you say the same? Miss Daphne Elliot's connections are impeccable.'

'And I will not hesitate to use them,' Miss Daphne whispered in an undertone. 'Have no fear, Louisa.'

'I am giving you the opportunity to retain your dignity, Mrs Ponsby-Smythe,' Louisa said, repeating the same words Mrs Ponsby-Smythe had used all those years ago when Louisa had begged for help in contacting Jonathon.

The woman blinked and took a step backwards. Clearly she was expecting Louisa to cower and beg forgiveness, just as she had done all those years ago when she had come looking for Jonathon with a baby in her womb. Mrs Ponsby-Smythe had another think coming. Louisa's days of being afraid were long over. What the woman thought of her and what she might have been able to do to her once upon a time had vanished. She had no power. She held no mystic key to make others think badly of Louisa. Louisa's shoulders felt lighter as she kept her gaze steady and Venetia Ponsby-Smythe turned away.

'That is up to you, Miss Sibson,' she said in a cold voice. 'But I suspect you seek an audience.'

Louisa squeezed Miss Daphne's hand, whispering that she would meet her in the drawing room. The elderly lady squeezed her hand back. Louisa waited until the sound of her footsteps faded.

'You have changed, Miss Sibson.' Mrs Ponsby-

Smythe said. 'I would have thought you would need an ally. You were always looking for someone else to fight your battles. A white knight.'

'Mrs Ponsby-Smythe,' Louisa began, gripping the banister for support as the enormity of what she was about to do swept over her. Whatever happened, she refused to show this woman how terrified she was of getting it wrong, of breaking down and crying.

'You think you are very smart, Louisa, returning this way. Seeking to recapture my stepson's heart and step into Clarissa's shoes. If she remained alive…he loved her, you know.'

Louisa kept her shoulders down and her head up. The well-aimed barb stung far less than she thought it would. Louisa released the banister and stood with her hands lightly clasped in front of her. She could do this. She was sure of it now.

'You lied to me. You lied to your stepson and to your daughter. You have lived a lie. If you had not lied, Jonathon would have been free to make his own choice.'

Mrs Ponsby-Smythe raised a handkerchief to her eyes. 'You have no idea of the crosses I have to bear. The trouble and pain they have caused me.'

'What crosses? When have you ever missed a tea, walked with paper in your shoes, or had to sleep under a bridge? Have you ever lost a baby whilst burning up with fever? Until you have had this happen, do not speak to me of crosses and deprivation. I was naïve, Mrs Ponsby-Smythe, but you were wicked.'

'How dare you speak to one of your betters like that! How dare you accuse me of wickedness! I did what I had to do for my family!'

'My better?' Louisa allowed her gaze to travel down the length of Mrs Ponsby-Smythe. Once she had considered Mrs Ponsby-Smythe the height of sophistication and taste, but no longer. She was simply a disappointed, ruthlessly ambitious woman. And pity for her flooded through Louisa. 'You are not fit to wipe the floor after me.'

'You are getting beyond your station, my dear,' Mrs Ponsby-Smythe said in a loud whisper. 'I warned you of what could happen if you became involved with my stepson, but you chose to disregard my heartfelt warnings. You have no one to blame but yourself.'

Louisa tapped her slipper on the ground. Heartfelt warnings indeed! The woman had no conception. The only heartfelt thing she believed in was her own social advancement. 'Your machinations will not work this time, Mrs Ponsby-Smythe. My one regret is that I respected you once upon a time. Remove yourself from my path. I have a dinner to attend.'

'As a servant to that old biddy?' Mrs Ponsby-Smythe's lip curled back and she stood squarely in the middle of the stairs. 'That woman wants her head examined for employing a woman with as loose morals as you.'

'As an equal.' Louisa lifted her chin and took a step towards the woman. 'I would watch what you say about Miss Elliot. Miss Elliot has friends and family who love her.'

'You? An equal? I would rather die!'

'That is your choice. For my part, what happened is in the past and has no part of my future.' Louisa reached the woman and stood toe to toe with her. Mrs Ponsby-

Smythe looked away. 'Stand aside, Mrs Ponsby-Smythe. I have a dinner to attend.'

Mrs Ponsby-Smythe moved out of Louisa's way, allowing her to pass.

'You will regret this, Louisa,' she said in a biting undertone. 'He will never love you. You can never take Clarissa's place. She is the mother of his son. His heart will never be yours.'

Despite everything, the barb stung. Louisa stopped. Slowly she regained control. She glanced back over her shoulder and saw a wild-haired old woman who had lost everything.

'You are deluding yourself, if you think I care about your opinion on the matter.' Louisa turned away from Mrs Ponsby-Smythe and walked down the remaining stairs.

*Her whole life in front of her.* Louisa stared at the closed study door later that evening as Miss Daphne's words echoed in her brain. After her confrontation with Mrs Ponsby-Smythe she had made it through supper and Miss Blandish's recital. Neither Mrs Ponsby-Smythe nor Jonathon had put in an appearance. There was no chance of encountering him in the garden either as rain fell steadily. It was as if he was avoiding her. There had to be a way of making him understand that she was ready to begin living her life properly. The past no longer shackled her.

Louisa took a deep breath, straightened the skirts of her green off-the-shoulder dress and forced her hand to grip the door handle and turn it.

She had been given a second chance and she had hung

on to the bitterness. She was not behaving like Annie Sims, seeking to romanticise the past, but was looking towards the future where there were no shadows. The man she was interested in was Jonathon Fanshaw, Lord Chesterholm, rather than the young and dashing Jonathon Ponsby-Smythe.

Her encounter with Mrs Ponsby-Smythe had shown her that she had allowed the past to have power over her, rather than taking charge of her life. From here on in she would live her life the way she wanted to. She was finished with hiding in the shadows and worrying what others thought of her. It was her life to live how she wanted and she wanted Jonathon.

Jonathon was in deep discussion with Roberts and his valet. The instant she entered the room, the conversation ceased.

'Am I interrupting something?' Louisa asked.

'Not at all,' Jonathon replied, dismissing the men. 'Stay, Louisa. There is nothing more that can be done tonight but in the morning, I want the search to begin again. This time, I want him found.'

'Very good, my lord.' The men bowed and left.

'Search? Has someone gone missing?' Louisa asked.

'Nothing for you to worry about. Everything is under control. This little adventure has nothing to do with the house party. There was a report that Annie's former lover had been spotted in the neighbourhood, but it proved false. As a precaution, though, I have had the snuffboxes and other valuables locked up in the new safe,' Jonathon said. He walked over to the fire and gave the coals a poke, sending bright sparks arching in the air. 'Is it thundering again? What disturbs your sleep this time?'

'You,' Louisa said, advancing forwards. Warm pulses coursed through her body with each breath she took. 'You disturb me.'

'Why are you down here? Are you going to try to seduce me into arranging a meeting with Venetia? You are too late. She left during dinner.' He held up a hand, stopping her words. 'She demanded a carriage and passage to the Continent. I saw no reason to stop her. You may despise me if you like.'

'Venetia and I have already exchanged words. We have nothing more to say to each other.' Louisa pressed her hands against the skirt of her gown. Venetia had run without ever telling Jonathon about the encounter. She had abandoned her daughter rather than face up to her crime. 'You were right about that.'

He dipped his head. 'When did this encounter happen?'

'Before supper, but there was no chance to tell you and then you disappeared…'

'Venetia never breathed a word.'

'Why didn't you tell me that she had gone?'

'I do have a responsibility towards my tenants. After she departed another matter claimed my attention.' He rubbed a hand across the back of his neck. 'I have spent the better part of the evening out in the freezing rain, trying to figure out what precisely happened at Middle Farm. But I am curious—how did you waylay her?'

'I did not plan on it, Jonathon. We met on the stairs. Miss Daphne was with me. Your stepmother confronted me. At my request Miss Daphne withdrew and I faced her on my own. In private.' Louisa glared at him. 'I did not seek the fight, but neither would I run from it.'

'Did my stepmother upset you?' he asked urgently. 'I wanted to spare you that.'

'Surprisingly, no—more than anything I pitied her.'

'Pitied?' His face showed his amazement.

'To be that consumed by ambition and hatred...' Louisa turned her palms face upwards. 'We have an understanding—the loathing is on her part. For mine, I want to live my life unhampered by the past. I have fought my demon and won. And, Jonathon, my demon was not your stepmother, but my fear of being inadequate and unworthy.'

Louisa waited unflinchingly under his amazed gaze, ready for when he stretched out his hand. He made no move towards her.

'Is that the only reason you have sought me out?' he asked, breaking the silence. 'I *never* had any doubts about your worthiness.'

Louisa took a great breath. She had to seize the opportunity. She had one chance to make it right.

'I came here on another purpose,' she admitted. 'To seduce you.'

'Seduction?' He gave an amused laugh. 'Or wishing I would seduce you?'

'I am aware of the difference.' Confidence bubbled through her. For this once, she would take what she wanted without apology or shame.

'So you say.' His eyes danced full of hidden fire. 'But I wonder...'

'I am a grown woman. I take full responsibility.'

Louisa worried her bottom lip. He needed to know that she was not expecting for ever. 'I am not looking for marriage, Jonathon. I want to live in the now.'

The shadow of a dimple shone in his cheek. 'Are you certain about this? Seducing me will not be easy.'

'Yes, I am certain.'

With three quick steps, Louisa reached him and undid his stock, throwing it on the ground. Without giving herself time to think or pause, she undid the buttons of his shirt. The shifting light from the fire turned his skin to red-gold, begging to be tasted. He did not move to touch her or help her.

Her fingers faltered and stilled. It was far harder than she had imagined. She willed him to respond, but he stood unmoving with his chin slightly raised, the shirt hanging loose about his body. 'Shall I go away?'

'No.' The word was drawn from his throat. He put his hands on her shoulders, held her from him. His sea-green gaze penetrated her being. 'What do you hope to gain from this little experiment?'

'Making love with you is not about gaining anything. It is about experiencing life.' She kept her head up and made her words sound firm. 'If a man might seduce a woman for no purpose, why can't an independent woman seduce a man?'

'I am in no mood for joking, Louisa.' He ran his hand through his hair, making it stand on end. 'If you start something, you must be willing to finish it no matter when that finish is. You must be prepared to accept the consequences.'

'I understand and I am not looking beyond the end of the night.' She rose up on her tiptoes and brushed his cheek with her lips. The daringness of it made her head swim. 'I want you to hold me. Please.'

His hands tightened on her shoulders and pulled her unresisting body towards him. Her breasts hit his chest. 'I am a man, Louisa, not some bloody hero.'

He lowered his mouth. She entangled her hands in his hair and pulled him closer. Her entire body thrilled with the power of his kiss.

His hands undid the small buttons at the top of her evening gown. The bodice sagged, revealing her chemise and the tops of her breast.

Slowly, reverently, he traced the outline of her breasts. Her nipples tightened under his touch and her back arched forwards. Now she wished that she had been simply dressed in her nightdress, rather trying to seduce him in her evening clothes. Her gown fell to the floor with a soft sigh, quickly followed by her petticoats until she stood in the firelight, clad only in her chemise, drawers and corset. Her carefully arranged hair fell in disarray about her shoulders.

'You wear your corset far too tight,' he rasped in her ear. 'I nearly had to destroy it.'

'I have a small waist.'

'But there is no need to faint.' His fingers freed the strings, unlacing her with a few expert twists of his hands. 'I enjoy you how you were made, Louisa, not conforming to fashionable dictates.'

'I thought this was supposed to be about me seducing you.' She leaned forwards and captured his fingers. She took each one into her mouth and suckled, rolling her tongue and holding them. 'You are slightly overdressed.'

She slipped her hand between the soft linen of his shirt and his firm chest. Using his actions as a guide, she teased his nipples, making them grow into hard nubs beneath her fingers. Then she pushed the material to one side, bent her head and tasted.

He groaned softly as his hands gently held her against him. Slowly she moved down his chest, nibbling and trailing open-mouthed kisses until she reached his belly button and felt his arousal against her cheek.

Her hands stilled on his trousers. Did she dare?

She pushed the thought away. The new Louisa, the Louisa she had become tonight, did dare. Later, she would think about what she had done, but tonight was for exploring and for feeling and remembering how good it could be. How much better they were together.

Her hand unfastened the button band and then she held him. Hot and strong. Alive. She ran one finger down his silken length and felt him surge upwards. She started to take him in her mouth, but his hands pulled her up, along his body until their mouths were level and his arousal pressed into the apex of her thighs.

'Let me pleasure you. I want this to last.'

She drew her hand back quickly. 'My touch fails to please you?'

'If you continue on, this will end very quickly and you will not enjoy it as much you should.' His fingers tilted her head back so she could see his passion-filled eyes. 'Your pleasure increases mine.'

Jonathon eased her down in front of the fire. He was no saint, he knew that and he wanted her. He ran his hand down her face, savouring her, and felt her flesh quiver under his touch. Surely her surrender after today meant she accepted that they were to be together. She was his.

He pushed the material to one side and laid her bare. He trailed his fingers down her abdomen and tangled them in her auburn triangle.

Immediately her body began to buck. His fingers slipped into her innermost folds, seeking her core. First one finger, then two, gently stroking her. She convulsed about him and his body surged, but he held on to his control. This time he would give her pleasure, so much pleasure that she would be tempted never to leave his arms.

He had always considered himself a good and thoughtful lover, but there was more to it this time. This was about Louisa and binding her to him. This time she would not leave.

She writhed her head on the floor, her red hair spilling out over the carpet. He put his mouth where his fingers were and licked, taking in the warm wetness that was her. Heat threatened to consume him as her body responded with great racking shivers.

Her hands clawed at his shoulders. 'Please, please.'

He lifted his head and stared directly into her passion-lit pupils. 'You are mine. You belong to me. Say it.'

'I am yours.' Her breath came in quick sharp pants. 'Jonathon. Please.'

He positioned himself and thrust as her hips rose to greet him. He marvelled at how she closed around him and held him. Her hips began to move, setting the rhythm. He matched it, feeling her breasts brush in time along the length of his chest.

Louisa grabbed his shoulders and held him. Kept him within her as the world thrummed about her.

She had nearly confessed her love for him, but this was far too soon. Love was not what this was about. This was about her choices in life.

She moved her hips faster and faster. And she knew that this was what living was about—being in his arms. Tomorrow or the next day, she'd consider the future but right now she wanted to experience and to be a part of him.

A great shuddering overcame her and then him. After, they lay tangled in each other's arms, skin touching skin. Louisa turned her head and saw the statue of Eros and Psyche, intertwined. Love and soul together, bathed in the firelight.

Physically Jonathon and she were as close as two people could be. But Louisa knew it was not enough. She wanted more. She wanted a true meeting of love and souls.

No shields, no excuses and no boundaries, he had said, but he kept them erected as well. If they were to have a future, she wanted to be in all parts of his life, not that little bit labelled Louisa.

'Did I do the seduction right?' she asked, raising herself up on her elbow and looking down at his face. His long eyelashes framed his eyes perfectly.

'You show promising signs.' He trailed a finger down the length of her thigh. 'You definitely meet all requirements. However, I wish to try it a few more times before giving you a definitive answer.'

It would be so easy to give in to him and to allow herself to be distracted from her purpose.

'And there are no rules between us?'

His hand stilled and withdrew. Louisa shivered slightly. She might be prepared to bare her soul, but Jonathon played by his own set of rules, just as he had always done. He gave a heart-melting smile and reached for her. 'I want you with me in my arms.'

She evaded his arms, hugging her knees instead. 'That is not the same thing. Even after this afternoon, you seem unwilling to share things with me.'

'What things?' He frowned. 'Oh, the break–in at Middle Farm? It is of no import. The farmer winged both men. They will not have escaped far. Allow me to handle it.'

Louisa did not give an answering smile back. Her guess was correct. He wanted to keep the estate and everything from her. He was not interested in the long term. Theirs was a meeting of bodies and no more. But she knew she had to try one last time. 'If it is unimportant, why didn't you tell me about it when I asked the first time?'

'Clarissa never asked about such things. They bored her to tears. She—'

'Understood? Let you look after her? Never questioned your decisions.' Louisa reached for her clothes. 'But I am not Clarissa. I can never be her.'

He gave her a long level look. Her insides twisted up tightly. He had to understand what she was asking and why. She wanted him as her partner, not as her master.

'Clarissa was my wife and she died having Arthur. She is in my past. What else can I say? You want everything, Louisa, but are prepared to give little in return.

Have you ever shown that you want to be part of my world, Louisa? Or are you always going to bolt back to your little cottage in Sorrento with its vines and lemons? Would you let me in your life there? Or is what we share for England only?'

'How can you ask me that?'

'I could ask you the same question. You will have to decide. But I want everything, Louisa. I want to be a part of your life. You need me.'

With as much dignity as she could muster, Louisa gathered her remaining clothes. She took a final look at the statue and knew she had lost. What Jonathon and she had could never be a true meeting of love and soul. Not until he was prepared to share his life with her as an equal. 'You have given me my answer. Thank you for setting me free.'

# *Chapter Fourteen*

A great hollow opened inside Louisa. It had grown ever since she had left Jonathon. The thought of not seeing him again filled her with horror.

The mist hung about the gardens, turning the spiders' webs into diamonds. The whole world was remade and waiting for her. Louisa walked along with a brisk step, rapidly putting distance between her and the house. It was what she wanted—independence and freedom. But why did her life suddenly seem so lonely?

A quick turn about the garden would settle her nerves. She knew she had lied last night. So much of her wanted this to be for ever, rather than for right now. She wanted to spend the rest of her natural life with him and for his smile to be the first thing she saw every morning and the last thing at night. But he had never followed her. She had bared her soul for him—now he had to do the same. He had to want to share his life instead of simply looking after her.

A faint shushing noise made her turn. 'Who goes there?'

'It is just me, miss.' Annie stood frozen against the skyline. Her eye sported a fresh bruise. In her arms she carried Arthur.

'Who hit you, Annie?'

'That don't matter, miss. You ought to go now, miss.' Annie gave a half-smile. 'You haven't seen a thing, right?'

'Why do you have Arthur?'

Annie's tongue flicked over her lips. 'I…I am looking after him for my aunt, Nanny Hawks. Everything is well, miss.'

'I didn't know you were that close to your aunt.' Louisa went towards the pair. 'Where is Nanny Hawks?'

'She's not well.' Annie's gaze slid away from her. 'I'm…I'm taking Arthur to my mother. You see, Lord Chesterholm don't have much time for him…and… please, we need to go, miss. It has been pleasant speaking with you and all.'

The back of Louisa's neck crawled. Annie was lying. Jonathon always made time for Arthur, despite his busy schedule. She had seen that time and again over the past few days. He was a good father, a father who cared, and he thought Nanny Hawks and her niece were not close. She doubted that he had given his permission, not with the house party on. 'Trevor found you. He hit you.'

Annie hunched her shoulders and hid her face. 'I had best be going. Arthur is getting a bit mardy.'

'Give Arthur to me, Annie. I will look after him.' Louisa held out her arms, but Annie tightened hers about Arthur. Louisa's heart sank. Annie needed Arthur for some reason, for something that was connected with her black eye. Right now, she had to get Arthur to safety and then she'd raise the alarm. 'Arthur and I are friends. I will look after him. Keep him with me until your aunt is better.'

At the sound of his name, Arthur began to struggle against the confines of Annie's arms.

'Ouch, the little beggar bit me.' Annie slapped Arthur's hand.

'Release him, Annie. Now,' Louisa said, glaring at the woman. 'He wants to get down.'

'That wouldn't be wise, miss...not when he is in one of his moods.' She shifted Arthur to her other hip. Arthur's wails punctuated the still morning air. 'Me ma...me ma knows what to do with him when he is in one of his moods. He ain't right in the head, see.'

Louisa's stomach revolted at the words. Annie lied with such ease. There was nothing wrong with Arthur.

'Your man did do that. He's back, isn't he? Why lie? You are taking Arthur to him.' Louisa quickly crossed the remaining distance. She caught Annie's arm. 'You have no right to do that. Give Arthur to me! Stop this while you still can!'

'You ought not to interfere, miss.' Annie shrugged Louisa's hand off. 'I know you mean well, but me mam needs him. My aunt gave permission. Truly she did. She has helped me out afore, like.'

'Did Lord Chesterholm know?'

'But, miss...I promised.' Annie's voice held a note of desperation. 'Aunt Mary understood.'

'Give Arthur to me and I will go with you to your mother's,' Louisa said slowly.

'You'd do that for me? Explain why I don't have things, like.'

'Yes, I would.' Louisa knew she should refuse, but what could happen to her? It was not as if she was a blushing miss; she had looked after herself for years and the streets of Naples were far rougher than the fields around Chesterholm. She would never forgive herself if she stood by and allowed Annie to take Arthur. 'First we will take Arthur back to the nursery. You know you do not want Arthur there. You do not want your man hitting a defenceless child.'

Annie gave a sigh and loosened her arms. Arthur jumped down. 'Go back to Nanny, Arthur, Go back now! Afore I change my mind.'

Arthur sat down in the dirt, looking up with wide grey eyes.

'We ought to take him back. To be sure that he makes it,' Louisa urged. If she could get Annie to return to the house, she could get help. Her arms ached to pick Arthur up, but Annie had positioned her body between Louisa and Arthur as if she were standing guard over him.

'There isn't time, see.' Annie gave him a shove. 'Go to Nanny, Arthur. There's a good lad.'

Arthur began to toddle off. Louisa started off towards him, but Annie's fingers closed around her wrist and held her tight, forcing her to walk away from the boy. Annie's strength surprised Louisa. She tried twisting her arm, but the woman only tightened her grip.

'Annie, what are you playing at?' Louisa brought her arm down sharply. 'Arthur's a little boy. I need to take him back to the nursery. You cannot be serious about abandoning a child out here in the gardens.'

Tears shimmered in Annie's eyes. 'I don't have a choice, like, miss. I promised. Me mam's life depends on it.'

'But he is only eighteen months old.'

'There, see!' Annie pointed towards the house. 'My aunt has him. See, I told you. My aunt looks after me.'

Relief flooded through Louisa as she saw Arthur reach Nanny Hawks and wave back. Arthur's ordeal was over. All she had to do was to free herself from this madwoman. Even now, Annie was pulling her towards the copse of trees. Surely Nanny Hawks would help her, but as Louisa watched, the older woman turned her back and strode briskly away. Suddenly the meaning of Annie's words became clear—*helped me afore*. Nanny Hawks knew the household routines. And what was it Nanny Hawks had said the first time they had met? Something about Annie meaning more to her than her own flesh and blood. Louisa put her hand to her mouth. Nanny Hawks had helped Annie by letting Trevor in. Nanny Hawks was the insider. The world tilted and then slowly righted itself.

'You are all right, miss? My aunt says that Lord Chesterholm is sweet on you and that you inherited a great deal of money from an elderly lady. Handy, like.'

'Annie, you must tell me what is going on. I can get help, but only if you trust me enough to know the truth. Nanny Hawks was the one who let Trevor in so he could steal the cameos and the snuffboxes. She did it for you.'

Annie gave a tiny nod. 'I didn't know he was going to do that. Not until after it were done, like.'

Louisa kept her voice steady and tried to ignore the tremors of fear coursing through her stomach. She had guessed correctly, but it also meant that she was in far more danger than she had guessed.

'I helped you before,' Louisa said quietly, willing Annie to remember the day they met. 'When you were frightened and alone. I can do it again. Lord Chester-holm is a kind man. He gave you a handkerchief to bind up your cut. Why do you want to steal from him?'

'No, miss, not this time. Lord Chesterholm has so much money. He won't miss a little bit.' Annie's back stiffened and a single tear went down her ruddy cheek. 'You come with me or I will get Arthur again. He sent me for the snuffbox and said if I couldn't get it, I was to bring Arthur to him because surely the boy's life was worth a snuffbox. He has me mam tied up. My aunt knows that. I can't go back without anything. Me mam…she is going to get hurt.'

Louisa thought quickly. She had to raise the alarm. 'You are amongst friends, Annie. No one can harm you here. You tell your story to Lord Chesterholm and he will get a rescue party for your mother.'

'It's too late, Miss. Trevor has come for me.' Annie shoved Louisa forwards and Louisa fell to her knees, losing her reticule amongst the bracken.

'You took your time about it, girl. Where is that blasted snuffbox and the other pretties I sent you for?' a rough voice said. A man who might have been hand-some once, but had run to corrupt fat, emerged from the undergrowth. A crude bandage was tied about his upper arm. 'You weren't going to cross me, were you?'

'I couldn't get them, Trevor. Honest. I brought her instead.' Annie dragged Louisa by the arm. 'Now let me mam go.'

Trevor sent a stream of spittle arching towards Louisa. 'A woman is worth less than nothing. His lordship will bargain for the boy, his own flesh and blood, but not this creature.'

'You are not having Arthur Fanshaw,' Louisa said, using her best governess voice. Her insides felt ice cold.

'She has money, that one. They will pay to get her back.' There was a note of desperation in Annie's voice. 'You see she is worth it. My aunt reckons that his lordship wants to marry her. And she inherited money.'

'You reckon?' The man stroked the stubble on his chin. 'You reckon she is worth the price of your mother's life?'

'And more.' Annie stuck out her chin. 'You gave me your word. I have brought you someone to bargain with.'

'Annie, don't pay attention to him. He is just using you.' Louisa held out her hands in supplication. If she could get Annie to help even the tiniest bit, Louisa knew she could escape and get back to Chesterholm. Surely they could run together. Two against one. Annie was not a bad person.

Two tears spilled down Annie's face. 'I have no choice, miss. I can't lose me mam. This is all my fault, miss.'

Before Louisa had time to react, her arms were

grabbed and bound, and a gag made from a dirty rag was thrust into her mouth.

Louisa kicked out with her feet but Trevor merely laughed at her, shoving her forwards so she stumbled. Her reticule was inches from her fingertips. Louisa glared at it. Her tiny pair of scissors, a nail file, everything that might be useful was in that reticule and she couldn't get it.

'What do we do now?' Annie asked. 'You will let me mam go now. She's no use to you.'

'We take her somewhere quiet until I decides. It was lucky you heard about the inheritance and the old lady. Else, your mam and you would not live to see the light of another day, I reckon.'

Ropes were slung around Louisa's wrists. She stumbled forwards as the rope was tugged. She wanted to believe that Jonathon would try to find her once he realised that she was missing. He had to know that she would not abandon him again. A stab of fear went through her. What if he didn't? What if she never had the chance to say how much she loved him and how much she wanted to spend the rest of her life with him? *What might have been.* They were the most depressing words in the universe.

Her foot hit a rock and she nearly fell. She bit back fierce tears. She refused to give Trevor and Annie the satisfaction of seeing her cry.

Jonathon regarded the morning room. Miss Elliot was in the corner with the younger Miss Blandish, but Louisa was nowhere to be seen. And without Louisa sitting there, sipping a cup of chocolate, it felt empty and desolate.

He had visited the nursery earlier, but Louisa had not appeared there either. And much to his annoyance, Nanny Hawks had taken Arthur for an early morning stroll. It was not really Arthur he sought, he wanted Louisa; not having her at his side made him jumpy. He had held out as long as he dared, hoping she'd relent and come to him but the feeling had grown. Something had happened to Louisa, something was far from right.

'Miss Elliot, is Miss Sibson still a-bed?'

The elderly lady looked him up and down and Jonathon was tempted to blush like a school boy. She knew somehow what had happened between him and Louisa and disapproved.

'Miss Elliot, I had only wanted to make certain that Miss Sibson was well.'

Miss Elliot drew her upper lip over her teeth. 'It is odd. I have not seen dear Louisa since yesterday evening.'

'I would wager that she has been kidnapped,' Miss Nella said with great relish. 'What this house party needs is a good kidnapping!'

'Nella!' her mother called.

'There is no doubt a logical explanation, Brother.' Margaret came up and linked her arm with his. Now that Venetia had departed, Margaret seemed far more relaxed than she had in years. 'Louisa is probably out on a morning walk. She used to be a great one for walking.'

'Yes, Louisa does enjoy her morning walks,' Miss Elliot confirmed. 'They help her to think.'

'Pa pa Lou la An.' Arthur burst in the breakfast room,

shouting his head off. He gave a little stamp of his foot.
'Lou An Go.'

'What is wrong, Arthur?' Jonathon knelt down beside
the boy. Arthur's eyes were wide, scared and his entire
body trembled. Jonathon forced his breathing to be even.
Louisa had said that Arthur spoke much better than he
gave him credit for. 'Slowly now. Try.'

Arthur burst into noisy sobs.

'Jonathon,' his sister said reproachfully. 'You ask far
too much of the child. He is a toddler.'

'Lord Chesterholm, Lord Chesterholm!' Nanny hurried into the room, her ample bosom heaving and her
cap askew. 'I am so sorry. Arthur got away from me.'

Jonathon put Arthur down and glared at the woman.
She refused to meet his eyes, pretending a deep interest
in the wooden floor. 'What happened, Nanny Hawks?
My son is upset. He has had a fright.'

She twisted her apron round and round. 'I would not
like to say, sir. We were out in the air, like.'

'You had best divulge what you know.' Jonathon
looked at her, hard. 'Tell the truth and shame the devil.
You are a good woman, Nanny Hawks, but something
has happened to upset Arthur.'

The woman twisted her apron. 'Miss Sibson has gone
with my niece, I think.'

'And Arthur doesn't like that. He's frightened for
Miss Sibson. Why?' Jonathon gave Arthur's soft curls
a stroke.

'I don't like it neither, sir, if truth be told. There is
something amiss. People could get hurt.'

'Why would Miss Sibson go with your niece?'

'Because Annie took Arthur!' The woman burst into

floods of tears. 'I do not know what to do, truly I do not. It was not supposed to be like this. They have Elizabeth. What could I do? Annie knocked me down and took Arthur and then…afore I could catch up, Miss Sibson was there. Arthur came back to me and Miss Sibson went. Miss Sibson is a right canny lass.'

'You had best tell me everything.' Jonathon put his arm about the woman's shoulders as the blood in his veins ran cold. The words Nanny Hawks spoke kept running through his brain. He was missing something, something big, and all because he kept his life compartmentalised as Louisa had accused him of. A place for everything and everything in its place. 'Who are you talking about?'

'That man of Annie's. He is a right danger. She thought him wonderful. He promised her the earth if I'd just let him in the house. Annie thought he might leave without her. I thought she'd stay if I did as she asked…'

'Nanny Hawks, did you let that man of Annie's into the house the day things were stolen? Did he threaten to expose Annie? Is that why you did it?' His head pounded when he remembered what Louisa had said on the carriage journey.

Nanny Hawks stood silent in the room with the clock ticking behind her. 'That man threatened me and mine. I was only doing what I had to do to survive. I thought he had gone away, but he came back and…and he has Elizabeth. Except you had locked up the snuffboxes…'

'Do you know where they have taken Louisa?' Jonathon fought against the urge to shake the woman. The law would have to deal with her. 'Think carefully. Any clue.'

The nurse shook her head. 'Honest, I don't know.'

Hard hands shoved Louisa to the stone floor. She did not want to think how long they had been walking, her hands tied, mouth gagged. Several times, her skirt had caught and snagged on brambles and thorn bushes. Once a branch had held her captive and her dress now bore a great rip along the hem. And it was one of her favourite dresses. Louisa gritted her teeth—another black mark against this couple.

And then they had come upon it—the stone hut down a dirt track, the same one where a few short days ago, she had sheltered with Jonathon and he had shown her what it was like to truly experience passion and to be alive. Everything was exactly how they had left it—the straw on the floor, the little wooden table where she put her reticule and the place where they had made love. And somehow it had made it worse, to be a hostage in the one place where she had felt loved and cherished.

On the other side of the table, a very frightened Mrs Sims cowered. When Trevor approached she gave a small whimper and curled up in a ball.

Louisa winced as Trevor's foot connected with Mrs Sims's back. A hostage? She might die here. She wished now that she had told Jonathon of her love for him, and how in the last few days she had rediscovered all those things that she had lost: laughter, joy and even tears. She had started living again. If she had tried to explain, would he have listened?

Her back straightened as Trevor bound her feet, tying

the other end of the rope to the table. Louisa knew she could easily become like Mrs Sims, cowering and whimpering. But she had a reason to live and fight—to be able to tell Jonathon how she felt and how she had never truly stopped loving him. She had only forgotten for a while and had allowed her doubts and misgivings to crowd out what was true and good about their relationship. He was right. She had been so worried about going back to the old Louisa that she had neglected to see that he had changed and that she had fallen in love with this new Jonathon, not her memory.

'There you goes—two women and my ticket to riches.' Trevor gave a leer as he tied the last knot.

Annie stood on her toes expectantly. 'Here, I thought you were going to release me mam.'

'Slight change of plan.' He rocked back on his haunches and nodded towards another man who lay on the ground. 'Old Tom was hurt bad in the fight. He needs someone to look after him, like. We stays here for a few days. Then we get out and starts a new life. His lordship is going to help us do that.'

'But you said...'

Trevor caught Annie's chin. 'You do as I say or else more people will get hurt.'

'I don't like you.'

'Too bad. You are stuck with me.'

Louisa took a deep breath and bid the panic to be gone. Calm, collected and reasoned. She knew her way back from the hut if an opportunity to escape presented itself. 'Let Annie and her mother go,' she said around the gag. 'You do not need them.'

'Listen to Miss Sibson!' Annie pleaded. 'Let her speak. She has money of her own, I tell you!'

'No one will hear her screams here.' His filthy hands tore the gag away. He held her chin between his meaty fingers. 'What do you have to say for yourself, Miss Sibson? How are you going to save yourself? What are you going to offer me...your virtue?'

'You promised to release Mrs Sims,' Louisa said loudly. 'You lied to Annie. She only brought me here because of her concern for her mother. You do not need either one of them. I can pay for your passage elsewhere if you let them go.'

'Just like that! You really think his lordship would not set the law on me.' The man laughed. 'Why should I release any of you without that?'

'Because you gave your word.'

'You were a fool to trust me.' He reached out and slapped Annie's cheek. 'I told her I wanted the snuffbox. But she brought an alternative. Now I am stuck with you.'

'It is my final offer—let everyone go and I will pay your passage,' Louisa said, twisting her arms behind her back. There had to be a way of getting the ropes to loosen. 'Did you use Nanny Hawks as well? Did you threaten to expose her niece as a loose woman if she did not let you into the house and turn a blind eye? She dotes on her niece.'

Trevor gave her a black look and she knew she was right. He had made the connection. It was why he had seduced Annie in the first place and then threatened Nanny Hawks. 'A man has to use his opportunities when he ain't born with a silver spoon.'

Louisa fought against her bonds, but the rope just drew tighter, cutting into her wrists. 'You are going to rot in hell.'

'I hope so!' He gave a crooked grin. 'Now, Annie, my love, you are going to do just what I say. And maybe your mam won't get hurt any more. You are going to deliver a little message for me.'

Tears started to flow down Annie's face.

'Annie, remember to do what is right,' Louisa called out as a massive fist connected with her jaw. 'Remember who looks after you and your family. And always will do. This man here lied to you and hurt your family. He does not deserve your loyalty.'

The only answer she heard was running footsteps.

'I have found Miss Sibson's reticule!' Nella Blandish called out from the long grass and Jonathon wanted to kiss her.

He ran over to where Nella stood. The reticule did indeed look like Louisa's. Annoyingly, Nanny Hawks could not say where Trevor had taken Louisa. Her only thought had been for Annie and her sister's return, rather than a rescue party. Jonathon had had Thompson lock the woman in the pantry so that she could not escape. When this sorry mess was over, and Louisa safe, he would turn her over to the Justice of the Peace. But that was for later. Right now, he had to find Louisa. 'Good work, Miss Nella.'

The young woman beamed. 'I did not think it possible for two adventures in the space of a few weeks, but here I am!'

'I doubt Miss Sibson would have abandoned her

reticule,' his sister said. 'She was most particular about such things when she was my governess.'

'Do you have any suggestions for how we discover Miss Sibson's whereabouts?' Jonathon longed to hit something. The world suddenly seemed a far lonelier place. There were so many things he should have done and said to Louisa. He had to find her before something happened to her.

'What about using the dogs?' Rupert Furniss shouted. 'Some dogs are good trackers. They can't have gone that far. They were on foot.'

'It is worth a shot.' Jonathon held the little purse out to Tyne and Tees. The dogs sniffed it, but sat down looking puzzled. Jonathon cursed and, ignoring Mrs Blandish's raised eyebrows, cursed again far louder. He knelt down and held the reticule out for the dogs again. They had to do it. By the time a rescue party was organised, Louisa could be dead. 'Tyne and Tees, try to pick up the scent. Find Louisa.'

'She went this way,' Nella called out. 'The undergrowth is stamped down and there is a bit of thread on one of the brambles.'

'Miss Nella, you may have found your calling!'

Jonathon guided the dogs over to where Nella pointed. They lifted their muzzles, barked sharply and set off. In the distance, he saw a woman running towards them.

Louisa watched with frustration as Trevor stalked the room. She had lost track of time since Annie had gone. The rope remained fastened about her wrists. Why was it in Minerva Press novels the rope always seemed to come undone easily and the heroine was free to save the day? The only thing she seemed to have done was to twist the rope tighter.

'That witch should be back by now,' Trevor said, coming back into the hut. Instantly Louisa stilled. 'If she has double-crossed me, it will go ill for the both of you.'

'If Annie has any sense, she will have confessed everything to Lord Chesterholm,' Louisa said. 'You had best allow us to go. Even now, a large search party may be coming for us. How do you think you'd fare against such an army?'

'If she betrayed me, you both will die. She knows it. Do you know how long it takes to cut a throat?' Trevor pulled out his knife and held it to Louisa's throat. 'Not so brave now, are we?'

Louisa closed her eyes and tried to concentrate as waves of helplessness washed over her. There had to be a way. Something she could do. She heard a faint noise. Her heart leapt. Someone was out there. She had to hope that it was not Annie back from her errand. 'Exactly how long does it take to cut a throat?' Louisa said in her loudest and most governess-like voice, the one she used when she expected to be obeyed. 'Will I have enough time to say my prayers? You will allow me to say my prayers.'

'Here, what is this?' Trevor spun around.

The door crashed open with a loud thump. Trevor started towards the door with his knife gleaming in his hand. Louisa stuck her legs out in front of him and he stumbled. Before Trevor had time to regain his balance, a fist connected with his jaw and sent him flying against the wall. Louisa's breath caught as Jonathon flew through the door and landed several more punches on Trevor's face. A group of stable hands and footmen armed with pistols and cudgels rushed in after him.

'Get up! Get up and fight like a man!' Jonathon grabbed Trevor by the lapels of his coat before hitting him again. 'Annie Sims has confessed everything! How you forced her to try to steal the snuffbox in exchange for her mother's life. She refused to let you murder two people!'

'I should have never trusted a woman!'

'It depends on the woman,' Jonathon said. 'I would trust Louisa Sibson with my life.'

He threw Trevor to the ground and gave the order for him to be guarded while his accomplice was rounded up.

Louisa collapsed back against the table. She was not going to die today. Jonathon had saved her.

She moved her hands and felt the ropes give way. *Now* it happened. 'Jonathon,' she called out.

Jonathon crossed the floor in a few strides and knelt by her side. His beloved face was creased with worry. He put his arms around her and held her tight to his chest. Louisa rested her head against him and heard the reassuring thump of his heart.

'Keep still, Louisa,' he commanded and quickly cut the bonds with a knife. Then he tossed the knife to his valet, who cut Mrs Sims's bonds.

His hands rubbed the blood back into her wrists and feet. 'Are you going to finally admit that you do need help from me?'

'Yes, yes, I will. I love you, Jonathon. I always will.

I want to be with you. I want to share my whole life with you.'

His hands stilled. 'You must only say that if you mean it.'

'I love you, Jonathon.' She lifted her hand and caressed his face.

He knelt down beside her. 'Now are you going to tell me why you tried to save the day?'

'It was not planned. I just knew that there was something not right.'

'You were willing to sacrifice yourself for my son. Do not deny it. Annie has told me everything,' Jonathon said with a loving smile.

Louisa shook her head. He had to understand the whole truth. 'I wanted to get away from Annie. I thought I could get her back to the house. Events overtook me. I am not brave.'

'I heard you taunting that piece of filth before we burst in.' His eyes grew sober. 'But next time…'

'There will not be a next time.' Louisa nodded towards where several of the footmen stood guard over Trevor. 'What will happen to him?'

He glanced over his shoulder. 'His days of thieving and violence are over, Louisa. He will be turned over to the law and will face justice for his crimes. I told you that I was a passable pugilist. It was only with great difficulty that I did not kill him. Has he hurt you?'

'A few bruises. That is all. It could have been much worse.' A shudder went through her. 'He held a knife to my throat.'

'I know.'

She grasped his fingers with hers and his hand

convulsed around hers. And she knew that she never wanted to let go. 'I suspect a good many people want to see justice done.'

'And it will be done, properly.'

A series of shivering convulsions went through her. Jonathon motioned to his men who removed Trevor. Then they led Annie and Mrs Sims from the hut. Suddenly the hut was empty and it was just them.

Jonathon placed his jacket around her shoulders and she drank in the warm scent that was uniquely him. Giving in to temptation, she laid her head back against his shoulder. He put his arms about her and steadily stroked her hair until the shuddering stopped.

'How did you find me so quickly?' Louisa asked.

'Annie came to deliver the message, but I already knew the full story from Nanny Hawks.'

'Nanny Hawks confessed to helping her?'

'With a little persuasion.' He cupped Louisa's face between his hands. 'You were right about me, Louisa. I have kept too much of life in separate boxes. I did not make the connection until today. It was wrong of me. You paid attention to little details and I just assumed...' He paused. 'But you are wrong about me as well. I want you in my life. All of my life. I want you as my life's partner, not as some doll who cannot do anything without consulting me first. I had that sort of marriage with Clarissa and I hated it. I thought you understood. I want a marriage of equals.'

She turned her face to his palm. Jonathon wanted what she wanted. She simply had not wanted to see it before. 'Jonathon, I was so frightened.'

'Frightened of dying?'

'No, not that. I was oddly calm about that. I was frightened of not seeing you again. Of never being able to touch you.' Her breath caught at the sudden look of tenderness that crossed his face. 'Of not being able to tell you how much I love you and how I have never stopped. You are the only man for me and I want to grow old with you. I never want to leave your side. I want you in my life…wherever that life takes us.'

'If that is what your heart desires. And we can live wherever you like, even Sorrento. It is my family—you and Arthur—who come first, not my inheritance.'

Louisa bit her lip, knowing what he was offering. He would give up everything to be with her. She did not need Sorrento. That had been an excuse, a way to hide from the beckoning future.

'I can grow lemons and vines in Northumberland, if we have a glasshouse.' Louisa stopped and struggled to get out of Jonathon's arms. 'Oh, no.'

'What's the matter?' His face creased with concern. 'Are you injured, Louisa? What is going on?'

'Miss Daphne.'

'Miss Daphne is safe with Mrs Blandish. She is anxious for you, but allowed me to conduct the rescue.'

'Miss Daphne is sure to be insufferable from now on. She will feel that she has had a hand in this.' Louisa leant back against his arms. 'Our marriage. She is sure to claim credit for it.'

'And why not let the elderly lady have her illusions?' Jonathon laughed softly and gathered her in his arms again. And she gave herself up to his kiss.

# *Epilogue*

~~~~~~~~~~~~~~~~~~~~~~

*Eighteen months later*

The bride wore ivory, a perfect foil for her radiant blondeness. The highly fashionable London church was packed with friends and relations as well as all the members of the *ton*. Much to Louisa's amusement, Susan Blandish had put her foot down and her groom backed her. They wanted their friends to share their day rather than the fashionable and had threatened to elope. Faced with such fierce opposition, both mothers put aside their differences, combined forces and booked a bigger church.

Now Susan Blandish's sweet clear voice filled the church, solemnly repeating her vows as she gazed up into Rupert Furniss's eyes.

A single tear trickled down Louisa's cheek as she silently mouthed along, remembering how slightly less than a year and a half ago she had said the same vows at St Cuthbert's in Chesterholm. Then, as now, she was surrounded by friends she loved. Jonathon's fingers curled about hers and she knew he was remembering the day as well.

She glanced up at him and smiled. He squeezed her hand. On her other side, Margaret stood, beaming, and next to her, the marquis whose proposal she had accepted only a few days previously. The pair planned a summer wedding. Margaret had blossomed now that her mother was convalescing in a small sanatorium in Switzerland for her nerves.

Miss Daphne sat a few rows in front of them with the bride's family. Even now her head was bent down as Nella Blandish whispered some new intelligence in her ear. Louisa knew the pair were busy concocting some new scheme. She was very pleased that Miss Daphne had decided to make her home at Chesterholm, rather than staying in Sorrento.

A little further back on the bride's side, Daisy Milton, now Viscountess Ravensworth, stood with her husband. Louisa and Daisy kept up a lively, almost daily correspondence, only seeing each other when they happened to be in London. Three months ago, Louisa and Jonathon had served as the godparents to Daisy and Adam's first-born son. And now Daisy's sister was busy preparing for her marriage to a wealthy farmer who lived on the estate next to theirs in Warwickshire.

Louisa fumbled for a handkerchief as Rupert Furniss began to say his vows. Jonathon pressed a large white handkerchief into her hand.

'A good wedding deserves a good cry,' he whispered in her ear. 'And your lace handkerchief would be sodden before Furniss gets to the "I do".'

Louisa smiled up at him, pleased that he had been so thoughtful.

The rest of the ceremony flowed over her as the handkerchief became increasingly damp.

As the happy couple walked out of the church, Louisa tucked the handkerchief into her reticule. 'Thank you for looking after me.'

A smile tugged at the corner of his mouth. 'Someone has to. Any idea on where they are going for the wedding trip?'

'Susan is hoping for Italy and I believe Rupert will oblige. I have offered the cottage.'

'It is a perfect place to honeymoon. Although I fancy their trip will not be as crowded as ours.'

Louisa smiled back at him. They had gone to Sorrento after the wedding along with Arthur, Margaret and Miss Daphne to close up the houses. There she had shown him the little grave and they had held each other for a long time, neither saying a word. Later that night, he had made tender love to her in the garden where the lemon trees and jasmine were in bloom. Louisa was convinced that it had been then amongst all that peace, tranquillity and love that their daughter, Mattie, had been conceived.

'Shall we stay at the wedding breakfast long?'

Louisa gave a quick shake of her head. 'Just until the cake is cut and then we need to get home to Arthur and Mattie. Our family.'

The word—family—still sent a thrill down her spine. Jonathon still took the time to tease her about her grasp of the Italian language. Louisa did not mind as she was just so happy that the Italian doctor had been proved wrong and she could have children. Their own little miracle.

'Arthur will be standing guard over his baby sister. He is absolutely besotted with her.' Jonathon guided her around a crowd of people.

'She is a dear little thing, but I do not know if it is a good thing to have Arthur so completely wrapped around her little finger...'

'He has to learn about managing women at some point in his life and where better place to start than with his baby sister?'

Louisa closed her eyes. Her life had changed so much in the past year and a half. She had rediscovered the joy and pleasure of being a woman. And while she would never be the idealistic and impulsive young woman she had been, she knew that that woman remained a part of her. She had been reborn and renewed, all because of the love she shared with this man.

'I am very glad I have you, Jonathon.'

'And I am never going to let you go,' Jonathon whispered in her ear. 'You complete my life.'

'And you complete mine.'

# HISTORICAL

*Regency*

## REBELLIOUS RAKE, INNOCENT GOVERNESS
### by Elizabeth Beacon

Notorious rake Benedict Shaw can have his pick of *ton* heiresses, but one woman has caught his experienced eye... governess Miss Charlotte Wells! And he isn't used to taking no for an answer...

## WANTED IN ALASKA
### by Kate Bridges

Outlaw Quinn can't risk doctor's visits—kidnapping a nurse is the only answer. But Autumn MacNeil is only dressed as a nurse for a costume ball, Still, there's no way he can let her go now...

## TAMING HER IRISH WARRIOR
### by Michelle Willingham

Widow Honora St Leger knows there is little pleasure in the marriage bed, so why should she care that the disturbingly sexy Ewan MacEgan is to wed her sister? Ewan finds himself drawn to the forbidden Honora—one touch and he is longing to awaken her sensuality...

## On sale from 1st April 2011
## Don't miss out!

0311/04b

# 2 FREE BOOKS
## AND A SURPRISE GIFT

We would like to take this opportunity to thank you for reading this Mills & Boon® book by offering you the chance to take TWO more specially selected books from the Historical series absolutely FREE! We're also making this offer to introduce you to the benefits of the Mills & Boon® Book Club™—

- **FREE home delivery**
- **FREE gifts and competitions**
- **FREE monthly Newsletter**
- **Exclusive Mills & Boon Book Club offers**
- **Books available before they're in the shops**

Accepting these FREE books and gift places you under no obligation to buy, you may cancel at any time, even after receiving your free books. Simply complete your details below and return the entire page to the address below. You don't even need a stamp!

**YES** Please send me 2 free Historical books and a surprise gift. I understand that unless you hear from me, I will receive 4 superb new books every month for just £3.99 each, postage and packing free. I am under no obligation to purchase any books and may cancel my subscription at any time. The free books and gift will be mine to keep in any case.

Ms/Mrs/Miss/Mr ——————— Initials ———————

————————————————————————————

Surname ————————————————————

Address ————————————————————

————————————————————————————

——————————————— Postcode ————————

E-mail ——————————————————————

Send this whole page to: Mills & Boon Book Club, Free Book Offer, FREEPOST NAT 10298, Richmond, TW9 1BR